100 Reasons to Celebrate

We invite you to join us in celebrating
Mills & Boon's centenary. Gerald Mills and
Charles Boon founded Mills & Boon Limited
in 1908 and opened offices in London's Covent
Garden. Since then, Mills & Boon has become
a hallmark for romantic fiction, recognised
around the world.

We're proud of our 100 years of publishing
excellence, which wouldn't have been achieved
without the loyalty and enthusiasm of our
authors and readers.

Thank you!

Each month throughout the year there will
be something new and exciting to mark the
centenary, so watch for your favourite authors,
captivating new stories, special limited
edition collections…and more!

Expecting a Fortune
by Jan Colley

ᘒ✤ᘍ

FORTUNE BABY ON THE WAY!

It's a landmark day in Sioux Falls – Nash Fortune is going to be a first-time granddaddy! But apparently Nash is blowing a gasket over the fact that his grandbaby was conceived out of wedlock. (Turns out his virginal daughter, Skylar, got knocked up by a mysterious New Zealander during her brother's wedding!) Too bad Nash's third wife, Patricia, ran out on him – she had a knack for putting a positive spin on their disgraceful family scandals!

Hmmm…we have to wonder why the dropdead gorgeous daddy-to-be is pressing so hard to get a ring on Skylar's finger and whisk her across the globe. Our sources whisper that Zack has a checkered past that rivals anyone in the Fortune clan. And history seems to be repeating itself for this charming bloke. Years ago, Zack was caught up in a messy situation with another pregnant girl who "coincidentally" also came from a wealthy family who liked to run roughshod over everyone. If I were Skylar Fortune, I'd get myself an iron-tight pre-nup before waddling down the aisle!

Fortune's Forbidden Woman
by Heidi Betts

GUESS WHO THIS FORTUNE SON IS SLEEPING WITH

Temperatures are rising in Sioux Falls – and so is the body heat…

In a town this small, secrets have a way of coming out. And do I have some dish for you! Turns out stepsibs Creed Fortune and Maya Blackstone may be getting a little too close for comfort as they comb the streets looking for her mother, Patricia. Everyone knows that Nash Fortune would do just about anything to get his missing wife back into his loving arms, but we wonder how he'd feel if he knew that there is hanky-panky going on between his "honourable" son and his virginal stepdaughter!

Apparently, Creed and Maya have had the hots for each other for several years. So we figure their legendary animosity is really just a smokescreen. You know what they say about forbidden fruit…

Available in March 2008 from Mills & Boon® Desire™

Thirty-Day Affair
by Maureen Child
&
The Prince's Mistress
by Day Leclaire

ᗝᏋᚷᏆᏢᏋ

Expecting a Fortune
by Jan Colley
&
Fortune's Forbidden Woman
by Heidi Betts

ᗝᏋᚷᏆᏢᏋ

The Millionaire's Seductive Revenge
by Maxine Sullivan
&
The Tycoon's Hidden Heir
by Yvonne Lindsay

Expecting a Fortune
JAN COLLEY

Fortune's Forbidden Woman
HEIDI BETTS

MILLS & BOON

Pure reading pleasure

First published in Great Britain 2008
by Harlequin Mills & Boon Limited,
Eton House, 18-24 Paradise Road, Richmond, Surrey TW9 1SR

The publisher acknowledges the copyright holders of the
individual works as follows:

Expecting a Fortune © Harlequin Books S.A. 2007
Fortune's Forbidden Woman © Harlequin Books S.A. 2007

Special thanks and acknowledgement are given to
Jan Colley and Heidi Betts for their contribution to
the FORTUNES mini-series.

ISBN: 978 0 263 85895 2

51-0308

Printed and bound in Spain
by Litografia Rosés S.A., Barcelona

EXPECTING A FORTUNE

by
Jan Colley

Thanks to Peter Mounce, brother-in-law and fount of knowledge on the thoroughbred horse-breeding industry; to Kelli Lowe, a friend who conveniently participated in the same phase of pregnancy as the heroine of this book and shared her "bump" stories with me (hello to beautiful baby boy Alex!); and to Debbie and Paul Thistoll of the Emerald Lodge Stud near Christchurch, who gave up their precious time to show me around their busy and successful stud farm.

JAN COLLEY

lives in Christchurch, New Zealand, with her long-suffering fireman and two cats who don't appear to suffer much at all. She started writing after selling a business because, at tender middle-age, she is a firm believer in spending her time doing something she loves. Jan is a member of Romance Writers New Zealand and Romance Writers of Australia, and she is determined that this book will be one of many. She enjoys reading, travelling and watching rugby, and would be tickled pink to hear from readers. E-mail her at vagabond23@yahoo.com.

THE FORTUNES

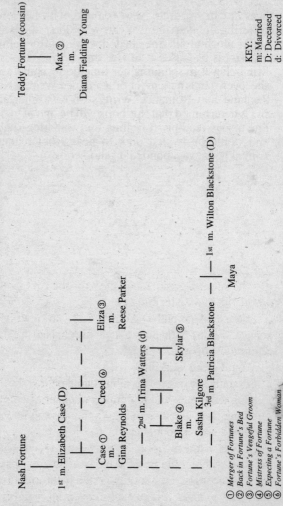

Teddy Fortune (cousin)

Max ②
m.
Diana Fielding Young

Nash Fortune

1st m. Elizabeth Case (D)

Case ①
m.
Gina Reynolds

Creed ⑥

Eliza ③
m.
Reese Parker

2nd m. Trina Watters (d)

Blake ④
m.
Sasha Kilgore

Skylar ⑤

3rd m Patricia Blackstone — | — 1st m. Wilton Blackstone (D)

Maya

① *Merger of Fortunes*
② *Back in Fortune's Bed*
③ *Fortune's Vengeful Groom*
④ *Mistress of Fortune*
⑤ *Expecting a Fortune*
⑥ *Fortune's Forbidden Woman*

KEY:
m: Married
D: Deceased
d: Divorced

One

Skylar pressed Send and waited for the personalized world clock to do its thing.

"Sioux Falls, South Dakota, U.S.A.," she read off the screen. "Friday, 9:06 p.m. Christchurch, New Zealand, Saturday, 4:06 p.m."

Would he be working?

Scraping her fingernails along damp palms, she drew in a ragged breath and hopefully a bucket of courage. Too long had passed, about three months too long, but she could hide it no longer.

Phone, address book...her fingers raced around the desk, tidying the jar of pens, straightening papers. Should she make a drink or go to the bathroom first? *If you want to make an easy job seem mighty hard, just keep putting off doing it. Who said that?* she wondered, then a knock at the door cranked up her heartbeat. A welcome relief? A stay of execution? But the butterflies stayed with her as she rose, tugging her long shirt down over her sweats.

It was easy to avoid people, living in the cottage by the stables, away from the prying eyes of the main house on the estate. No one had noticed a thing, but that wasn't surprising. After all, who ever noticed Skylar? But the concern in her brother's eyes on a rare visit from Deadwood last week came back to her now.

"Coming." Skylar yanked the door open and nearly passed out on the spot.

Zack Manning opened his mouth then closed it again with an audible snap, or that might have been the sound of her knees buckling.

He stared at her, the beginnings of a smile on his handsome face fading fast.

Her worst nightmare. Adrenaline flooded her system and she could not look away. She felt her lips move in a soundless prayer, felt the tension in her fingers, balled into fists by her sides.

After an age, he lowered his gaze, straight to her midriff. Released momentarily, she sagged against the doorjamb, but her relief was short-lived. Incredulous gray eyes shot back to her face, pinning her again, and she watched his tanned face leach slowly of color.

Skylar swallowed. "Zack," she said, her tone just above a whisper. *Deny everything.* He couldn't see what she had hidden under her long checked flannel shirt.

"When did you think you might put me in the picture?"

Skylar's head dropped and she stared at her feet. "I was just— I just got off the Net. The world clock…" Her voice trailed off. Did she expect him to believe that when she was four months pregnant and hadn't bothered before now?

The crown of her downcast head prickled under his glare. Sighing, she moved to the side so he could enter. Skylar closed the door as he brushed past but did not turn immediately. Instead she leaned her forehead on the door, gathering her jumbled thoughts, but the truth of it was, she had no idea what to say.

Slowly she turned. Zack prowled the lounge of her cozy little cottage and he looked furious. Tightly controlled, but furious. His tall rangy form bristled with tension, his mouth was set in a harsh line.

She hovered by the door, hoping she didn't look as tragic as she felt.

Zack suddenly came to a halt and leaned forward with his large hands spread on the battered leather of her old sofa. "We used protection." His voice was flat.

Skylar's first thought was surprise that he did not question the baby's paternity, that he automatically assumed this was his child. Then she bit her lip to stop a rogue smile. Who would want her? After all, she'd been a virgin that night back at the beginning of February.

"The…it broke, I guess." She kept her face down, unable to even say the word. Her face felt hot enough to fry an egg on. How excruciating, to be discussing this with him. "I thought—" her breath hitched "—it might have, when Maya was here."

Her best friend had burst into the unlocked cottage almost the moment they'd finished. Skylar had panicked, vaulting from her bed, pushing at him while throwing a robe on. Maya had a habit of just walking up the stairs and into her bedroom.

"I think I would know!" His voice was low with an icy undertone.

Her shoulders jerked as she recalled the desperate whispers, how she had pushed him into her bathroom and closed the door. There was just enough time to kick his clothes under the bed and straighten the covers before a tearful Maya walked into the room.

Aside from the fantastic sex, it was a pretty lousy end to her first time.

"I would have known!" he insisted.

"The light was out," Skylar whispered. Images of herding him into her bathroom played through her mind like a film clip. His hand reaching for the light switch. Her hand slapping it away. "You probably couldn't see."

"And you didn't think to mention it at the time?"

"I wasn't sure." She rubbed her forehead, sighing wearily. It was her first time, how was she supposed to know? And even if she did, there was no way she could have broached such an intimate subject. Not with him. "I didn't—didn't think I knew you well enough."

"Didn't *know* me well enough?" He made a harsh sound that might have been a laugh.

"It wasn't like we were in a relationship," she mumbled. "It was just too embarrassing, talking about— stuff like that."

She flicked him a nervous glance and a ray of hope soothed her a little. His mouth was more relaxed. A wash of anger still mottled his cheeks but his brows creased more in confusion now. Maybe he believed her.

"I couldn't see a thing," he said, as if to himself. "I just disposed of it and waited for you to get Maya out of the bedroom." He glanced at her sharply. "You were pretty keen to get rid of me then."

Skylar walked over to the dining table and sat. "I thought I'd be spared—" she clasped her hands, prayer-like, on the table "—since it was my first time."

His tone was incredulous. "Skylar, you breed horses. Virgin or not, surely you understood the implications of unprotected sex."

Squeezing her hands together, she nodded miserably.

Zack leaned on the couch, his eyes boring into her. It was done. The worst was over. She cast him some furtive looks and his well-remembered features began to make an impact on her already heightened senses. Skin like his loved the sun and her own pale arms, bare from the elbow, looked insipid compared to his healthy tan. New Zealand's seasons were the opposite to here and South Dakota was just out of a long, cold winter. His sandy hair was still short at the back but longer than she remembered at the sides and front. The deep dimples that traced a line from his well-defined cheekbones to his strong chin were not in evidence tonight. Skylar had fallen head over heels for those dimples almost at first glance.

"Does anyone else know?"

She shook her head. Avoiding the family and her monthly nights out with Maya wasn't difficult when it was the busiest time of the year for the Fortune Stud.

"When were you thinking of telling them? After the birth, or…"

His sarcasm intensified her guilt. "I'm sorry."

"You're sorry." Zack began pacing the room again, as if he was circling his prey.

"I don't—hold you responsible or anything."

"What?" The tension in his quiet voice screamed through her nerves.

"I mean, financially…"

There was a long, excruciating silence.

She sighed, still not looking at him. "I mean, this doesn't have to encroach on…"

Zack sat down suddenly, as if all the air had just gone out of him. "No," he said dazedly, "I'm only the father."

He was ashen. Skylar rose, guilt clawing at her throat. "Do you want something? A drink?"

"Are you seeing someone?" He peered up at her in a lightning change of tack.

She ducked her head with a disbelieving smile, as if he'd said something ridiculous. "No." She twisted her hands together. "Who?"

His suspicious appraisal was unwarranted.

"What are you doing here, anyway? I thought you weren't coming back till the fall."

"Blake called," he muttered. "He was worried about you, said you weren't yourself."

"He shouldn't have done that."

"Done what?" he asked.

"Gotten you involved."

Zack bared his teeth mirthlessly. "Since I'm only the father."

"He doesn't know anything."

"Makes two of us!" he barked, and Skylar jumped. There was an indeterminate slide inside that she'd only felt a couple of times before, and her hand instinctively went to her stomach.

"What is it?" Zack leapt to his feet. "What's wrong?"

She looked up and blinked at the concern in his eyes. "Nothing."

"Why are you holding your stomach?"

"The baby moved."

The look on his face shocked her, as did the jerky movements of his big hands as they dragged through his sandy hair.

"I can't believe this," he grated, "You're—what? Four months pregnant, the baby's moving and I've only— I didn't know a thing."

That was pain darkening his eyes, she was sure. Pain making his voice sound raw.

"And I'm not to have any part of it?" Zack clipped out. "You want to cut me out of everything?"

Skylar twisted her hands together. "It's not like that." She shuffled on her feet, not knowing what to do or say to make things right, or if not right, better.

"I think I will have that drink," he told her curtly, after long moments had passed.

Why had she offered? The only alcohol Skylar had ever kept in the house was the odd bottle of wine if Maya was coming by. The day her pregnancy was confirmed, she'd thrown out a half-empty bottle in her fridge.

She peered at a dusty bottle of some apricot liqueur that must have been there for three or four years, then closed the cupboard and poured him a glass of water.

As soon as he'd taken it from her, she moved back, turning away from the waves of anger she sensed building in him again. She tottered a few steps, turning from him and heard his hard swallow.

What a mess. The word *sorry* danced around and around her mind, along with *clumsy, clueless, stupid.* The silence dragged on and she chewed on her thumbnail. "Where are you staying?"

Zack rapped out the name of Sioux Falls most prominent hotel, the Fortune's Seven, one of several her brothers owned.

Sleeping with him was the dumbest thing she'd ever done, although at the time, it surpassed all her amassed curiosity and fantasies. She should stick to horses for company. She'd never had a problem talking to horses. They didn't judge or reduce her to a quivering mass of nerves and resentment at her clumsy social skills.

"I'll take care of everything," she blurted, unable to take the silence anymore.

She heard another hard swallow. "That's great. That's just great, Skylar."

She spun around, stung by the bitterness in his voice. His searing eyes told her it was anything but great.

"The baby won't want for anything," she told him defensively. He must know that. She made good money doing what she was doing, quite apart from her heritage as one of the Fortune family. The city of Sioux Falls was practically owned by the Fortunes.

"Nothing but a father."

She sighed. "My father and Patricia will be crazy about a baby. And my brothers, well, they'll come around. The baby will be knee-deep in male role models."

"And you don't think that a biological father has any part in this warped family scene you've cooked up?"

"Zack, if you want to see it, have access, that's— that's okay."

"*Access?*" he snapped, prowling around her in an ever-decreasing circle.

Skylar flinched, blinking. "If you want. What *do* you want?"

He gave her a withering look. "Thanks for asking.

Pick a date. We'll get the whole family around tomorrow and tell them we're getting married."

"What?" It was her turn to be shocked.

"Make it quick, Skylar. I can't be away from home for long."

"Married?" she whispered, her head spinning.

He drained his glass and banged it down on the table. "My child is going to have two loving parents, not just one."

"I'm not marrying you, Zack." A hiccup escaped her throat. "Not marrying anyone."

He leaned down, his face inches from hers. "You may have cut me out of this till now, the worrying, the morning sickness, the movements. But that changes as of right now." She'd never seen his gray eyes glint like steel before. "We *are* going to be married, so get used to it."

She made a pitiful attempt at a smile. "That's just—dumb."

"What's dumb?" he demanded. "Pretending it hasn't happened? Hiding it from everyone? I suppose you could have delivered it in the stables and told everyone the stork left it."

His flippant remark stirred an unusual lick of anger. "Maybe this is why I didn't tell you. I was afraid you'd want to take over, have it all your way."

Her voice rang out, clear and strong, making them both start. Skylar seemed to have lost her stammer. Normally she was hard-pressed to string five words together around Zack Manning.

He recovered first. "You've had your way. It isn't good enough."

"I'm not marrying you, Zack."

"No kid of mine is going to be brought up without two parents and a wedding ring."

"This child will want for nothing," she repeated, stung at the assumption she couldn't provide for the baby.

This wasn't like her, to argue back. It must be her hormones kicking in. Her baby-protective hormones.

"No, it won't, because I'll take care of the both of you."

Incredulous, she just stared at him, shaking her head. "I don't believe you."

"Whatever." He shrugged and headed for the door.

"Where are you going?"

"If I'm not back in an hour, your father has used his shotgun on me."

"No!" Skylar leapt after him. "Zack, please. Let me tell him, my own way."

"You've had your way for four months. The next five are mine, I reckon."

She attempted to scoot around him to get to the door first. "He's an old man and he has problems of his own right now."

Zack blocked her with ease. "Your father is tough as an ox."

"Zack, Patricia has left him. He's devastated."

"Then a wedding to look forward to and a baby on the way should be just what he needs to take his mind off things."

"Will you please," she implored, "leave my father out of this until I've had a chance to think?"

Zack nearly combusted, his knuckles on the doorknob turning white. "A chance to think?"

"Just until I tell everyone. I'll keep you informed—"

He yanked the door open, rolling his eyes. "Yeah, right!"

Skylar was hot on his heels and having to run to keep up.

Zack turned on her. "Get back inside."

"I'm coming with you."

"Skylar, this is man's talk. You don't want to be there."

"Don't you patronize me!" Much as the note of panic in her voice disgusted her, she had to stall him.

"Calm down." He turned her, his hands surprisingly gentle on her shoulders and at odds with the harshness of his voice. "I'll be back soon."

"Dad's not at the house," she lied, desperate. "He had to go look for Patricia."

"Forgive me if I don't believe you."

"You're impossible!" she wailed.

"No, I'm a lamb." He propelled her back inside. "And you are a lying, conniving… Sit down." He settled her gently, insistently, into a chair. "And wait for me."

"When did I ever lie to you?" Skylar wondered if she could faint on cue. Any stupid female trick would do, just to keep him here.

He bent toward her, his face so close she felt his breath on her skin. "How about my twice-monthly phone calls, when I would ask how you were?" he suggested.

She bit her lip, her eyes wide. Trust him to bring that up.

"Did you not think to say, 'Fine, Zack. Pregnant. It's yours, but fine.'" He glared down at her then turned on his heel.

She slumped. It was true. She'd had ample opportunities to tell him he was going to be a father. How excited she'd been, the first time he called, yet embarrassed, too, at the less than perfect ending to their night of passion. In subsequent calls he'd suggested she come down to check out his new stud and also dropped hints about his return in September for the Keeneland Sales: "Maybe you could take a couple days off and come with me…" She was ever the blithering idiot, too shy to talk of anything other than horses.

Naturally, after she discovered she was pregnant, those conversations were torture and she wondered why he bothered. But to give him his due, he had always shown an interest, always asked after her.

A car engine started up outside, rousing her.

Her father! She had to warn him. Picking up the phone, Skylar quickly dialed the house and begged her father not to talk to him. "Get Peggy to say you're out," she demanded. Goodness knows she asked for little enough from her father.

Curious, Nash Fortune agreed, telling her to come up directly after Zack had gone.

A few minutes later, Zack returned, thwarted in his attempt to speak to her father. Grim and determined, he pushed his face close to hers. "If you are not here in the morning," he warned, "I will track you down. Count on it."

As soon as he left for town, Skylar drove up to the big house and her father opened the door. "What is going on, Skylar?"

He looked so tired. She hated having to dump this on him, after the day or so he'd endured. It wasn't a lie about her father's wife leaving him. "Any news on Patricia?"

Nash shook his head sadly. "No. What's Zack Manning got a bee in his bonnet about?"

"Sit down, Dad."

Two

Never again!

Zack swung the rental car out of the hotel parking lot and headed toward the Fortune Estate, about twenty miles west of the city of Sioux Falls.

Never again would he allow himself to be shafted by wealth and power. That was his domain now. He had more than enough to make Skylar's family squirm, should they play hardball.

His eye was drawn to the twenty-three-story Dakota Fortune building a block away, where Case and Creed, her half brothers, conducted their business. No doubt he'd have to deal with them at some stage, but his focus was on Nash Fortune this morning. Regardless of the man's marital upheaval, his daughter was four months' gone—four months!—and it was past time Nash knew what Zack's intentions were.

He rubbed his eyes, a sleepless night exacerbating a whole hemisphere of jet lag.

Focusing on what to say to Nash helped ease the burn of anger. Skylar clearly thought so little of him, she couldn't even tell him of the life they'd created. Sure, they barely knew each other, but he bristled at the notion that he was unapproachable where Skylar was concerned. He'd made a concerted effort to be pleasant to her on his visit here earlier in the year, especially when it became apparent how shy and uncomfortable being around him made her. Zack knew when someone was sweet on him.

His cell phone rang. It was Max Fortune, his closest friend and business partner in Australia and Skylar's cousin.

"What in blazes? You knocked up my little cuzzy, you bastard?"

Zack grinned. The Australian rancher was all bark and no bite where he was concerned. They'd been through a lot together.

Then he sobered. These big rich families moved quick. He hadn't said a word to anyone and already the southern hemisphere family grapevine was abuzz. "What do *you* want?" he drawled.

"To knock your block off, mate." There was a pause. "What are you going to do?"

Zack blew out a breath. "I'm on my way to see Nash now about making an honest woman of her."

There was a lengthy silence. The two men's self-imposed bachelorhood had come to a sticky end a few months ago when Max wed his old flame Diana. Zack imagined the sound of necks cracking as his friends and enemies did a double take at this second blow to confirmed bachelor status Down Under.

"What does Sky think about that?"

Zack had his own ideas about that. While tossing and turning in his hotel bed, he'd concluded that he'd walked into a setup the night of Case Fortune's wedding four months ago. Skylar's setup.

"She'll come around," he said shortly. "Who told you, anyway?"

"Nash called Dad. Gave us all a shock, that's for real. Dad told him, 'Don't trust that Kiwi, he's got sprogs all over the world and he's only out for your money.'"

Zack let out a bark of laughter and nearly missed his turnoff. "Tell the old reprobate thanks." He knew of Teddy Fortune's warm regard for him.

But there were some things the Australian Fortunes didn't know. Like the mistake eighteen years ago, when Zack had gotten his young sweetheart pregnant. Like the anger that had burned in his gut all these years, born of his helplessness as a penniless boy from the wrong side of the tracks who had been virtually run out of town. Helpless to stop Rhianne from giving in to her rich family's wishes to abort his baby and not ruin her life.

Never again…

"You'll, aah, you'll be nice, won't you, Zack? I like old Freckles, she's a good sort. I wouldn't have her hurt."

"I like her, too, Max," Zack reassured his friend quickly. "Wish me luck or I won't ask you to be best man."

He hung up, thinking with surprise that was true; he *did* like Skylar, more than he'd liked any woman in a long time. There was something about her right from the start, even though she did nothing to lead him on, until the night of that family wedding.

Shocked nearly senseless at the news he was going to be a father, there was not a shadow of a doubt in his mind that he and Skylar would marry. Even now, about to confront her father and cause this family all sorts of upset, there was only one course of action.

Love didn't come into it.

Just ahead, he saw the stone pillars that announced Fortune Estate land. Instead of turning off to Skylar's cottage in the stand of trees by the stables, he drove toward the big house, as she called it, thinking it was better Nash was prewarned, had had time to think about it.

Despite that, his stomach tightened as he approached the huge old mausoleum the Fortunes called home. A little too gothic for his taste; Zack preferred a more contemporary residence. The dark gray stone made it appear almost black and very forbidding. But inside, it was comfortable and homely, reflecting Patricia's warm personality.

He parked the car and took the steps leading up to the house two at a time. Peggy, the housekeeper, showed him into the dining room. Zack was surprised to find only Nash present. He'd expected one or two of the large family here at this time.

The older man looked up from his breakfast, his glum expression lightening. "Zack! Sit down. I hate to eat alone."

The two shook hands and Zack helped himself to juice and toast from the ample buffet and tried, unsuccessfully, to prevent Nash calling to Peggy to fix some fresh eggs.

"Where is everyone?" he asked, part of him disappointed he could not settle with the whole family in one sitting. They chatted for a couple of minutes about the whereabouts of the other residents of the house. Since Zack had left in early February, Nash's older daughter, Eliza, had moved to Montana to be with her husband, Reese. The other two sons, Case and Creed, divided their time between apartments in town and the estate.

Then Nash fixed him with a stern gaze. "So you're about to become a daddy."

"That's why I'm here."

"Congratulations." Nash's gaze narrowed as if trying to read his mind.

"Not sure that's appropriate, under the circumstances."

"New life is precious, whatever the circumstances." Nash finished his pancakes just as Peggy slid a plate full of freshly scrambled eggs in front of Zack. His mouth watered. He'd eaten nothing but plastic airline food in the last twenty-four hours.

"I like you, Zack," the older man continued. "You're a straight shooter. I believe your intentions are good."

"They are." Zack sent up a silent thanks to Teddy Fortune in Australia. "I asked her to marry me."

"Asked?"

Zack paused, a forkful of eggs on the way to his mouth. "More or less," he affirmed with a quick nod. "She won't have it."

Nash leaned back, his expression fond. "Skylar is a complicated girl," he said slowly. "It's hard to know what she's thinking. Her mother—well, she wasn't the mothering type."

Zack knew a little of the history. Skylar and Blake's real mother, Trina, was run off the Fortune Estate, sans children, when Nash discovered her cheating on him.

By all accounts, Patricia, Nash's third wife, was more of a mother to them than their own.

"I don't know Skylar as well as I should." Nash lifted his coffee cup. "She bottles things up. She's close to her brother, and Patricia and Maya, but doesn't seem to need the rest of us much." He gave a sad little smile. "We all think the world of her, but it's true, we're a family that doesn't talk easily about feelings."

"I'll take good care of her, sir. I know it'll be strange at first, a new country, being away from her family. But I'm in a position to give her anything she wants."

"What she wants? I think what she wants is her independence. And her horses. Girl always loved her darn horses."

"I have more than enough horses to keep her happy." Zack pushed his plate away and leaned his arms on the table. "It'll be a good life, Nash, and I'll bring her and the baby back whenever she wants."

"It's not me you have to convince." The older man sighed heavily. "There's too much goin' around in my old brain at the moment. Thing is, I don't think Skylar knows a lot about the ways of men. She's an innocent."

Not that much of an innocent, Zack thought grimly.

A flash of blue through the window caught his eye. Their subject mounted the steps outside. "Do I have your blessing, sir?" he asked quickly.

"My blessing?" Nash stuck his thumb in his belt, his tired blue eyes peering out under thick graying brows. "If you can get the girl to agree then…" He nodded slowly, then raised his head.

Skylar entered the room, looking mutinous. They both watched her approach and Nash inhaled sharply.

"How the heck did we all miss it?" he murmured. "It's as obvious as a poke in the eye she's expecting."

Both men stared at her candidly, though doubtless Zack's reaction was vastly different than her father's. To an outsider, she was dressed as normal: jeans, a longish flannel shirt with a shapeless navy jacket over the top. Her light brown hair shone in braids, what he could see of it, with her signature baseball cap jammed on top.

The moment she'd opened the door last night, the knowledge that she was pregnant hit him like a sledge-hammer between the eyes. *Wham! She's pregnant. Wham! It's mine.*

Wham! Not again...

He'd always considered her pretty. Her wide mouth turned up at the corners with a sweetly pronounced bow in the middle. Arched brows dipped low in the middle of her forehead in that interesting way some women had that looked like they were on the verge of frowning. The old adage about pregnant women glowing was true, the proof of it standing in front of him now. A luster to her creamy skin, freckles seemed more pronounced, her eyes more blue. In his mind, the shy and scruffy tomboy who never looked him right in the eye, had been replaced by one hellishly attractive woman.

One very ticked off woman. As if she could read his thoughts, she glared at him, her chin tilted up defiantly. "What are you doing here, upsetting my father?"

Nash raised his hand. "Now, now. He's not upsetting me. We're just having a chat."

She kept her eyes on Zack. "About me, naturally."

Zack folded his arms, torn between a worrying stab of desire and annoyance.

"Get yourself some breakfast, girl," her father ordered. "Let's talk this thing out."

Skylar narrowed her eyes even more for good measure then stalked to the buffet and poured some juice into a glass. She returned to the table and sat.

Zack looked pointedly at the glass. "Shouldn't you eat something?"

"Don't start," she retorted.

Both guns blazing, he thought with wonder. Where had this spitfire been hiding?

Nash looked at her daughter. "Zack has asked me for your hand."

She scowled. "How quaint. Is that a New Zealand custom?"

"Skylar," Nash hushed her. "Do you like him at all?"

She exhaled and looked away with a shrug.

"Well, I assume you liked him well enough to make a baby with him," Nash rumbled.

Skylar's eyes shot around the room, resting on Peggy clearing a table over by the window. "Dad!" Her freckles almost disappeared in the crimson glow. "I've told him I'll take care of everything," she said in a low voice. "He can see the baby whenever he wants. *If* he wants."

Zack swallowed his scathing reply. He would deal with that when they were alone.

Nash cleared his throat. "See, I think Zack might be a little like me. When I asked your mother to leave, it was on the proviso that she leave you kids here. I couldn't bear to be parted from you, any of you."

"Lots of people are single parents," she began. "Statistics say…"

Nash cut her off. "*Not* in this family, girl. You're a

Fortune. I would ask you to consider the implications of that in all you do."

Skylar's eyes widened.

Nash continued in a softer tone. "Just because it's the modern way doesn't mean it's right for everyone."

She glanced meaningfully at Zack. "If you want to be more involved, then you're just going to have to spend more time in the States."

He frowned at her. She seemed to have left the stammer behind, as well.

Then she did something that rocked him to the core. She leaned right back in that age-old pose of pregnant women everywhere, one hand cradling the bottom of her belly and the other moving slowly, lovingly, just under her breasts.

Something slammed in his chest. Man, he'd never wanted to touch something so much.

"Zack?"

Nash's voice cut through his longing. Zack cleared his throat for the second wave of attack. "We can come over two or three times a year. I know you'll want the baby to grow up knowing family."

Skylar's sweet mouth compressed and she huffed out a sigh. He frowned at her, annoyed with himself for being distracted, even charmed by her. "Skylar, I'm offering you marriage. Security. A good life for that baby of ours. There will be no stigma about single parents, or why Daddy doesn't live with you. You and I aren't romantics. We are sensible, well-grounded people. We'll damn well make this work for the sake of the child."

Her mouth still a straight line, she put her nose in the air and looked away.

Nash rested his elbow on the table, his fingers moving through his graying hair. "I wish Patricia were here. She'd know what to say."

Skylar looked at him, concern softening her lips.

"After we talked last night, Sky, I made a couple of calls, to Teddy and another business contact I have in those parts," Nash commented, eliciting startled glances from both of them. "Zack is wealthy, successful at what he does, and if there are any skeletons in his closet, they're so far back, it doesn't matter a damn. He is well liked and respected. He has never been married, has no children. Teddy and Max are behind him one hundred percent. You could do a lot worse, you know."

Skylar looked at him, smudges of betrayal darkening her eyes. "You're talking about the rest of my life here."

Nash's head rolled back, his broad chest rising on a deep inhalation. "Where does it say marriage is forever? Ask me."

Her eyes shone with sympathy. "Oh, Dad. She'll come back. I know she will."

"She will or she won't." Nash sighed and his stern gaze moved to each of them in turn. "But I have bigger things to worry about than two young people who are very well suited, even if they don't know it yet." He leaned forward and put his hand on his daughter's shoulder. "Love grew for me and Patricia. It didn't happen overnight. Now you have a baby to think of and a family name that has been besmirched once too often for my liking. And I'd like to tell you differently, girl, but there are no guarantees in this life."

Zack watched Skylar's face fall. He actually felt a pang of sympathy for her, even though her father was on his side. But he kept silent. This salvo was between her and Nash.

"Just tell me you'll think about it. Don't set your mind against it on some girlish notion." He put both hands on the table and pushed himself up, sadness evident in his stooped shoulders. "Give me something good to tell Patricia if she calls. She's got a real soft spot for you. She'd love to see you expecting. A marriage in the family is just what's needed to bring us all together again."

"That's blackmail," Skylar whispered.

"Whatever works for you," Nash said comfortably. "Just promise you'll consider it, Skylar. It's not a bad proposition." He turned to Zack, putting out his hand. "Shall I tell Peggy to air out the empty apartment upstairs? No sense wasting time and money on a hotel."

Zack shook his hand. "Maybe in a few days. I'd appreciate it."

The silence lasted minutes after Nash walked heavily from the room. Zack was torn, wanting to comfort her, guessing she felt let down. The temptation was there to go in for the kill while she was vulnerable, the words of her father fresh in her mind. But sometimes, as in business, it was best to let the opposing party lead and hang themselves.

"You can stop looking so smug," she muttered, suddenly, drawing herself up in a tense line.

Her eyes flashed, warming his blood. How could he have forgotten the fire in her? He recalled having the skin of his back raked when he'd realized she was a virgin and momentarily pulled back. That straightened his spine and made him grin. No way would spitfire Skylar allow that!

Catching her eye, he arranged a more sober expression on his face and put his hands behind his head.

"What are you looking at?"

"It occurs to me I've been a bit insensitive."

"Really?" Her mouth curved in what she probably meant to be a sneer, but Skylar's mouth didn't *do* sneer. It was still a sweet smile.

"So I'm asking. Skylar Fortune, will you marry me?"

The indignation drained out of her. Her eyes were troubled, her mouth turned down. "Oh, Zack."

He leaned toward her, taking one of her hands before she could pull back. "It's not the perfect start, I give you that. But a child should have two parents. We are responsible, independently wealthy, sexually compatible..." He smiled at the blush scooting up her throat and face. "And we like each other. We always did."

Skylar bit her lip briefly, drawing his eye. In lieu of kissing her there, where she was so troubled, he raised her hand, laced their fingers together and kissed the tips of hers.

"It's not enough," she mumbled.

He nodded reassuringly. "It's enough."

She squeezed his hand. "Zack, I never ever expected to get pregnant. And I never expected to fall in love and get married and walk off into the sunset, either. But why should you settle for second best?"

"I don't consider you second best," he admonished. "Far from it."

Skylar pulled back from him suddenly, wrapping her arms about her torso. This was all moving too fast. He was too easy, calm, while she felt like screaming and gnashing her teeth. She knew a hustle when she saw one. Her father and Zack were bonding together...and she had a fair idea of what her brothers would think about all of this. Case and Creed, her half brothers, were carbon copies of their father. The scandal this pregnancy would cause would be their main concern. She imagined lots of male posturing and talk of dragging Zack down the aisle.

Gulping air, she rocked back and forth, trying to quell a rising panic. "Oh, I don't know what to say…" she wailed, not caring that Peggy was still in the room.

"Say *yes,* Skylar." Zack's voice remained calm and constant. "I won't let you down."

Why should she believe him? She'd always felt so apart from everyone, like an afterthought. Did no one else see how impossible this was?

It had hurt to hear her father's glib words, passing her fears off like she didn't know her own mind. No guarantees, do what's right, don't surrender to girlish notions…such as love?

A tear welled up. A tear! Skylar Fortune didn't cry. She swiped at her eyes, succeeding only in dislodging it and starting its journey. "He can't force me," she said through clenched teeth. "*You* can't force me. I need the time to make my own decision."

His easy smile and dimples faded. She saw disappointment in his face where, a second ago, victory had lurked. He thought she'd just go along, do as she was told. Skylar didn't make waves, hell, not even a ripple. Everyone would no doubt think she'd be lucky to snare him.

"Don't you think we've wasted enough time?"

She met his accusatory glare and upped it. He wasn't easy now, but he'd backed her into a corner and, like one of her stallions, she was apt to kick.

"If you'd informed me a couple of months ago," Zack said tightly, "we'd have had all the time in the world to get to know each other."

"What difference does it make?" Skylar demanded. "Two months, five months, nine…why do we have to decide about marriage right now?"

Something in his gray eyes shifted. "My baby will not be born illegitimate."

The quiet intensity of his words, each carefully enunciated, the warning in his eyes, made the air throb between them. Skylar inhaled, almost afraid to speak. This wasn't the Zack she knew.

Then he blinked and she couldn't be sure she had seen anything. He was still grim, but he was Zack. New Zealander. Razor-sharp businessman. Vintner and new studmaster.

Sexy. Charming. Considerate.

Father of her baby.

Skylar sighed. She wanted him, she had from the first. But not this way. Not shackled to him because of a broken condom. "I can't give you an answer right…"

"When?" he demanded, cutting her off.

Her jacket rustled with the rise of her shoulders. It was hard not to be disappointed when the intensity he had just displayed suggested it was more the baby he was concerned with, not her. She raised her chin and put some steel into her spine.

Zack inhaled. "I'll have to go home for a few days to sort out some things." He frowned down at the table. "Make arrangements for a longer absence. We need to spend time together, Skylar."

Or then again…Skylar nodded hopefully, her breath hitching when he reached for her hand.

"This is my first baby, too," he told her, his tone softer now. "I want to be there for it. The whole thing."

Or maybe not. Her shoulders dropped, but at least

she would have some peace, some thinking time. "I'm not going anywhere."

Zack suddenly pulled her toward him, squeezing her fingers firmly. "I want you to swear, on the baby's life, that you'll not do anything stupid while I'm gone."

Her heart lurched. "Wh-what?"

"Like run," Zack grated, "hide. Let your family talk you into getting rid of the baby."

"They wouldn't…I would never…"

She was shocked that he could even *think* that…from the instant she had first felt pregnant, that was an option that had never entered her head.

"Swear, Skylar." Zack's grip was just short of painful. "I have no intention of losing this baby."

"Zack, I would rather die than…"

"I won't be cut out of this, do you understand?" His voice was low, almost menacing. "I may not be quite in the league of the Dakota Fortunes but I've got enough behind me to make things very nasty, and very public, if you do anything to hurt my child. Do you understand?"

Skylar nodded woodenly. "I swear."

Well, at least everyone knew where they stood. Zack Manning had no interest in her. It was the baby he wanted. She was only the incubator.

A movement over his shoulder caught her eye and Skylar stiffened and snatched her hand from his.

Three

A clawing tension descended as Maya Blackstone walked into the room. Skylar straightened her spine, folding her arms protectively around her middle.

"Hi." Ever curious, Maya scooted around to the side and beamed when she saw who was sitting with Skylar. "Zack! I didn't know you were back."

"Gidday, Maya." Zack slowly got to his feet, a genuine smile on his face. "Just leaving actually, but I'll be back in a few days." The smile faded as he turned back to Skylar. "Take good care, Skylar. You have my number."

He nodded at the two women and walked out.

"Want something to eat?" Skylar felt almost giddy with relief at his leaving, though that was tempered by the knowledge she now had the task of telling everyone about the baby. At least she could do that her own way, without Zack breathing down her neck.

Maya shook her head. "I'm relieved to hear you talk about food," she said, looking thoughtfully after Zack. "Since you missed our last two dinner dates."

Maya didn't come to the house if she could help it so they usually got together once a month at her place in town.

"What brings you here?"

"I came to see if there was any word on Mom. Blake tells me Nash has hired an investigator."

Blake! He should be first to know, really. She owed him, Skylar thought darkly, for instigating Zack's visit. And then there was her mother…

Sensing she was the object of avid attention, Skylar looked up into Maya's curious face.

"So, the handsome Kiwi is back. How do you feel about that?"

May as well get it over with. While she was choosing her words, Maya tilted her head and narrowed her eyes.

"Don't tell me, I can see. Your usual slobby attire aside, you look great, Skylar. The picture of health."

She blinked, frowning. "What do you mean, slobby? These jeans are only a year old."

Her friend grinned. "Come on. You wear your clothes like a shield." Her nicely manicured fingers flicked toward the front of Skylar's jacket. "Your wardrobe could do with a complete overhaul."

"Excuse me for living," Skylar protested. "Just because Eliza is in Montana with Reese doesn't mean you have to take over as chief nag." At least she was spared being dragged all over town to replace her wardrobe and having her half sister camped on her doorstep, making sure she took care of herself.

Anyway, back to the task at hand. Skylar hadn't told

her best friend she'd slept with Zack, though she had mentioned liking him—a lot. "Maya, do you remember the night of Case's wedding?"

Maya nodded. "The night Eliza got her wish and finally talked you into a dress."

What a monumental disaster that turned out to be. "And later you barged into the cottage after the fight with Creed?"

Maya's mouth compressed. Creed was the main reason she didn't like coming to the house, Skylar suspected. Those two brought out the worst in each other.

"Maya, I was," she cleared her throat self-consciously "*with* Zack. That night in the cottage."

It should have been funny, the openmouthed gape, the dawning horror, but for the life of her, Skylar could not dredge up a smile.

"I didn't…" Maya stammered, "Oh, no, please, tell me I didn't interrupt…"

Skylar shook her head glumly. "We made it to the finish line. Just."

Maya flopped back in her chair, blowing out a long puff of air. "So it's official. I am now the only virgin left in all of South Dakota."

Skylar didn't smile. In fact, for the first time since she'd had the pregnancy confirmed, she put her face in her hands and burst into tears, shocking them both.

Six days later, Skylar heard the screaming from her office and leapt to her feet. Without even knowing how she got there, she hurtled in through the entrance of the stallion barn, yelling for the grooms, then abruptly skidded to a halt.

The main stable housing the twenty-five broodmares

she accommodated was ten meters away and most of the mares were out in the pasture, enjoying the spring weather for a few hours. The stallion barn had four stalls, two on one side opening out onto handsome land-scaped gardens and a lane that forked and led to two grassed yards, set diagonally apart. The other two stalls opened into the breezeway. That way, even when the stallions were both in residence, they didn't have to see each other or be led past the other's stall.

Demetrius, a large fourteen-year-old chestnut, had stood at Fortune Stud for two and a half years. He was middle of the road, his crop placing quite regularly on the track. He was not particularly unruly for a stallion, but when Skylar purchased the prized Black Power a year ago, Deme resented the young usurper. Hence the modified barn. They may have to room together but they did not have to like looking at each other.

Demetrius wasn't in his box. Over the years, he'd caused great amusement by nudging and nibbling on the bolt of the top Dutch door to his stall until he opened it. Deme's party trick, they called it, and everyone took special care to check the bottom half was securely latched after mucking out or returning him to his stall.

Both the top and bottom halves of the door were wide-open. An ominous bashing from inside Black Power's stall down the end told her that her most valu-able asset was in trouble. Skylar spun and raced down the outside of the barn.

As she feared, the big chestnut had gone visiting. His ears were back and he lunged his head and neck inside the open top door of the stall. A crunching bang from inside, accompanied by a high-pitched roar drowned out Skylar's renewed calls for help. Demetrius lunged again, showing his teeth. She glimpsed a flash of black as Ace, Black Power's stable name, reared up in his prison, his legs flailing in the air around Deme's head.

"Deme, no!" She leapt toward the horses, wincing when one of Black Power's legs pounded against the top of the door.

Suddenly an iron grip on her arm hauled her sharply back against a hard wall of muscle.

"No!" Zack Manning said in a low snarl. "Get back." His eyes blazing, he yanked her roughly to the side of him. "Stay."

Air jetted from her lungs as she lurched to a standstill.

Stripping off his suit jacket, he flung it at her and began rolling his shirtsleeves up. "Deme, right?" He jerked his head toward the two horses. He'd met both back in January.

"Careful, he can be…"

Zack gave her a scathing look. "Get outta here. Find someone to help, *now*." He advanced toward the stallion.

Skylar raced back into the stallion barn to look for a lead and yelled again for Bob, the head groom. Hearing voices, she stuck her head out the door. Her four workers were walking back from the mare's barn. Urging them to hurry, she rushed back to Zack with them hot on her heels.

Zack had a tight hand on Deme's halter and was bringing his head down. She saw his lips moving, talking, soothing. The others moved slowly around the horse. She gave the lead to Bob and watched with relief as he clipped it on to the halter. Deme gave another toss of the head and finally was coaxed into taking a backward step.

Her attention was on the stall now. There was another crunching blow that shook the building. Skylar covered her mouth with her hand and prayed. Ace was ten million dollars' worth of horse, syndicated to the Fortunes and two other parties. Skylar's biggest gamble, and he was due to serve a mare in less than two hours. The standing fee for this seven-year-old stallion was twelve thousand dollars. *Please, God, don't let him hurt himself.*

Her growing reputation amongst breeders in this part of the States was mostly due to the huge investment in Ace. He was a young sire but with fine lineage and his first crop two years ago was already making an impact on sales all over the States.

Bob, the head groom and stallion manager, released Deme into the care of the others and stepped up to the stall. Ace was still playing up, smashing up the stall. Skylar took a couple of anxious steps forward but Zack moved in front of her, shouldering her away. He stood next to Bob who leaned into the Dutch door, talking quietly to the agitated beast.

Her relief overwhelmed her but she wouldn't be satisfied until she'd had a good look at her pride and joy. She stretched and strained behind the two men, subsiding when Zack flicked her a scornful glance before turning his back again.

Frustrated, she bent and scooped up his suit jacket. His arrival had been a surprise. All she'd known for sure was he'd be here before the weekend. She had expected him to phone with more specifics. She hadn't expected him to just show up at the stable, still in his business suit.

Bob was still talking to Ace. She stood behind them restlessly, trying to peer between Zack's broad shoulders and the older man's tall, thin form. Standing on tiptoe, she caught flashes of a sweat-darkened flank as the stallion paced and blew, trembling with rage and fear.

"Is he all right?"

"Let's give him a few minutes," Bob muttered, "till he's calmed some."

Zack turned abruptly and took her arm. "What the hell were you thinking?" he muttered, propelling her a few feet away.

The adrenaline drained away, leaving impatience and a feeling of defensiveness. "What was I supposed to do? Let him kick himself to…"

"Get help," he grated.

Skylar frowned at him from under the peak of her cap. "Do you know how much he's worth?"

Zack stepped up to her, close. She was not short, being five foot nine in her stocking feet, but she sure felt small with his lean body, rigid in anger, looming over her.

"Not as much as that baby you're carrying," he said in a deceptively soft voice. "The one you swore an oath to protect."

Her head dropped. He was right—she should never have gone near the stall. It was instinct driving her. In all honesty, and it was hard to admit it even to herself, she had completely forgotten about being pregnant when she'd heard the screams of the sparring stallions.

"I know. I'm sorry. I just didn't think—"

Zack glared down at her. "That's the last time you don't think. Starting now, you don't go near these horses, any of them."

Her head snapped up and she roasted him with a

scowl that matched his own. This was a new side to him, and Skylar didn't like it one bit. "It's the busiest time of the year…" she bit out, struggling to hold her temper. Another surprise since she didn't think she had a temper to hold.

"We'll manage." Zack's eyes were like granite and he stood, legs braced, like an immovable force. "Won't we, Bob?"

How dare he undermine her authority like that? She heard Bob's grunt, saw his large ears turn pink and recognized he'd made the judicious decision not to turn his head.

"I have to call the vet," she muttered, wrenching her arm from his grip. Okay, she was sorry, but when all was said and done, nothing had happened. She and the baby were fine. Pebbles erupted in angry little spurts under her boots as she stomped off toward her office.

Who did he think he was? He and her cousin Max had come to *her* for help a few months ago, not the other way around. This was her life's work, for Pete's sake! Lost in a spiteful exchange that was only in her head, she was suddenly aware he had followed when her office door banged with enough force to rattle the windows.

"While we're on it," he said, striding up to her desk, "that goes for riding, too. Till after the baby is born."

Skylar stopped like a slap and turned slowly to face him. "What?"

He leaned back, folding his arms.

"Zack, I can handle horses. I've been riding since I could walk."

"I ride, too," he said evenly. "When's the last time a horse shied on you?"

Her lips parted with a scathing retort. Like a flash, the remembered pain of being dumped unceremoniously on her rear end a few months ago sent the retort up in a puff of smoke. Her hand crept behind herand she gave her backside a quick rub. Roscoe, her ancient gelding, had never liked surprises and a well-camouflaged snake slithering over a log certainly surprised him that day.

Skylar's shoulders slumped and she gave the unkempt surface of her desk a thorough scrutiny. She was honest enough to admit to receiving her fair share of bruises, even broken bones, over the years from shying horses.

With a downcast face, she saw Zack's fingers relax a little where they curled around his biceps.

Skylar sank down into her chair. "Is this what it's going to be like?" she asked quietly.

There was no answer, forcing her to look up.

"Demanding this…demanding that?"

"Horses are unpredictable."

"I meant you. Not asking. Not talking, just…"

"Where the safety of the baby is concerned, yes." He punctuated that with a nod, then unfolded his arms and sat. "I'm still learning but you showed me your system in January. With your supervision, from here—" he waved a hand around her office "—and Bob in charge, me and the boys will keep things running smoothly."

"We're still covering most days. The summer mares are arriving and there are still half a dozen late foals to come."

"Well, it'll be good practice for me when we kick off in our spring." His tone and gaze did not waver. "Skylar, this is difficult for both of us."

She nodded sullenly, tapping her desk.

"We need to spend time together, get to know each

other. That means I'll be here every day under your feet. It would be easier if you'd give us a chance."

Irritated by her tapping fingers, she twisted her hands together. "I don't like being given orders."

"I'm not an unreasonable man. I'll listen to your arguments and concerns. But I won't let you take any chances with our baby."

Our baby. He was right, she supposed. This life inside her was precious and fragile, and although she'd like to tell him to mind his own business, this was his business.

She rocked forward, still clasping her hands together. "I guess I can understand that."

There was a long silence while she swallowed her resentment, let her mind concede that his requests and demands were not so unreasonable. She had already relinquished a lot of her more physical workload over the last weeks in deference to her pregnancy.

"You look good, Skylar. Are you?"

She nodded. Now that the morning sickness had passed, she felt energized by a feeling of well-being and good health. Her mouth softened, remembering yesterday's ride on Roscoe down by the lake. She'd dropped the reins and just buried her face in his mane, arms around his neck, chattering like a moron. Just because she needed to share the exhilaration, the burgeoning love for this tiny life inside, even if it was just with an old horse.

Could she share with him, the father of her baby? Skylar wanted to, but she didn't know how to take this grim stranger. He was so different from the attentive, respectful man she had fallen for a few months ago.

Zack's impending return had filled her with a mixture of excitement and trepidation. Would a week see him reconciled to the pregnancy, more reasonable about his insistence on marriage to a virtual stranger?

If today was anything to go by, she was inclined to think not.

Zack arched his spine, acknowledging his body's exhaustion. He'd crossed umpteen time zones in the last week between the States, New Zealand and Australia and then back to the States. There were arrangements to make for an indefinite absence from his substantial franchise conglomerate. Luckily his winemaker had completed harvesting in Zack's absence and there wasn't much going on at the new stud right now as the foaling and breeding seasons were the opposite of the northern hemisphere. Managing the weanlings comprised the main business at this time of year.

He looked down at his three-hundred-dollar shirt and the expensive suit pants that were now streaked with horse sweat and dust. It was fair to say it hadn't been a good week.

The rage seeped away but there was enough residue to narrow his eyes when he looked at her. It would take a while to get over seeing the expectant mother of his baby walking up to twelve hundred pounds of loose and agitated horseflesh.

But she did look good, more magnificently pregnant than a week ago. There was no mistaking it now.

A wave of fatigue made him light-headed. Every muscle, every sinew, had jumped to attention and been stretched to the limit. It was adrenaline, jet lag and a measure of stress. He was dead on his feet.

"The doctors are happy?" It was an effort to un-clench his jaw.

She nodded, relaxing a little.

"How did your family take the news?"

Skylar sucked on her bottom lip gently then released it with a small smacking noise. "With varying degrees of amazement."

That's what her brother had told him when he phoned two days ago. Zack respected Blake's direct-ness. He was almost friendly once satisfied of Zack's intention to marry his sister and that he had no interest in milking the family's coffers. He even suggested they double up, as he and his fiancée, Sasha, were planning a winter wedding.

Blake had also warned him to tread carefully with Trina, his and Skylar's mother. Apparently she liked to meddle in the Fortune's affairs, even to the extent of supplying the tabloids with false information about her own children.

"What about yours?" Skylar asked.

His head raised. The jury was still out on how much to divulge about a rather unusual family situation with his soon-to-be wife. "Surprised," he told her. "But in-creasingly happy about becoming a granddad."

She looked as if she expected more. Less was more, especially concerning his father. "He's not in the pic-ture much."

"Is your mother…"

Zack nodded. "She died four years ago after a long illness." He paused, watching her face carefully. "They hadn't been together for some time." What would she feel about that? Skylar Fortune was, after all, a horse breeder. Lineage was important to her, although her own parents did not have a great track record in that respect.

He found only honest curiosity there. Her clear skin and eyes, the slight parting of her wide, shapely lips had him struggling to believe what Blake had let slip on the phone. It was an innocent enough comment, but it confirmed Zack's suspicions that he was set up four months ago at the wedding. Set up for seduction by this innocent-looking woman.

Why? Was it just about the baby? Did she want the baby, not the man?

He hardened his heart. No one, not Skylar nor her wealthy family was going to cut him out of his baby's life and run him out of town.

He exhaled and pushed himself slowly to his feet. "I'm beat. I'll see you tomorrow. Do the boys log on at six or…"

Skylar nodded.

"So you get to sleep in," he commented, picking up his jacket.

"It's not necessary, Zack." She rose also. "The boys can manage. They've been doing so for the last few weeks, mostly."

"Shall I walk you back to the cottage?"

She declined. "I have some calls to make. I think I'll postpone Ace's cover this afternoon. I can't risk him hurting a mare. And I'll get the vet out to have a look."

"Don't you go near him," Zack warned.

She shook her head. "I won't. Are you staying up at the big house?"

Zack's eyes moved slowly over her. "I'm open to a better offer."

She rewarded him with a blush. "How long will you stay?"

"Depends on you. But just so you know, we have weeks, not months, Skylar. I have pressing business commitments right now."

Her shoulders drooped and she looked away.

This wasn't the way it was meant to be. Their reunion should have been pleasant. So far he'd given her ten different reasons to turn him down. But he was tired. He was angry for what she'd put him through today and for the inadvertent comment Blake had made on the phone. He was deeply worried that his own father was spinning wheels on the other side of the world that would have a devastating impact here.

A yawn caught him unawares. Zack was in no shape to go five rounds about a wedding right now. It would be enough to make the ten-minute walk up to the house without collapsing. "Don't reject us without giving it a go," he murmured, then hoisted his jacket and felt the lump in the pocket. "Here's a DVD I made of my home and the vineyard and the stud. Forgive the quality—I haven't had much practice at home movies." He handed her the disc and headed for the door, his head spinning with exhaustion.

Four

"I did not!" Skylar's voice rose in indignation. There was no way she'd canceled the Clendon mare.

Her head groom, Bob Keen, slid his cap back and scratched his forehead.

"What did he say, exactly?"

Bob had called the Nebraskan breeder when the maiden mare hadn't arrived as arranged.

"That a woman phoned yesterday claiming to be you and left a message that Black Power's season was cut short because of a paddock accident."

Skylar shook her head in bewilderment. "That's baloney. I postponed his afternoon serve because of Deme's little stint but I definitely haven't canceled anyone." She sighed. "I'd better call him."

"Don't bother," Bob told her, rising. "He's already

made other arrangements. She's been palpated and she's ready to go. He didn't want to risk waiting."

Dammit, she was looking forward to doing business with the man from Omaha. His broodmares were well regarded and he rarely dealt with stud farms outside a select two or three in Kentucky. His approach was made on the recommendation of another Nebraskan breeder. Whatever the misunderstanding was, it left her operation looking less than professional.

"While you're here," she said to Bob as he turned to go, "did you find out who left Deme's stall unlatched yesterday?"

Bob sighed heavily and screwed his face up. "Could've been any one of us," he said in his slow drawl.

Skylar gave him a skeptical look as he left her office, knowing he wouldn't rat on one of the boys. It was worth mentioning only because she needed to remind everyone she was still the boss around here. Truthfully, she hadn't been pulling her weight since she'd learned she was pregnant.

But she wasn't overly worried. She trusted in Bob's authority. Whoever left that latch open would hear it from the sharp end of his tongue and it would be a whole lot worse than if she said anything.

Hearing voices, she wandered over to the window, not for the first time today. It had only been one morning and Skylar was sick of four walls already. The allure of paperwork lost its appeal while *he* was barely ten feet away, bending his long back over a shovel or broom, bantering with the boys.

Zack Manning looked like he'd slept well. Looked like he belonged here, mucking out stables, leading the horses out to pasture, washing down the mares for their stints in the receiving barn. She strained her ears as the unfamiliar accent drifted in through her open window, startlingly different from the other men's lazy drawling dialect.

One thing was plain: the boys liked him. Everybody did, including her family. Most likely they were surprised that he'd even bothered with her, let alone want to sleep with her.

Certainly no one had thought to ask what she wanted. All the talk centered on weddings and reputations. Her family was probably fearful that, if she didn't hurry up, she'd lose the only guy who would ever ask her.

Dragging her jacket on, she chose an apple from the fruit bowl on her desk—apples were her only craving so far—and decided to stretch her legs. Zack looked up from his shoveling, midsentence, and watched her pass.

"Keep your shirt on, Manning," she said snippily as she breezed past the men in the yard. "I'm just going to give old Roscoe a treat." Ignoring the curious stares of the grooms, she tugged the peak of her cap down and must have even tossed her head, because her long braid thumped on her back a couple of times.

Behind her, Zack said something to Ben, the youngest and newest member of her team of workers. She heard a snort of laughter then the clang of a shovel hitting the fence. Her heartbeat ratcheted up a notch when she sensed determined footfalls coming after her but she did not slow.

Roscoe raised his head and ambled toward her. She took out her pocket knife and began to cut the apple into slices, taking a bite from one.

"How old is he?" Zack's frame leaned on the fence beside her.

"Twenty-one."

The old bay blew softly as he drew near and rubbed his face and ear against the fence, inviting a scratch from Zack.

"Since I'm not allowed to ride, I hope you figured in some exercise for old Roscoe here." That would teach him for being so dictatorial, she thought, amused. "A bit of a jog for an hour every other day should do it."

"Ben's lighter," Zack pointed out.

"Ben only has one speed, flat-out."

There was a burst of laughter from the men over by the stable. Skylar looked around. The three faces were turned their way.

"It's about me being the father."

"You *told* them?"

He shrugged. "I confirmed it. They'd noticed you…" his eyes flicked down to her midriff "…weren't yourself and they're wondering what I'm doing here." It was his turn to sound amused.

"What's so funny?" she demanded, her eyes still on the men.

Zack exhaled. "I told Ben to spread the word. If any of them see you near a loose horse," he paused "shoot the damn horse."

Skylar's eyes shot back to his face. He hadn't smiled but there was a sparkle in his eyes as he squinted into the midmorning sun. She decided not to give him the satisfaction of a response so she turned back to slicing the apple and offering it to Roscoe. Her old faithful had his nose buried in Zack's sleeve, eyes closed in bliss as his ears were given a good old-fashioned scratch.

She sighed. Just because every living thing on this estate had taken a shine to Zack Manning didn't mean she had to go along. Holding out the apple, she took three or four steps along the fence, coaxing Roscoe toward the new automatic livestock waterer. "Come on, boy, have a drink." He hated freezing cold water so she'd given him a treat and had his own heated water trough installed.

"What are you up to today?" Zack asked, taking a slice of fruit from her fingers and offering it to the horse.

"I'm going into town shortly. I've got some grain and stuff to pick up."

"Want some help?"

"Nope." She needed a few things that weren't exactly on her supply list.

"Don't you be lifting…"

"I won't," she told him quickly, turning to reassure him.

He was closer than expected when their eyes met. Skylar sucked in a breath, unprepared for the shake-up her nerve endings were getting.

It was not the first time. Her quick slide into a one-sided magnum crush began in January when she, Zack and Max, her Australian cousin a couple of times removed, had spent a few days flying around the Midwest. They were looking at horses for a stud farm the two men were setting up in New Zealand. Had he guessed of her infatuation? Was he planning to railroad her into something she wasn't ready for by laying on the charm?

She recalled the first time she'd met her cousin after Nash and Patricia had told the Australian Fortunes of her small breeding operation. They hit if off immediately, with Max ribbing her unmercifully from day one. She enjoyed his irreverent and quirky humor and, if Zack hadn't been there, would have given as good as she got.

But he *was* there, quiet, alert, respectful. From what Max said, he was a sharp businessman who had amassed a fortune in a very few years. His desire to learn the breeding business and admiration for her knowledge was enough of an attraction from the start.

But Skylar's uncharacteristic fascination with his dimples, watchful eyes, muscular build should have set the alarm bells clanging. They were forever in close quarters—tiny planes, stalls, cabs. Just a couple of days into their visit, she morphed into a breathless, red-faced wreck every time he looked at her. The instances where they brushed hands or arms nearly paralyzed her.

Like now. He watched her as if he knew the hairs were doing the quickstep on the back of her neck.

"I, um, better go," she stammered, pushing the remaining fruit into Roscoe's soft nose.

"Let's get together later."

"Wh-why?" God, she was such an idiot.

Zack sighed, his eyes on her face. "Talk. Drink coffee. Get to know each other."

"Oh. At my place?"

He nodded.

Okay, she could handle that…if she kept reminding herself it was her turf.

"Did you watch the DVD last night?"

She wiped the blade of the pocket knife and closed it. "You have a…" she shrugged, not used to giving compliments, "…nice home." Maybe tonight would be a great idea, serve as an icebreaker. "And some beautiful horses." Reminded, she smiled at her drooling, chomping pet. "Who lives there with you?"

"Just me."

That was a lot of house for one person. "Where does your father live?"

"Not far away, but don't worry. He's not on the door-step every five minutes."

Why should she be worried? "No brothers or sisters?"

He shook his head. Roscoe nibbled on his sleeve while he told her about the skiing and beaches all within a half hour of the valley and the nearby city of Christ-church, a couple of times the size of Sioux Falls.

"A city in training," he said with a smile. "But there're theatres and nightclubs, if that's your bent, and plenty of good eating places. There are some closer smaller towns. You don't have to go far for supplies, whether for entertaining or business."

"Do you entertain a lot?" She was so unsophisti-cated. Her relations, especially Eliza, were much more comfortable in social situations than she was.

Zack grinned. "Yeah, it's pretty racy. We have a Christmas party for the workers and other farmers around the district. It's the talk of the tabloids for months."

Skylar broke into a reluctant smile. She liked him so much…the old feelings returned full force. "Front-page news, right?"

He reached out and slapped the old horse on the flank. "I had my share of action when Max and I were out conquering the world. About three years ago, I'd had enough of the rat race and public attention and retired myself to the quiet country life."

"Are you and Max famous?"

"He's a lot more famous, or infamous, than I am. We

have had some spectacular successes over the years and one or two gigantic failures. I'm not unknown down in my neck of the woods but it's fairly unobtrusive." He paused. "Would you miss that? Being gossiped about?"

Her braid flopped over her shoulder as she shook her head. "No, sir. Though I haven't exactly set the papers on fire." Skylar looked down and caught sight of her bulge pushing out under her jacket. *Until now,* she amended silently.

"Publicity can be a double-edged sword," Zack said, his expression becoming serious. He fell silent, looking out over the pasture.

Skylar picked up her supplies then parked her car in the shopping district, intending to spend ten minutes refreshing her wardrobe. With an armful of low-waisted jeans, bib overalls and large-sized T-shirts, she headed for the checkout but paused at a rack of spring dresses. Some of the colors were out of this world, not that she would have a clue what suited her. "Where are you, when I need you, Eliza?" she muttered under her breath, It wouldn't hurt to try a couple on, especially as she was now effectively an office worker.

Some time later, she found herself in the beauty salon. Trying on dresses was all very well but it was painfully obvious that the last—and first time—she'd had her legs waxed was Case and Gina's wedding.

It made good use of time to allow Roz to fuss with her hair while she was there, clucking over its dry condition. Things escalated from there. There wasn't much she could do while the foul smelling foil-tips color developed so she did not demur at the suggestion of a manicure and pedicure. "It's a slow day," Roz told her, "lucky for you."

Two and a half hours later and several hair shades lighter, she emerged from the salon, tingling all over. Luckily there was an old rubber band in the lining of her pocket, so with that and her cap, she was able to hide a lot of the damage. But on the way to the car, she passed the boutique Eliza had dragged her into the week before Case's wedding.

The dress in the window was the most fantastic shade of russet. She stood there gawking for so long that the assistant came to the door.

"Nice to see you again, Ms. Fortune."

Skylar mumbled something as she was drawn into the shop, unable to take her eyes off that dress.

"That burnt sienna color would look gorgeous on you. How did the jade outfit go a few months ago? Your brother's wedding, wasn't it?"

Eliza obviously shopped here a lot for this woman to remember her one encounter with Skylar.

The woman slid the dress off the hanger. "Do you have a strapless bra?"

She couldn't help sniggering. Luckily, the boutique carried a range of designer undergarments. This day was turning into a roller coaster she seemed unable to stop. Why was she doing it? Did she want to make herself more attractive for him?

"I need new clothes, that's all," she muttered, patting her bulge. "Nothing fits."

The assistant's eyes lit up.

Much later, she slid her battered black leather wallet into her back pocket and hurried to the car before her credit card vomited all over her purchases. At home, it took two trips to lug all the bags upstairs. She dumped them unceremoniously onto her bed and flopped down herself. "Impossible," she moaned, kicking off her Doc Martens and rubbing her nicely pedicured but aching feet. Some women actually found shopping pleasurable. Apparently, pregnant women left their modesty at the door. Skylar's tingling-all-over body reminded her that a great deal of it had been stripped, scrutinized and sometimes painfully attended to today.

A knock at the door galvanized her. Checking that not too much weird-smelling hair showed under her cap, she hurried downstairs, wondering if her depleted eyebrows still looked as surprised as they felt. If he said so much as a word…

Zack leaned on the door, tilting his head to peer at her face. "You've done something to your hair."

Skylar heaved a sigh. "Just a trim," she lied and stalked into the kitchen without extending an invitation. It was difficult to walk normally after a bikini wax, another first.

Zack watched while she self-consciously made some coffee. She wasn't used to being watched. Wasn't used to any of this. Her nose twitched at the delicious aroma of his real coffee. Instant decaf just wasn't the same.

He sat at her kitchen table and she brought the drinks over and cleared a place amidst the clutter.

Zack's eyes followed the progress of a book she tossed on top of the pile and his tan seemed to fade. He reached across and picked it up. "Baby names," he read before looking up into her face.

A rush of embarrassment heated her skin. "It's a little early for that, I know," she mumbled.

He exhaled slowly. "I haven't given it any thought." He searched her face. "Have you?"

"Not really."

"Do you know what sex it is?"

No, and that suited her fine. "I had a scan last week but I asked them not to tell me. Do you want to see the picture?" She rose and found the ultrasound picture in a drawer in the kitchen. Zack's eyes widened when she placed it in front of him. It was a long time before he looked up again.

Skylar studied his earnest expression over the rim of her cup, feeling guilty. Last week it had occurred to her to reschedule the scan so he could attend but her nerve failed her. The image of lying spread out and bare bellied in front of him was way too personal for the current status of their relationship. If it *was* a relationship.

He shrugged helplessly. "You'll have to show me."

Skylar scooted her chair closer, not close enough to touch him, and pointed out all the important bits.

After a long time, Zack leaned back and put his hands behind his head but his eyes remained on the photo. "How often do they do the ultrasound?"

She stood and moved her chair back to the head of the table. "That's it unless there are problems." To avoid witnessing the disappointment on his face, she transferred her attention to sorting through a stack of mail on the table.

"Speaking of doctors," he finally looked up at her face, "I had the works done while I was home last week. Blood tests, HIV, X-rays and a complete history. There is nothing genetic for us to be worried about."

That was something she had not even considered. She opened her mouth to tell him she had no idea about her family genetics when he fixed her with a very intense look.

"That means I'm safe."

The air whistled in through her nostrils and she blinked and looked away. Sex. He was referring to sex, between them, in the future. Unprotected sex…

Her heart started thumping.

Zack's mouth dried. He knew when a woman was thinking about sex, with him. He'd seen this before from her, months ago. But then she changed the game plan after the event. Backed off and closed up completely.

He supposed that to a woman, especially a shy woman like Skylar, her first time would be a lot to process. So despite his surprise and disappointment, he'd allowed her to avoid him the day after they'd made love. But then he got called home urgently and did not even get the opportunity to say goodbye. Instead he made plans to return later in the year for the Keeneland sales in Kentucky, knowing that she and Nash always attended. He kept in contact by phone and decided that, unless he met someone else that touched him the way she did, he would push matters then.

Circumstances had changed. Whether by accident or design, she was carrying his child. No one would run him off this time.

What had Blake said? That she must have set her cap for him that night because no one had ever seen her take the slightest interest in her appearance before. The whole family had been as shocked as he was when she walked into the wedding reception looking so glamorous.

If this whole thing was a plan to get him into bed and get pregnant, why not tell him as soon as she knew about the baby? Unless a baby was the prize she coveted. The objective.

Zack did not have the time to be considerate and patient. "The night of Case's wedding," he said, watching her closely. "Did you plan it so we'd end up together?"

Her cornflower-blue gaze skittered away from his face. "Not planned, exactly." Her fingers twisted together. "Hoped, maybe."

There was guilt all over her face. Even her eyebrows looked inflamed. "Is this what you wanted, Skylar? Was I just the means to an end?"

She did look at him then, a real look, not the usual over-the-left-shoulder look. "It was your condom, Zack," she told him softly.

Hell, of course it was. "I know."

Her shoulders jerked. "Dumb luck, that's all." She rubbed her eye with a knuckle and gave a self-deprecating smile. "I can't even get sex right."

She must be joking! Memories of the passion and pleasure they'd shared flashed again in his mind, like a hundred times before. If it wasn't for Maya's untimely arrival— Which reminded him. "Did you forget to lock the door that night or does Maya have a key?" Zack had been so consumed with lust at the time, intent on unlocking much more intimate doors, that he hadn't considered the possibility of an intrusion.

"I hardly ever lock it. It's private land."

He wrenched his thoughts back to the present. "You will from now on," he warned, holding her gaze. "You're too isolated out here between the stables and the house."

He made a mental note to check the lock on the way out. "Independence is one thing, Skylar, but you don't have to go through all this on your own."

Her cheeks puffed out a breath. "Well, now everybody knows, I'm guessing I won't be left on my own for a minute."

He sharpened his look.

Skylar raised her hands. "I only meant that I'm not used to the attention. No one notices me usually. I'm just little Skylar, playing houese with her horses." She wrinkled her nose. "Eeww! That sounded tragic, didn't it?"

"You sure got my attention," he said with feeling.

"How did you see it, my attraction, so quickly, Zack? No one else noticed but you knew straight away."

He'd wondered about that, himself. "It was written all over your face."

She looked down and passed her hand over her eyes. "I was so embarrassed about that night. I couldn't believe it when you called. And kept calling."

"I liked you right from the start, Skylar. You knew that."

"How'm I supposed to know? I've never even had a boyfriend before."

Zack put his elbows on the table and steepled his hands. "And now you're going to be a mother."

"It feels…" She leaned back and laid her hands on her belly. "How can you go your whole life and not know how much you wanted something?" She looked up at him with wonder. "It just feels right."

His eyes glued to her hands. A longing so deep, so wrenching, assailed him. "*This* feels right, Skylar. Us. Come home with me."

Apprehension chased the wonder on her face away. "I want you to be involved, Zack, but you must see that marriage is just too big a step."

"I'll make up for whatever you lose by moving away," he vowed.

"You'll make up for my family, my business?"

"You just said your family never notices you. As for the horses, you can be equal partners with Max and I. Call it a wedding gift from us both."

"He might have something to say about that."

"Max would be delighted. You'd not be coming empty-handed. With your knowledge and contacts here, we'll make it the best stud operation in the country. Bring Ace, if you want."

"He's syndicated," Skylar mumbled. "It's not just up to me."

"We talked about shuttling him a few months ago and you were all for it. Skylar, we can work all this out later. You write your ticket, your prenup, whatever. Just let's get it done."

She looked up from under her lashes and set her mouth in a stubborn line. "You've got an answer for everything, haven't you? Zack, I need more time."

"If you'd told me earlier of the pregnancy, we could have had all the time in the world. The way things are now, my business commitments don't allow me the time." He inhaled and swallowed the frustration he heard creeping into his tone. "Is this because you haven't had a boyfriend before? You want romance. I can do that, Skylar, after the wedding. But right now, I want you settled and happy well before the baby is born."

"Settled and happy," she murmured, as if to herself. "You know, Zack, you're right. I haven't had much of a love life. I should probably be grateful to you for saving me from certain spinsterhood." His exasperated sigh didn't move her. "And it's true that I like you better than I've ever liked anyone."

She met his eyes now and hers were resolute, reminding him that he would not get things all his way with this woman. Shy little Skylar was growing in more ways than one.

"But I have a baby to consider now. I will be making decisions with this—" her hand moved over the swell of her belly "—foremost in my mind." She jutted out her chin defiantly. "I am Skylar Fortune from South Dakota. You need to give me a bunch of reasons why I should become a New Zealander in such an all-fired rush."

Well, well. She was certainly beggaring his first impressions. Pregnancy had upped her confidence and, although part of him wanted to shake her, his admiration grudgingly grew. "Your own father thinks we have a lot to build on. *I* think we have a lot to build on."

There was a ghost of a smile on her face, but she directed it at her stomach. "That's because I have something you want. At least be honest about it, Zack."

His eyes narrowed. "I *am* being honest about it."

"You're well traveled, sophisticated. Used to going out to nice restaurants and parties and probably have a dozen beautiful women you can call up at anytime. Zack, I'm not one of those women. I'm not like that. This is me." She swept her hands down in front of her. "Not that girl at the wedding."

"I'm not asking you to be the girl at the wedding," Zack argued. "I liked you before that. I think you're gorgeous in jeans, or out of them, for that matter."

She huffed impatiently, flushing. "It's the baby you want, not me."

Zack rose abruptly and leaned over her chair, sliding one arm firmly around her waist. "Are you sure about that, Skylar?" Lifting her so that her backside was right off the seat and only her stocking toes touched the floor, he crushed his lips down on hers.

He remembered her mouth. Wide, sweetly curved and irresistible. Her name smiled through his mind like a warm welcome. He felt again what he had months ago, that she fit. That he wanted to be with her in some way that was important and bewildering. Anticipation was sweet on his tongue.

It took a few seconds but she responded with tentative acceptance. He pulled her more firmly against him and felt her hands clutch at his shoulders and the weight of her body shift, as if she flowed up into him. Desire pumped loudly in his ears and he nearly forgot his purpose. Easy does it, don't scare her, he reminded himself. This is just a taste.

He pulled back from her mouth and opened his eyes. She released a strangled breath from the back of her throat and it sounded like a protest. Because he'd kissed her or because he'd stopped? Regretfully, he set her gently back on the chair and her hands slid off his arms. She swallowed.

"Did that feel like a man who doesn't want you?" Zack was still bending over her, only an inch away from her face so his question was just above a whisper.

Skylar's long dark lashes fluttered open at the sound of his voice. She sucked her lower lip into her mouth, shaking her head.

He straightened and frowned down at her. "Okay, then. Romance it is, starting with dinner tomorrow night, just the two of us." He would sweep her off her feet, but at the end of it, he would have what he wanted. His ring on her finger and both of them winging their way back to New Zealand.

"But I warn you, I don't have time to play games. I need to be back home in New Zealand and I need you there with me."

He walked to the door, jiggling the lock a couple of times. It seemed to be working fine. "And just for the record—" he paused, waiting for her to look at him "—you got the sex perfectly right that night. Your only mistake was not locking the door."

Five

Nothing was going right! Skylar pouted at her reflection in the mirror. She couldn't find the butterfly clip of one of her only pair of earrings. There was barely a scrape of lip gloss left in the pot and the expensive perfume Eliza had given her for her twenty-first birthday wasn't her taste.

But the dress looked good. Better than good, she decided, turning this way and that in the big bathroom mirror.

Like the flesh of a russet apple, the rich color did something for her skin that made even her stupid freckles look okay. The split was indecent but worrying about that diluted her self-consciousness about the soft crepe fabric hugging her middle.

Personally she thought that looked beautiful. Seventeen weeks of pregnancy poked pridefully out against the dress, demanding attention.

And then her courage deserted her. Men liked flat tummies and big boobs, didn't they? The push-up strapless bra certainly enhanced her chest but she doubted Zack would even notice. All he'd see was that she appeared to have swallowed a small cantaloupe.

Why the heck hadn't she bought a tent to wear?

Close to tears by the time he knocked, she had a mind to turn out the lights and pretend not to be home. Darn pregnancy hormones. Darn Eliza, too, for being so far away. She could always rely on Eliza to make a silk purse out of a sow's ear.

Resigned, she picked up her shoes and the lovely raw silk wrap she had borrowed from Maya and tiptoed down the stairs. A full minute ticked by while she stood with her hand on the doorknob, squeezing her eyes shut to contain an unfamiliar panic.

Is this what you want, Zack Manning?

He'd raised his hand to knock again when she opened the door.

"I thought you'd—" his eyes moved from her face slowly down her body "—stood me up." He swallowed when his gaze reached her belly.

He was still staring when Skylar laughed nervously. "You have no idea how close I came." She moved aside and motioned him in.

Zack carried his jacket hooked in one finger over his shoulder. She tossed her shoes on the step and followed, thinking he did not look much like her stable hand tonight in dark pinstripes and a crisp white shirt. In fact, he was so handsome, she was reluctant to look at him out of fear that he'd see how much he affected her.

Zack turned at the fireplace and gave her another long look that seemed to soak through her skin and drug the flapping butterflies in her stomach. For a second, anyway.

"Wow!"

It sounded like "Whoa."

"You scrub up pretty well, Ms. Fortune."

Skylar twisted the wrap in her hands. "I'm a little worried." She looked down, grimacing. "About…" Her fingers fluttered in a nervous pass over her stomach.

His smile faded fast. "Worried?"

She warmed at his concern. "Not worried. Nervous." She took a quick breath and met his eyes. "I seem to have gained about a ton today."

Zack looked at her, his eyes crinkling at the corners. "You look…" he shook his head, as if he couldn't believe it "…amazing."

And suddenly, it was all right. The butterflies subsided and she realized how much she was looking forward to tonight. She *did* want to be seen with him, to sit in a fancy restaurant and have every women in the room envy her. To have his eyes focus on her all evening, ulterior motive and all. Just for tonight, Skylar wanted to try romance.

"Can I ask a favor?"

He looked at her expectantly.

"Can we just have, like, a first date? No talk of the future or weddings or even babies. Just two people trying to get to know each other."

Zack nodded. "We can." Then he pulled his jacket over his shoulder and reached into the inside pocket. "Almost forgot."

He drew out a long flat box covered in midnight blue velvet. Her heart stuttered. She'd never received a gift from a man before, unless you counted her family. She stepped forward shyly and their hands bumped as she shoved her wrap at him and took the box.

It was like nothing she had ever seen. Shades of sea-green and indigo and sunrise smoldered in front of her eyes. The colors of the necklace glowed like the shell of the mollusk depicted on a blurb pasted to the inside of the lid.

Skylar pursed her lips and breathed out the letter *P*.

"Paua. It's a species of abalone found down our way."

"And these are like pearls?"

Zack lifted the exquisite white gold chain. "A man-made particle is embedded by hand under the shell." He indicated she turn around. "Two or three years later, the pearl is harvested. The paua are farmed just for this process and like the real pearl, you don't always get a result."

His hand, roughened from his labors at the barn, brushed her hair from her nape, making her tingle. The three vertically set shimmering discs, interspersed with three small emerald-cut diamonds, nestled against her breastbone.

With his hands on her shoulders, he maneuvered her in front of the mirror above the fireplace. The person who stared back was a stranger. The necklace lent her a simple elegance she'd never possessed, complimented not only the structure of her neck but the texture of her skin and shape of her face.

Even more astonishing was Zack's face behind her, filled with pride and a hint of tender surprise, as if he'd been the one given an unexpected and cherished gift. They stared at each other for several moments before he bent and kissed her bare shoulder, a soft, lingering kiss that reassured and aroused at the same time.

Then he raised his head and looked at the necklace. "Uniquely New Zealand," he said softly, laying her wrap around her shoulders. "I had it made just for you."

She floated out to the car, feeling like Cinderella on her way to the ball. Her fingers hardly strayed from the beautiful necklace on the drive into town, loving the rich smoothness of it on her skin and fingertips.

They waited to be seated. This was not the most exclusive restaurant in town but it had built its reputation on romance and intimacy. It was dim and the tables were set around partitioning walls, bars and large potted plants, so once seated, the diners did not feel they were in a room full of other tables, because they were mostly hidden.

Zack's hand pressed on her lower back as they were led to their table but she checked at the sight of a familiar brown head.

"Creed!" The sole occupant of the table looked up, his mouth dropping open.

"Skylar." Creed half rose. "Wow. You look…"

Zack leaned toward him, hand outstretched.

"Hello, Zack. We haven't caught up." They shook hands.

Creed obviously hadn't been out to the estate since Zack's return.

"You have really come out of the closet," he commented with a pointed look at her midriff. "Are you sure it's wise to advertise?"

Skylar was busy checking out his table for signs of a companion. What was Creed doing in the most romantic restaurant in town, eating alone? "What do you want, to cram me into a girdle?"

"A little discretion goes a long way in this town when your surname happens to be Fortune." He paused, his eyes flicking from Skylar to Zack. "Unless of course you're about to announce your engagement."

You could always count on Creed and Case to have the best interests of the family reputation closest to their hearts. "You would have me locked up with my head shaved if you could," she retorted. "Talking of being discreet, what are you doing in this den of discretion? Is this where you bring your women?"

Creed gave a melancholy smile and glanced at the lone glass and solo setting.

She grinned. "Don't tell me you've been stood up?"

He shook his head. "I often eat here, alone or otherwise."

She immediately felt sorry and put her hand on his arm. "I guess it's not easy for you, seeing Sasha with Blake."

"Sasha and I were just friends and colleagues. She was helping me out."

They referred to his ex-employee who had accompanied Creed to public functions and social events for the last year or so, until Skylar's brother Blake swept her off her feet and they announced their engagement last month. Was Creed missing her? It was hard to tell. No one could accuse Creed of being lighthearted about anything.

"You'll find someone nice soon." The second the words were out of her mouth, she thought how patronizing and smug she sounded. Just because, for once in her life, she had *someone nice* take her out tonight and buy her precious jewelry.

Her guilt intensified when Creed looked positively glum. "Someone nice? I doubt that's possible."

Her curiosity bubbled up. Creed was often stern but she would not have described him as without hope.

"Don't worry about me," Creed said. "I'm just feeling a little sorry for myself." He gave her a wry grin. "Unrequited love is a terrible thing."

This was a night for surprises. Skylar's eyes widened and she opened her mouth but her half brother held up his hand. "And before you ask, no, I don't want to talk about it."

"Oh, but…"

Zack came to Creed's aid with an easy grin. "I'd ask you to join us, mate, but I'm working on that engagement you mentioned."

She forgot all about Creed and frowned at Zack. "You promised."

He nodded his head toward the maître d' who still hovered, waiting to see them to their table. "Shall we go eat?" he asked, an amused smile on his lips.

She turned back to Creed, who also looked amused. "I hate to see you sitting here, being miserable on your own."

"I'm not miserable. You run along." He turned to Zack. "The salmon is excellent here."

"What about the unrequited love?" She pouted. "Spill."

"Good night, Skylar. Zack. Enjoy your evening."

Zack tugged on her hand and she reluctantly moved off.

"Oh, and, Sky?"

She turned back.

"Pregnancy agrees with you. You look stunning."

Her mouth dropped open for a second. A compliment, from Creed. Almost unheard of. She let Zack lead her away, deep in thought.

They sat and ordered wine for Zack and a spiced tomato juice for Skylar. Her mind raced with possibilities about her half brother's heartache. Who was the mystery woman? It would be too terrible if it were Sasha, despite his claims to the contrary.

"Hey, you." Zack's gently chiding voice brought her eyes back to his face. "We're supposed to be having a romantic dinner together, not wondering about your brother's love life."

"Sorry." She smiled at him. "I've never wondered about his love life in the past. He always seems so distant."

He shrugged. "So the man has a heart."

"And it's hurting. Poor Creed. He makes out like he's got it all together. Maybe I've misjudged him."

The drinks and menus arrived. Skylar was suddenly ravenous and her mouth watered at the descriptions of the dishes, although fine dining was nothing new for someone brought up on the Fortune Estate. However, sitting across a candlelit table from a man who set her heart vibrating like wheels over a cattle guard, was a unique experience. Her eyes flicked around the room. There were probably thirty or forty people here but the clever arrangement meant she could only see two tables clearly. Both couples, both quite young. She wondered if they were in love or breaking up, discussing business or cheating on their wives.

"You grew up with Creed and Case, didn't you?" Zack asked after the waiter finished taking their orders.

"And Eliza, yes."

"Why are you so distant?"

"Blake and I always felt like the poor cousins." She played with the swizzle stick in her juice. "They never forgave my mother for cheating on Dad. It was us against them." Her hand came up and fingered the lowest set pearl. "At least, it seemed that way when we were younger. I get on okay with them now in a sort of disconnected way. I know they're all concerned about me, as I am about them."

"My impression is they're all very fond of you. Now Blake, he's a different kettle of fish."

"Blake's always been confrontational. Especially after Dad handed the reins of the business to Case and Creed. He really felt that."

"He blames them?"

She nodded. "They offered him a place but he could never work under them. Still, he's done well for himself. I'm proud of him." She looked in the direction of her brother's table but could not see him. "I think Case and Creed are impressed by his achievements, too, even if they probably wouldn't say it."

As they ate, the talk mostly centered on horses and New Zealand. Zack kept his word and did not push her about weddings or the future. The meal was exquisite and Skylar reveled in his attention. She talked more about herself than she had ever done, due mostly to his skillful questioning.

"Have you always had a love affair with horses?"

"My father has always loved the track. He goes to all the big ones and the sales, too. My very first horse was a thoroughbred, Roscoe."

"Yet thoroughbreds are not that big here," Zack remarked.

"That's why it's such a thrill to have Black Power. Dad has a lot of contacts. He persuaded a big Kentucky breeder it would be a win-win situation to sell him to us for a fair price." She took a sip of water. "The breeder would get bragging rights and the industry would be better developed here. Nebraska and Minnesota are expanding their breeding and racing industries so they a good source of mares for me."

"And for Ace." He grinned.

After dessert, he sat back in his chair and just watched her for a minute or more without speaking. It was a measure of how comfortable Skylar felt that she did not mind his quiet study at all.

Finally, he spoke. "What gives, Skylar? Why is it that for the whole of the time I knew you until Case's wedding, you were this shy, stammering little thing who backed off whenever I looked at you and never dressed to impress—me or anyone?"

Dress to impress, one of her mother's mantras. High-impact impressions. That was Trina all over.

"Then the wedding," he continued. "You walked in with your head held high and made a beeline for me. We talked all night...danced." He raised his glass. "How do you do it? Go from one to the other?"

"Which do you prefer?" Her question was quiet but her heartbeat thumped in her ears.

"I can live with either," he replied seriously. "But it'll be a lot of fun guessing."

Max had once said his Kiwi friend was silver-tongued. Not in the smooth, glib, traditional sense, she decided, but he did often say exactly the right things.

"I blame you and Max for the night of the wedding." Skylar wrinkled her nose. "I liked you. I guess you knew that. Remember that day trip to my friend in Grand Island to see that stallion you were interested in shuttling? Max kept joshing me about not having a boyfriend to take to the wedding. Anyway, he said something crude and because you were there, I nearly died of embarrassment."

She glossed over it now but as much as she liked Max, she could have cheerfully throttled him that day.

"Freckles, you're too picky. Not surprising, given your occupation and proximity to the equine male reproductive organ. How can a mere man ever measure up?"

Skylar wouldn't have cared had Zack not been there. But given the infatuation that had gripped her by the throat over the last couple of weeks, her discomfort was intense. Through a haze of fire-engine red, she'd punched her cousin smartly on the arm, cursing him under her breath.

That wasn't the end of it.

"Then he said I had better watch out, that Eliza was after me to get all titivated up for the wedding."

"And I said—" Zack's eyes were bright with humor "—you wouldn't hold any truck with that rubbish, would you, Skylar? Fancy dresses, makeup, smelly perfume?"

She grimaced, recalling his muttered "give me horse sweat any day" comment.

"I was only trying to help," Zack insisted. "I could see you were embarrassed."

"Huh!"

"You stomped off then." He raised his eyes to the ceiling with an air of bafflement. "I said to Max I thought he'd offended you. He told me he thought what I'd said was much worse."

"Idiots, the pair of you," Skylar muttered.

That had been the catalyst. After a couple of weeks of wanting him to notice her. but feeling too shy to let him know, Skylar knew it was time to act or forever wonder. She was a twenty-four-year-old virgin. She had to sleep with someone, sometime. Why not the only man she had ever met who made her blood boil? "So, I thought, I'll show you. I can be grown-up and look good if I want to."

"So you let Eliza corner you."

"She's been trying most of my life to get me to look after my skin, cut my hair, get a manicure." Skylar smiled fondly. "I actually think Trina, my mother, had more of an influence on Eliza than she would own up to."

The best part of the whole plan was that he lived in New Zealand. Should Skylar miscalculate his interest or prove inferior in bed, then she didn't have to see him again. Her plan was perfect.

And to her surprise, things panned out so much better than she expected, until Maya's unfortunate interruption. For some reason, her brain functioned and she was able to conduct a conversation, even dance a step or two. For some reason, he seemed captivated by her. It was the best she had ever felt: knowing that she had turned his head, stole his breath, transfixed him for a few short hours.

He was as frantic with lust as she when they sneaked away from the post-wedding party at the big house and she dragged him upstairs to her bedroom. Their love-making would live on in her memory forever. Intense, four-hundred times more exciting than anything she had ever experienced and mind-numbingly satisfying.

Skylar looked down at her tummy. There was no way in the world she could have foreseen these consequences that night. What was it about getting dressed up that lent her confidence and poise and made her interesting to the opposite sex? A pretty dress was like a magic cloak, borrowed for a sliver of time. No doubt tomorrow, she would appear as tongue-tied, boring and scruffy as usual.

"I suppose I threw myself at you," she said wryly.

Zack shook his head. "You didn't have to. I came running." The smile faded. "And I didn't protect you that night. I feel bad about that."

She sighed, rubbing her bare arms. "It's not how I thought things would turn out. I wanted you to show me what it was all about, that's all."

"But you didn't want anything to do with me afterward."

"I did," she insisted. "I was ashamed. I wanted to believe I could carry off this cool, sophisticated rendezvous." She smiled down at her glass. "Instead, I ended up making a big mess of things."

Zack reached for her hand with both of his. Surprise and anticipation shivered through her, intensifying when she felt his feet under the table sandwich both of hers between them.

"Uh-uh." He shook his head. "I wouldn't have missed that for the world."

That rocked her. Part of her, a big part, fell in love with him right then. Even so, she worried she'd be burned. If he only knew that, should he mention marriage at this very minute, Skylar would probably clamber right over the tabletop to acquiesce.

The whisper-light touch of his fingers on her upturned palm sent a lick of excitement shooting up her arm. He shifted closer to the table and darned if she didn't, too, so that one of her knees was firmly trapped between both of his.

Zack laced his fingers with hers. "Why did you leave it so long to tell me?"

"I was a coward," she murmured, and looked away but her fingers squeezed his gently. "I've never been good with words and this was the biggest thing that ever happened to me. I wanted to keep it safe…I don't know. But I really was going to call you the night you arrived."

His thumb stroked along the inside of her wrist and their eyes met. He believed her, she could see that, even through the dizzying array of emotion and fear and rising excitement. His touch branded her and she shivered, wanting more.

Suddenly, everything seemed shiny and new. The flowers and candles on the table. The muted voices and low musical tones of some hidden stereo…the respect of the waiters. The man sitting opposite her with his sharp, wanting eyes. This was the stuff of her dreams since the moment Max introduced them. Would he clasp her hand and tell her quietly that he loved her?

The waiter slid her cup of decaf in front of her and she reluctantly pulled her hand from his, before she dissolved into fantasyland. "How did you and Max get together, anyway?"

Skylar knew her cousin and Zack were business partners but that was about it.

"We played rugby for university in Sydney," he replied, stirring his coffee. "Went traveling for a bit. When we came home, we pooled our resources…" He chuckled. "Mostly Max's resources, I would have to say, and set up a backpackers' bus company. It went off like a rocket. Pretty soon, there were thirty buses wandering around the country with our logo on them. It made sense to expand into New Zealand since most back-packers would travel both countries if they were going that far."

She frowned. "I'm confused. Are you a New Zeal-ander or an Australian?"

Zack paused, monitoring his thoughts. There was a limit to the amount of information he wanted to divulge at this point. "I grew up in Australia but my mother was a Kiwi and New Zealand feels like home now. I spent a couple of months setting up the bus company there and then we discovered franchises. It looked like a good opportunity to make a killing for half the work."

Both had been amazed at the roll of successes they accumulated in a very short time. With Max's sharp eye for a bargain and seemingly unlimited resources and Zack's cutthroat instincts toward marketing and eco-nomic trends, the pair were soon ensconced as a parent company of twenty or thirty different franchise compa-nies. They moved into the lucrative arena of the stock market. By then, they were household names.

Zack had, for a while, enjoyed the cut and thrust of business and gambling on the market. In all, they had spent less than a decade setting up an explosion of small home-based franchises that needed little guidance. There was a head office in Sydney and another office in Auckland.

Then Max wanted to take on more responsibility at his ranch and Zack suddenly found himself with a very good reason to tire of the publicity their risky and en-trepreneurial exploits attracted.

But he wouldn't go into that right now.

"I needed another challenge," he told her. "So I

moved down south and bought a winery, one that was just starting out and needed some decent marketing to make it fly."

"And the name Greta?"

Greta Wines and now Greta Stud were now the most important things in Zack's life, along with the woman and the baby she carried sitting across the table from him. "It was my mother's name." His mother's real name, as he found out when she died after a long battle with cancer.

Gill Manning was really Greta Thorne. All his life, she had adamantly refused to talk of his father, saying he was either in prison or dead. She told him he must never try to find out about him or great harm would come to both of them. Zack believed she really was afraid because they packed up and moved on every year or so. As he grew old enough and then rich enough to find out for himself, she made him promise to leave it alone. Only harm would come to both of them if he meddled in the past, she said. Later, when she fell ill, he didn't have the heart to go against her wishes.

But the day she died, his responsibility for her died, too. He needed to know. So he hired a private investigator to map out her life.

It was a shock to find his mother's family was *the* prominent family in New Zealand politics. There were two former prime ministers, and even now, his mother's oldest brother was the leader of the main opposition party.

But his reception with that esteemed family was anything but warm. They turned their backs, saying Greta had died for them the day she ran off to Australia.

"I thought it might be a girlfriend's name." Skylar folded her arms and leaned on the table, her eyes down.

Zack watched her chew on her bottom lip. The perfect out to change a subject he needed to keep under wraps for now. He lowered his head so he could see under her downcast face, encouraging her to look at him. "If you want to know, just ask," he told her, amused.

She looked into the flame of the candle and raised her shoulders.

"I was seeing a woman in Australia every month or so for a couple of years, but it was a very casual, open-ended thing. It suited both of us that way."

He had to strain to hear her question. "Was?"

"I finished it." He paused, then added, "The other day."

The flame of the candle wavered drunkenly with her exhalation but still she did not look at him. "Was she upset?"

"Not overly. We'll probably remain friends. I always seem to stay friends."

"What was she like? Pretty, I bet."

"Well, she didn't have your cute smile," he teased. "No freckles, poor thing, and her eyes were kind of muddy looking. Not like your baby blues."

She smiled and rested her flushed cheek in one hand. "You're making fun."

"Maybe." He was discovering he liked making her blush.

"So you bought the vineyard. Why the stud? They don't exactly go together."

"Max's idea. Over a few beers last year at the Melbourne Cup, we decided it would be fun to breed a winner."

Her brows furrowed. "You must be rich if you can afford to throw millions at a bit of fun."

"I do all right," he told her. "If that's what's worrying you."

Her lips curved a fraction. "We nearly made it through dinner."

Zack stroked his chin, wondering what it was about her smile that pulled at him. She was pretty, quite beautiful tonight, but nice dinners with lovely women weren't new for him. Forging closer personal ties was, and sometimes she made it difficult for him to remember that he was here for one purpose only—to secure a part in his son's or daughter's life and make up for all the years of being denied a family.

Sometimes she also made it difficult to remember when he'd ever wanted someone so badly... "But will we make it home before I kiss you?"

The drop of her necklace rippled as Skylar swallowed. She had no answer to that. Zack crossed his ankles around hers, trapping her again. She looked away but he saw the tremble in her fingers as she picked up and drained her coffee cup. When her other leg pressed tentatively against his a few seconds later, he could not help his satisfied smile.

Zack signaled the waiter for the check. He brushed her arms, settling her wrap around her shoulders and held her hand while they waited for the car to be brought around. As he leaned over her to open the door, their eyes met and held. Skylar finally broke the connection, by looking down at his mouth. Zack tipped her chin up with his index finger, employing his other hand to caress her skin under the foam of silk around her shoulders.

She was perfectly still, her arms by her sides, her lips slightly parted. Zack moved his bottom lip over the seam of her mouth until she raised her eyes to him. "I guess not…" he whispered. She did not move back and so he took her mouth, watching until her eyelids fluttered down.

He pressed her closer, kissing her deeply. Her hair was silky between his fingers. This wasn't just a taste now. Her night of romance, all wrapped up and tied with a bow. He used all his so-called expertise to show his desire and stoke hers.

But the joke was on him. Suddenly, he was starving for her, as if he hadn't just spent a couple hundred dollars on food. It was her mouth and skin he wanted and he feasted until the moment when he felt her knees began to buckle. Only then did he pull back and let her slide into the car.

Six

Barely breathing, she held herself still so she could not feel anything but the memory of his mouth on hers, his warm hand caressing her shoulder and pressing on her back, his fingers combing through her hair.

She had so little to compare his kisses to. A couple of uncomfortable fumbles at college and then that magical night a few months ago.

But tonight his kiss was quite different to the fire and passion he had overwhelmed her with before. Back then, he'd given her no room to move, no time to think. And that was just the way she wanted it. Tonight, he was much more measured—a planned seduction.

And again, that was just the way she wanted it.

His mouth had just the perfect touch of firm and a hint of need. The spread-out hand on her back suggested control and his fingers used her hair so gently to coax her head back to just the right angle to be kissed.

His kisses were intoxicating. How could she resist? And why would she want to?

Because time did not seem to register, it jolted her to hear the crunch of the estate's gravel driveway in her ears. Even louder was the silence when he rolled to a halt.

He'd turned the engine off. She had a decision to make.

And in her mind, Skylar had probably made the decision when he gave her the necklace.

So she took her keys from her purse and offered them to him, still staring straight ahead. "Because—I don't know how to say—" she faltered, feeling his eyes on her "—what I want…"

Seconds dragged by. She held out the keys like she was passing the salt. Wouldn't it be hysterical if he turned her down?

Finally, finally, she felt his warm hand on hers.

"Loud and clear," Zack said in a gruff voice and took the keys from her fingers. He got out of the car and she followed, waiting in an agony of nerves while he unlocked the door. She moved forward into the darkened hallway and heard the sharp double click of the door being closed and locked.

And then she felt his hands on her arms, his lips brushing her ear from behind.

"Can you—can you take the necklace off?" she whispered. "I don't want to break it."

His hands stroked up her arms and she shivered. She felt him release the catch and the slow slide of the chain and then his mouth on the top of her shoulder, chasing down her butterflies, whipping them into a frenzy.

Zack turned her gently to face him. His hand came up and cupped her face. "Nervous?"

Skylar nodded, swallowing hard.

"More than the first time?"

"Yes." She gulped, berating herself. It was a bit late to play the blushing virgin now. But four months ago, she'd had a couple of glasses of wine and several dances pressed up against his body. The knowledge that he'd be leaving in the morning. She was so eager, she'd practically torn his clothes off.

But this was another night. He bent his head. "Kiss me." He tapped the corner of his mouth with his index finger. "Here."

Skylar hesitated then rose up onto her toes and dusted a closed-mouth kiss where his finger had been. He smelled sexy and expensive and all male.

"Sweet." He slid one arm around her waist. "And here." He tapped the other corner of his mouth, his chin raised expectantly.

She did as he asked, recognizing that he was allowing her to set the pace. Emboldened, she raised her hands and caged his face, kissing him squarely on the mouth and lingering now. Parting her lips just a little. Tasting and breathing him in.

And suddenly, the nerves slid away and she felt comfortable enough to explore and indulge her curiosity. Her hands snaked around his neck and played with his hair, combing her fingers through. She kissed him a little harder then tried fisting her hands in his hair and tugging his head down with the slightest of pressure.

He slid his other arm around her waist and, still with her mouth locked on his, she pressed up against him, sighing with pleasure. And it was a pleasure. With her arms up around his neck, her whole body melded the length of his, soft curves against lean, tight muscle. His legs braced firmly as she leaned into him, her bulge between them the only scrap of distance.

The kisses deepened and her excitement grew. His tongue probed and now there was nothing tentative about her response. The thrill made her feel like a billion champagne bubbles, steeped in exhilaration. By the time he dragged his mouth off hers and backed up, leading her to the bottom of her stairs, Skylar had to force herself not to race him, just as she had that first night.

The bedroom was dark but she stayed his hand from the light switch. Zack took both ends of the wrap and slid it sideways, back and forth over her back and shoulders. The sensuous feel of the cool silk on her hot flesh warmed her and she arched, her tummy bumping him. To steady herself, she put her hands around his neck again and he moved forward and took her mouth.

The one or two times she had tried openmouthed kissing had been unmemorable, even distasteful. Not with Zack. Now she yearned to be invaded, to taste and test the texture of him on her tongue. She sank into his hot mouth and plunged her hands into his hair. His hands stroked down her sides and then up her back and he pressed her in. Her soft curves melted against his hard and tightly muscled form. She gasped at the feel of his erection rubbing just above her pubic bone at the swell of her tummy. She wanted more. Wanted everything. Her whole body tingled with impatience.

His hands found her zipper, which ran from the middle of her back down to the provocative split of the dress. In the back of her mind, she felt the zipper coming down, the fabric loosening. But when the fabric whispered over the tips of her breasts and kept moving southward, she stiffened and clamped one arm around the top of her abdomen, halting its progress.

She didn't want him to see her. Over his shoulder the light from the hall spilled into the room through the open door.

She could still see his features, the blaze of desire, the questioning look. But she didn't want to see his face when he finally saw her naked. Yes, he had made her feel beautiful tonight with his gift and his wanting eyes. But this was down to the nitty-gritty now. "You won't—you won't be shocked at my big belly, will you?"

His mouth turned up. He leaned forward and nuzzled her neck. "I'm looking forward to introducing myself." He nibbled kisses on her throat and at the base of her ear and she tried so hard to rise to the same heart pounding excitement again and nearly succeeded. Until he unfastened her bra. She flinched. Her breasts quivered at the withdrawal of support.

Zack leaned back and looked at her again, concern in his eyes. "Are your breasts sore?"

"Sensitive."

His kisses glided down her throat, while his hands supported and lifted her breasts. His fingers rubbed and squeezed and she arched her spine, needing more, needing something else and finally she felt first his palms and then his fingers circle her nipples, touching every tiny bump in her engorged areolae like Braille.

He knew just what to do to blow her mind. Cupping her firmly, he licked first one then the other aching tip, blowing on them and the chilly air was torture. With relief she saw his head move forward and he took one large dark nipple into his mouth. She gulped and pushed forward insistently, inciting him to suck. The pleasure was exquisite, one click short of pain and she wondered if she was supposed to want this so much when she was a few short months away from having her baby suckle her.

But this distraction couldn't stop her clamping her arm against the dress when his hands began smoothing it down again. Instantly Zack pulled back. "Still nervous?"

What he must think of her! "It's just—" she ducked her head, knowing he could see her embarrassment "—It's big, bigger than you think. And the belly button looks funny, not out, just flat. And there's this weird line down the middle that goes right from my belly button to my…"

"Linea negra," he murmured.

"No, to my…" And then her face burned with embarrassment as his words sank in.

Stupid to think he wouldn't have read up on every stage of her pregnancy.

Zack tilted her chin up and brushed her lips with his mouth. "Sky, nothing is going to happen that you don't want."

He thought she didn't want him? "Oh, but I do want. I do. Only, can we close the door? Do it in the dark?"

If he was disappointed, he didn't show it. "The first time, then." He released her and closed the door then drew her close and kissed her tenderly. "Do you have any idea how beautiful you are to me?" He tapped her nose with his index finger and she opened her eyes. "All of you." As he spoke, he ran his hands up her spine.

She inhaled, weak with relief that now he was just a

dark outline and she couldn't make out his features. Her overriding desire now was to touch him, all of him. So she set about undressing him. But it proved tough to undo buttons one handed so she had to let the dress go.

Her eyes closed with deep sensuous pleasure as she skimmed over the skin of his chest and shoulders and arms. The shape of him flowed into her fingertips, like a piece of music or a great film, taking her where she wanted to go. A little scared, a lot curious and overwhelmingly excited, she breathed a sigh of relief when she managed to get his zipper down without mangling him.

He leaned into her. Overcome by the unfamiliarity of her skin pressing against his, she swayed a little. "You okay?"

She nodded and put her hands on his hips and they kissed, deep and carnal. Soft against hard, her blood pounded as he moved his mouth down her body, inch by inch. Insecurities faded away as an erotic charge flooded her senses. She swayed and squirmed and pleaded for more as his hands stroked over every inch of her. Through a rapidly building haze of excitement, she felt the slow slide of her panties down her legs, legs that were being coaxed apart by a thousand nibbling kisses and his thumbs pressing purposefully up her inner thighs.

She came apart at the very first touch, but Zack showed no mercy. He licked and sucked until her body stopped cramping, the initial white-hot blast washed by a wave of ecstasy that slowly ebbed away.

Her knees buckled when he took his mouth away, as if that was the only thing holding her up.

"I've got you," he murmured, pulling her close.

Boneless, she sagged against him, curling her toes at the aftershocks that continued to ripple through her.

Zack turned his head and licked the corner of her lips. She opened to him and they kissed deeply, his need giving an edge to her satisfaction and leaving her wanting, too. Like chocolate, she couldn't get enough.

He pushed against her and she jolted as that hot, velvety length slid against flesh still absorbing and throbbing with prickles of intense pleasure. She gripped him between her legs and moved back and forth, slick and burning. He grunted and backed up toward the bed, pulling her down on top of him.

This was completely new for her but somehow it all seemed so natural. A natural progression from feeling so vulnerable about her nudity to standing while he pleasured her intimately to now levering herself above him, torturing him with slow teasing slides of her body over his. She found the power to tease was its own aphrodisiac.

But her own excitement was her undoing. Bold now, she teased him just an inch too far, a slight and mostly unintentional miscalculation. She'd known he was quick and she could, in all honesty, have reneged on the deal, but the sensation of him slipping just inside and the anticipation of lots of hot, hard flesh filling her, was irresistible.

Skylar eased down, slowly at first, adjusting to the fiery heat. She began to rock, raising up a little, changing angles to build and prolong the pleasure coursing through her. His hands firmed on her hips and he moved inside her with a delicious friction, molten with a centre of steel. Tension built quickly and warmth flooded her body and mind. And when Zack felt her tremors begin he thrust up strongly, pulling her hips down and she tumbled into an ecstasy that was relentless and mind shattering in its power.

* * *

Zack opened his eyes when he felt her face bury into his shoulder. He huffed in a gathering breath and turned to look at her—what he could see of her. A curtain of light caramel hair covered most of her face, along with his shoulder, but a little patch of creased forehead told of her screwed up eyes.

She wasn't going to block him out again. Zack did not sleep with women he didn't like. Just as important as arousal was the aftermath. It bothered him that bonding with Skylar after their first time had not been an option. That was not going to happen tonight, especially with so much riding on it.

"Hey, you." He blew on her hair, sending a section rising sharply and then flopping down. "Wake up."

She screwed her face up harder and rubbed her nose on his skin. "Not asleep."

Zack eased over onto his side so he was facing her. "Don't you go all shy on me again." Reaching out, he brushed the hair off her face. "Wasn't so bad, was it?"

An expulsion of air escaped her nostrils and she shook her head. He leaned toward her and dropped a kiss on her nose.

"Was it—different?" she asked, finally looking at him. "With the bulge and all?"

Too right, it was. An amazing, magical feeling making love to a woman growing big with his child—either that, or the lack of a rubber, a rare occurrence over the years.

"Different? Yeah, it was special." He brought his hand down between them and laid it on her belly, feeling a rush of emotion. "More of a connection because of what's in here."

That's what he'd missed since Rhianne, the tenderness. And it wasn't just tonight, because of the baby lying between them. Their first night together had also given him that feeling, though he'd supposed at the time that was because he'd been her first. Virginity was a gift and carried responsibility, in Zack's mind.

"But physically?"

"Physically, it was great. What's worrying you?"

"Just that, because of the baby, you feel you have to be gentle. Would you normally be gentle?"

Zack considered. "There's a place for gentleness, just like there's a place for fun and intensity and sometimes just out-and-out hot sex." He tilted her face up to his and brushed her lips with his own. "It's all good, Skylar, as long as you're both on the same wavelength at the same time."

She squirmed a little under his gaze. "But what if, when I'm not pregnant anymore, you don't feel the same connection?"

Zack smiled at her reference to a future for them. At least she was entertaining the thought. "I already had the connection. I have had for months."

Her mouth twisted. "Really?"

Zack bristled at the note of skepticism in her tone. "I don't make promises I won't keep, Skylar. I wanted you before, I want you now, and I see no reason not to keep wanting you."

She looked away, but he gripped her chin firmly, forcing her to look back.

"Where does this insecurity, this lack of self-esteem come from?"

No response, which was going to get her exactly nowhere, Zack decided. "You're pretty, you're intelligent.

You're successful at what you do and have a fantastic rep in breeding circles. Why is it so hard to believe someone could want you?"

"I believe what you want is this." She cast her eyes downward, to where his hand still rested on her stomach.

He frowned. "I do. Very much. Listen, I know you'll be an amazing mother. I know that this baby will have a great life and not want for anything. But you're nuts if you think I would marry you if I didn't want to be with you. If I didn't think we were a good fit."

It was dark in the room but Zack thought he saw her eyes light up with hope. In the silence that followed, he castigated himself for turning the aftermath of lovemaking into another demand. He had intended to keep his promise not to talk about the future or the baby. This was supposed to be her night, her one perfect night. The gift, the meal, the lovemaking—he could afford one night.

"One thing about pregnancy," she murmured, pushing away from him. "The pressure on your bladder. S'cuse me."

Zack turned a bedside lamp on, plumped up the pillows and lounged back with his hands behind his head. Surprised, he realized he hadn't noticed last time how feminine her room was. She gave the impression she didn't give a damn about her sexuality but her room was nice. Tasteful, elegant, understated. Come to think of it, the furniture and decor downstairs were elegant and comfortable, too.

Skylar returned, rubbing her hands together and making a Scottish laird proud with her rendition of *brr*. He made a tent with the covers and she clambered in and snuggled up, shivering with theatrical comedy.

"I like your room." He rested his chin on her head and inhaled a fresh burst of toothpaste. "Not what I expected."

"Too girly, you mean. Eliza helped. She loves decorating."

"You make out that you're not girly," he teased, "but I sense a latent femininity."

"Maya says I wear my clothes like a shield," she mused, spreading her fingers on his chest.

"They do shout 'back off!'" he agreed. "Why is that?"

Skylar sniffed. "Dunno. I wasn't without role models. Eliza." She paused. "My mother."

Zack was curious about her mother. "I met her once when Max and I spent a night at Blake's casino in Deadwood. She's a beautiful woman." *Beautiful but shallow. Brittle temperment, calculating mind.*

"Did she come on to you?" Skylar raised up, a suspicious twist to her mouth.

"No. She was preoccupied." With a white-haired high roller, Zack recalled. Older, exuding wealth and flashy gold on his fingers and wrist.

"Humph." She subsided, nestling back down and put a tentative hand on his chest. "She usually is."

It sounded like Skylar did not wholly approve of her mother. Maybe that's why she dressed the way she did, to avoid the comparisons. Because there were comparisons. High cheekbones, creamy skin, the sweep of a wide, shapely mouth. But Skylar was taller, more solid, more earthy and real. "Don't you get on?" He covered her hand with his and began to move it in slow circles on his skin, encouraging her to feel.

"I'm a disappointment. Not glamorous or sophisticated."

He smiled at the small hitch in her breath and the resistance in her wrist when he directed her fingers over his nipples.

"I don't go out with any of the guys she tries to hook me up with."

No, from what he'd observed, Skylar would definitely not be interested in the crowd her mother ran with. *Thank God.*

Under his hand, her fingers curled as the tips circled lightly over his nipples. Little tingles of awareness chased his interest in her mother away. He eased their hands over his chest and abdomen moving from side to side in a slow exploration.

"Zack?"

"Mmm?" The slow dance on his skin was lighting fires everywhere. Her head was still on his shoulder, looking down but he was covered by the sheet.

"I'm curious."

"Curious is good." He rubbed his chin up and down in her hair. Tracked the enthralling journey of their hands down to where he felt most powerful, yet willing to beg.

"I've never seen—or touched—a naked man before. Not really."

He sucked in his stomach as their hands continued lower.

"That's a terrible shortcoming," he murmured into her hair. "Let's remedy that."

It seemed no time at all until the alarm buzzed in his ears. Zack woke with a bursting bladder and an equally insistent erection. *Down, boy!* In her condition she needed her sleep. They'd had precious little in the night, where Zack found, to his delight, that lying with a curious and inexperienced woman had its advantages.

Skylar could be in no doubt now about how well they were suited. The whole evening was a resounding success and moved him that much closer to his goal. And it had been no hardship at all.

"We were lucky with the alarms," Skylar mumbled, allowing herself a catlike stretch.

She was referring to the foaling alarms. Because of the lateness of the breeding season, the pager had only sounded once, and when Skylar called in, Bob told her he could handle things.

"Up and at 'em." He groaned then leaned forward to nip her shoulder. "As my mother used to say."

She snuggled even deeper under the covers while he dragged himself out of the bed. "Did your parents divorce, Zack?"

He tensed. "Why do you ask?"

A hand escaped the covers and she rubbed at her nose. He relaxed a little, seeing she was seconds away from falling back to sleep. Idle curiosity, that's all. He bent and scooped up his suit trousers, grimacing when he realized he would have to make the walk to his room in the big house to change.

"You always say 'my mother,' 'my father.' Never 'my parents.'"

Zack zipped up his pants and sat on the edge of the bed to drag on socks. "Your parents are divorced," he reminded her. "What our parents did has no bearing on us. I for one, don't believe in divorce."

He turned to look at her. Only her face showed above the covers. "Wouldn't it make sense, Skylar, for me to come and go to the stables from here?"

She kept her eyes closed but he noted the swallow and the almost imperceptible shake of her head.

Not yet. She didn't trust him yet.

Disappointment dampened his earlier smug cheer. He got up and shrugged into his shirt. So there was a bit more work to do yet.

He took a last look at the sexy, tousled woman in the bed. "It's a poor show," he told her, "when a man has to sneak into his lover's parent's house to find his pants."

Her delectable mouth curved in a wicked smile. "Want me to come and hold your hand?"

"Stay." He leaned forward and kissed the smile away.

Seven

Later in the afternoon, she sneaked into the breeding shed to watch Ace at work. The teaser had been and gone and the mare stood quietly awaiting the arrival of Black Power. She was a pretty thing, even with the twitch on her upper lip and padded booties on her hind legs to minimize any damage she may try to inflict on her beau.

Oh, he was beautiful, she thought as Bob led him in, sleek and high stepping through the woodchips carpeting the floor. Even at this late stage of the breeding season, he was the total professional. Led to the mare, he introduced himself, nuzzling her neck and shoulders, moving down her body with lips turned in and nibbling gently. It was brief and fairly unimaginative as foreplay went but seemed to have the desired effect on both parties.

Once Ace got down to business though, the tenderness was out the window as he carried out his duty with his teeth embedded in the mare's neck.

She watched proudly as her team moved unhurriedly around the breeding shed, carrying out their appointed tasks. All of them except for young Ben had worked at Fortune Stud since Skylar started and they were a pretty efficient and well-oiled team.

The owner was from New York City, although his mare boarded in South Dakota close to Rapid City. He was new to the breeding game and had made the trip especially to see Black Power at work. "Is it always so quick and brutal?" he asked, wide-eyed, as the stud heaved himself off the mare's back.

"Every stud is different," Skylar told him. "Demetrius, my other stallion, is more your *wham bam thank you, ma'am,* sort of guy, but he's nicer than Ace at the finish. He'll always rest his neck on hers for a few seconds afterward."

Zack, who'd been given the job of soothing and distracting the mare, chose that moment to give her a long slow look that made her giddy. So giddy that she wasn't watching when Ben, charged with washing the stallion down, inexplicably kept the handheld shower nozzle pointed up as Bob led Ace away, soaking the hindquarters of the mare and the astonished owner. Despite Skylar's and the white-faced boy's repeated apologies, the man turned decidedly frosty and stomped off to his horse van, brushing at his expensive damp suit.

Skylar was peeved at Ben's lack of concentration. A lot of her business was word-of-mouth. There could be expensive consequences if the disgruntled breeder from

New York put the word around. At least Black Power had performed with his usual consummate professionalism.

Later she walked home and took a shower, changing into a long peasant skirt and one of her new long-sleeved T-shirts. When she'd left, Zack was busy loading the mare back into her van and setting up for Deme's cover. He hadn't said when or if he would come again and Skylar was too shy to ask in front of the men.

She was studying the meager contents of her fridge, thankful she hadn't invited him for dinner when he knocked. He'd come straight from the stables, still dusty, his clothes streaked with horse sweat and peppered with flakes of sweetfeed. The moment the door closed behind him, he dragged her into his arms and kissed her until she was breathless.

"I've been thinking about this all day," he growled, propelling her toward the stairs. She gasped at the feel of his rough hands on her skin as they slipped under her top. The smell of sweat and grain and horse fed her need. She loved that she was clean and fragrant and he wasn't, but now wasn't the time to analyze her weird appetites. Now was the time to celebrate and indulge them.

Mouths locked, they crab-walked up the stairs, both sets of hands fumbling with buttons and zippers. Their clothing littered the short corridor to her room, forlorn shapeless shirts with noodle arms, her bra still fastened, dragged over her head and hanging drunkenly by one strap from the doorknob. Zack hopped on one leg to the bed, battling jeans that had snagged on his shoes. Noses, teeth, foreheads, elbows all bumped to the music of labored breaths and the odd giggle from Skylar.

Finally they were naked, stretched out against each other on the bed and Skylar thought her heart would explode out of her chest. So this was his idea of out-and-out hot sex. Edgy, desperate, irresponsible when she thought fleetingly of the unlocked door downstairs.

But one thing she found, when he snagged her wrists with the fingers of one hand and loomed over her, was that trust beat in the roaring of her blood. He filled her in one long restrained slide, careful to keep his weight off her body. And then he rolled so she lay on top and she drew her knees up until she straddled him and began to move.

"I have no idea what I'm doing," she whispered, her legs scissored around his waist. She drowned in a desire she had never dreamed of and then a wash of pleasure that was impossible in its intensity. He felt beautiful moving inside her—she felt beautiful draped around him. She pulled away from his mouth and sat up, uncaring about her bulge of a tummy, all self-consciousness gone. He made her feel beautiful.

But when she felt the tremors start and swell and crash over her, her body collapsed down onto him and his rigid flesh and strong hands gripping her hips were the only things that kept her from shattering.

A couple of hours later they finally made it downstairs to eat. Skylar pulled her hair back in a damp ponytail as they walked down the stairs. Zack smelled a whole lot better after their bath but unfortunately had to don the same clothes he'd arrived in.

Skylar heeded this and tried to figure out an opening to say she had a spare key should he feel like going to his room in the big house and bringing a few things back for the morning. But out of a pretty dress, or out of bed, it seemed she would always be dogged by shyness.

They ate grilled cheese sandwiches in front of the gas fire. Zack put his empty plate aside, pulled her down in front of him on the sofa and wrapped his arms around her middle. "Do you see how good we are together?"

His breath tickled her ear. "Mmm." Her skin tingled in remembrance. "If I'd known how good it could feel, I wouldn't have waited so long."

Even without seeing his face, she felt the change in his mood, the leap from lazy fulfillment to steely determination.

"It could be like this every day," he told her, his voice deceptively soft.

"Could it?" Her eyes flicked around the room while she struggled to formulate a reply. "I feel like we're just getting started."

Zack exhaled and slipped his hands under her T-shirt, cupping her bulge. "Skylar, I've missed enough of this pregnancy. I want to be there every step of the way from here on in."

His meaning was clear: she should have told him earlier. But she so loved the newness of this, the novelty of having someone desire her. He was asking her to leap from excitement and passion straight into marriage. Would the fire they seemed to ignite in each other fade once he had what he wanted?

"I just wish it wasn't so far away," she hedged, staring at the blank TV screen.

"You will like it there, I promise." He covered her hand with both of his. "What are you scared of?"

Being stranded in a strange country when you decide you don't want me anymore. "I don't even know what the law is. We could split up and maybe I won't be allowed to bring the baby home."

"Wouldn't you rather consider the probability that we'll be very happy together?"

He had no idea how much she wanted that and if another life wasn't involved, she might risk it. "I'd rather consider that probability when I've had a bit more time to get used to the idea."

Zack stopped rubbing her tummy. "You know what my situation is. I have two new businesses, which I'm still learning about, and I can't do that from here. Once they're fully up and running and I've got the marketing on track, I can be more flexible. What I don't want is to be going backward and forward every other week while you make up your mind." He shifted behind her. "You owe me, Skylar, the next few months. Don't deny me the chance to watch you growing big with our child."

She leaned back into him until she felt his cheek on hers. It was very tempting. Her infatuation was so much more advanced. She forced her mind to consider the possibility of him leaving her now.

It left a black hole of despair.

Skylar knew it was impossible to have exactly what she wanted—Zack living here with her and her baby. He was a man. She was supposed to want to follow. Women always had to make the sacrifices.

But it was asking a heck of a lot to give up her safety net. "Who runs my place in the meantime?" Somehow she knew he would have an answer for that, too.

He did. "There are management agencies for that sort of thing, or you could promote Bob. He's managed bigger operations than this before."

Her pager bleeped. Relieved, Skylar rose and turned it off then pressed the speed dial on the phone.

"I'll call if I need you," Bob's voice said. "There's possibly two more to go off tonight." The foaling alarms attached to the mares went off once the animal had been down for twenty seconds, activating a receiver which then paged Skylar and Bob.

She excused herself to use the downstairs bathroom and on the way back, the spare key hanging on a hook by the back door snagged her attention. Would that placate the impatient man in her living room for the moment? It was a compromise. She took the key off the hook.

But the moment she walked back into the living room, the pager bleeped again. "That's number two," Bob said. "I'll call Zack up at the house."

"I'll call," she said quickly. The other boys had the night off so Zack, standing in for her, was on call. "You carry on, Bob. I'll alert the vet, too, in case we need him."

Zack was already pulling on his boots.

"I'll grab a jacket." She turned and started for the stairs but Zack grabbed her hand.

"No, you won't." He leaned forward and kissed her hard on the mouth. "Get some sleep. We'll continue this tomorrow."

It wasn't until after he'd closed the door that she realized she still had the key in her hand.

Skylar and Bob were in her office when Zack poked his head in the office door. "All set?" he asked Bob.

The two men were flying to Minneapolis to meet a friend of Bob's near Canterbury Park Racetrack. The man had a couple of well-bred broodmares for sale.

"Sure you won't come?" he asked as she walked them out to the truck they were taking to the airport.

Skylar shook her head. She wasn't keen on leaving the farm with Bob and Zack away. Anyway, she had paperwork to catch up on.

"Everything's done, the vet's happy with the foaling shed so you keep away," Zack ordered. "Dean's around. You've got my number, right?"

Sheesh! "Yes, Grandma," she drawled.

He opened the passenger door while Bob slid behind the wheel. "You cooking up anything tonight?" he asked in a sultry undertone.

"Hot dish, maybe." She grinned. The famous South Dakotan term *hot dish* referred to anything gooey cooked in one dish with cheese on top, but they both knew that wasn't what she meant.

"Ooh, baby," he whispered, and before she could slap him away, he leaned down and planted a firm kiss right on her lips. She took a quick step back and gave a furtive look around, feeling the heat burning her cheeks. With a wicked grin he climbed into the truck.

Tidying up the office might hopefully be an antidote to rampant sex hormones. Now was as good a time as any with Zack Manning glaring at her every time she got within a mile of anything with four legs.

She tore the tatty desk pad off to throw it in the trash but noticed the name *Burke* and a phone number, circled in Zack's handwriting.

She knew it was Zack's handwriting because of the note he'd taped to her front door when he'd finished foaling in the small hours. Her face lapsed into another dreamy smile. Not wanting to wake her, he'd said he and Bob would be starting late but she was not to help with the mucking out, the boys could handle it.

Talk about overprotective.

She leased some land from John Burke for her summer mares. The use of one hundred and fifty acres of pasture from the ex-hog farmer next door was good income. One day she hoped to be able to extend the twenty-eight stall broodmare facility so she could winter over more mares.

What could he want? She dialed but there was no reply.

The spring-cleaning took longer than expected but since Zack was going to be late anyway, Skylar was in no hurry. It was dark when she locked her office. She passed Dean and asked him to check that the foaling alarms were switched on; there were still a couple of mares close to their time.

It was usual for her to stop at Roscoe's paddock on the way home, but as she drew near, her ears picked up something weird. Nash had installed two or three lights along the driveway and they glinted dully off the stainless steel of the automatic livestock waterer.

She concentrated and then picked out a large dark shape on the ground, a couple of yards in from the fence.

Roscoe was down. Her first thought was colic. She'd seen it a hundred times. If it was just a bellyache, caused by change of feed or not drinking enough, a colicky horse sometimes lay down or stood stretched out, turning its head to nip and nuzzle its flanks.

"What's up, old boy?" she called to warn him she was coming. Roscoe lifted his head to peer at her, then dropped it again. His breathing wasn't particularly labored and she couldn't see if he was sweating. Probably just a mild case.

She climbed the fence, thinking to coax him up and

give him a bit of a walk around. It wasn't until she was squatting down beside him and put her hand on his stomach that the first real concern stirred in her gut. He was soaked in sweat. His upper lip curled right back and his eye gleamed white in the darkness.

She started to rise, hoping to catch Dean before he went up to the big house where Peggy always set dinner aside for him in the kitchen. It never occurred to her that the trusty old gelding she'd owned since she was three would hurt her. As the horse blew and then heaved himself toward her in a desperate effort to roll over, a front hoof caught her at the base of her neck and knocked her flying. Just as well, she thought in a crazy burst of lucidity, or he'd have rolled on top of her. That was her last thought before the back of her head caught the edge of the waterer.

Zack stopped the truck, his forehead creasing at the lack of lights on at the cottage. Dinner was definitely mentioned and Skylar was not so sensitive she would cancel just because he'd teased her.

He tapped the steering wheel, peering through the windshield at the dark windows. They'd arrived back a little earlier than expected and Zack was looking forward to seeing her. He'd already driven by the stables when he'd dropped Bob off. Her office was locked up and in darkness.

So he turned the truck in the direction of the big house. Maybe some news had come through about Patricia. It wasn't like Skylar to let people down. She had his number.

Case Fortune opened the door as he was about to ring the bell. Skylar's oldest half brother looked stern.

"Zack. I just knocked on your door."

"What's up?"

"My father and I were just discussing the gossip pages of the *Tribune* today."

His gut tightened. As far as he knew, the story his father had instigated hadn't broken yet.

"My sister's condition is attracting attention," Case continued. "It would be nice to think some progress was being made on an engagement announcement, sometime before the baby comes."

Zack swallowed with relief. "I'm working on it." His foot nosed the step as he tried to curb his impatience.

"Dad has got enough on his mind at the moment," Case continued. "The last thing he needs is the spotlight on the family. You are going to do right by Skylar, aren't you, Zack?"

"Is that because you give a damn or you're just worried about the gossip rags?" He squared up to the bigger man.

Case raised his hands in peace. "Keep your shirt on. Of course I give a damn, she's my sister. But as CEO of Dakota Fortune, I also have an obligation to see that the reputation of the firm and my family members doesn't suffer."

"The way I see it, the Fortune name is dragged through the mud about once a week." Zack's voice crackled with annoyance.

"You might think about that next time you frequent one of the top restaurants in town," Case rumbled.

"Point taken." Zack peered around the other man's bulk at the open door. "You'll be the first to know when it happens, Case. In the meantime, it'd just be good to see her. Is she inside?"

Case shook his head. "I haven't seen her. Maybe she's gone to see Maya in town."

Zack turned in the direction of the stables, scowling. "She invited me for dinner but she's not home."

"Not like Skylar to renege on an invitation."

Zack started down the stairs at a brisk trot. "I'll go have another look at the stables. If she's gone against her word, I'll throttle her."

Case followed him swiftly down the stairs, looking concerned. "I'll come with you. What do you mean, gone against her word?"

They sped down the driveway. "I asked her to keep away from the horses and to stop riding till the baby was born. Too many hidden dangers."

"Gina and I are trying for a baby. The sooner the better, as far as I'm concerned."

Zack grinned wryly. "Well, congratulations, Case. Welcome to all this worry."

"Old Roscoe is having a roll in his paddock," Case commented as they slowed on the approach to the stable complex.

Dean and Bob were talking outside the mare barn. The stable hand told them he'd last seen Skylar five-to-ten minutes ago, on her way home. Bob made the comment she usually stopped by to see Roscoe in the evening.

Zack's heart dropped to his knees. He took off running toward Roscoe's paddock. They found Skylar groggily trying to drag herself away from Roscoe's thrashing body. Praying there were no spinal injuries, Zack vaulted the fence, grabbed a handful of jacket and pulled her a few meters away. The rest passed in a blur. It seemed an age later before he was in the backseat of

Bob's car with her cradled in his arms. Case was driving, the others staying back to tend to Roscoe.

Skylar squirmed and arched her spine.

"Keep still." Zack wrapped her up in his arms, tense as rock. "Where does it hurt?"

"Head," she mumbled. "Neck. Roscoe?"

"He'll be fine. Bob's with him." He felt a stab of pure hatred for the horse. He half hoped Bob would put a bullet in him.

"Zack?" Skylar's voice suddenly rang out clearly. There was no mistaking the fear.

He hugged her tighter. "Shh, baby. I've got you."

She moved her head slowly as if her neck was a piece of wood. A single tear slid down her cheek. "My baby?" Her voice broke.

He squeezed his eyes shut for a second. It was easier thinking about her or the horse than what might be going on with the baby. Forcing himself to be gentle when really he wanted to explode, he stroked her hair.

But she was disoriented and confused and kept mumbling the horse's name and the word *baby,* over and over.

White-faced and more terrified than he had ever been in his life, he bent his head and rested his lips on her hair. "It'll be fine, Sky. I promise."

They made the hospital in double-quick time. Case had driven one-handed while calling their predicament in on his cell phone. The second the car came to a halt, he leapt out and met the small cluster of nurses and doctors and they loaded her onto a gurney. With Case up ahead, loudly issuing orders, Skylar and Zack were soon inside an Emergency Department treatment room. They took all her vital signs and questioned and prodded her endlessly. Skylar was silent, fearfully so. Zack was frightened, too, right down to his marrow. He could not stop looking at her white face but he wouldn't let her see his fear, looking away every time she met his eyes. He knew she would not be taking much in and that he had to listen to the doctors for both of them.

Skylar was unable to say for sure if she'd been knocked out but her slightly confused state convinced the doctors that she had a concussion. The top of her shoulder and side of her neck were red and swelling and there was an egg-sized lump on the back of her head.

Of more concern was a possible abruption. A sharp jolt such as falling onto her back violently could have ripped part or all of the placental sac away from the womb, meaning the fetus would not be getting the blood and nutrients it required. But apparently there was no bleeding and did not appear to be any leakage of amniotic fluid. The doctor ordered an ultrasound and she was hooked up to a fetal monitor. Both of them were comforted to hear the mushy quick tones of their baby's heartbeat.

"That's a good sign, surely?" Zack squeezed Skylar's hand while tears of relief poured silently down her face.

More time passed. He told Case he may as well go home as there would be no news for hours.

"I'm probably far enough along that the ultrasound will show us what sex it is," Skylar suddenly said, her voice subdued.

Zack nodded. "Are you ready for that?" Personally, he couldn't bear knowing if the worst happened.

She considered the question, and incredibly, her mouth softened in a small smile. "Amanda, if it's a girl." She sniffed. "Don't know why."

Zack felt her nails digging into his palm and so many conflicting emotions tore about inside. His daughter. Amanda. Would she be tall, like her parents? Fair? He squeezed his eyes shut, trying to shut off the images of a small girl with Skylar's blue eyes and wide mouth. *Don't lose it now.* He had to stay focused and calm.

"Is that all right?" Skylar asked, and he heard the hope in her voice. He knew she was trying to distract them both.

"Amanda it is." He squeezed her hand.

"How many should we have?"

He stifled a groan. He would be happy with just this one, should the powers that be grant them a healthy baby. But he played along, wanting to comfort her. "At least a rugby team."

What started out as a watery smile soon dissolved into heartbroken tears and she squeezed her eyes shut.

"Hey, hey. Keep positive, love." He kissed her hair while she did a reasonable impression of being in labor, judging by the savage pressure she put on his hand. "You're in good hands here. I promise you it will be okay."

But really he knew that this was out of his control. He had never felt so helpless in his life. And although everything in him wanted to rage at the world, her misery and dependence on him kept him from doing so.

She let go of his hands and covered her face. "I can't bear it, Zack. I let you down. I couldn't keep your baby safe."

She apologized time and again for going into the paddock. "He was quiet, I thought he just had a bellyache. He didn't try to roll until I was beside him." A fresh bout of tears erupted. "I would never have…"

He took her hands in both of his and brought them

to his lips. "I know you wouldn't have." Yes, he was angry about that, too, but she didn't need guilt compounding her fears. "Sky, I can be strong for you, but you've got to be strong for the baby." He shook her hands lightly. "You hear me? There's no one to blame. It's just life." He stared hard at her, willing her to take heart.

Finally the ultrasound equipment arrived and the preparations were tense and silent. But then Zack saw the most beautiful thing he'd ever seen. Life, with its thumb in its mouth and unlikely looking extremities and features. The ultrasound technician considerately asked if they wanted to know the sex.

Zack felt Skylar's involuntary jerk, took in her wan, wanting face. Recognized that she needed this, needed the distraction of planning and hope. He nodded and it was hard to do, because he *so* did not want to know, did not want to bond any further with the baby should the worst happen.

They turned to the technician and the tears flowed down her face when they were told to expect a girl.

All the energy drained out of her then and she slept. By six in the morning, Zack's eyes burned with fatigue. He disengaged her hand, walked to the window and stretched.

Would she get over it if the baby died? He hated not being able to comfort her. It reminded him of his mother at the end when the drugs could not subdue the pain ripping her to shreds and she couldn't understand why they weren't working anymore.

Skylar's guilt was eating her alive. If the baby didn't make it, would she push him away so he didn't remind her of it? Should the unbearable happen, would she let him nurture her, take care of her? Give her more babies?

Zack realized with a jolt that his future happiness depended on her being there, baby or not.

Whoa! The lightening sky outside seemed to float through the window and fill his mind with cotton wool. Everything paled into insignificance. The scandal that was about to erupt back home, his fear that her family would keep her from marrying him, even the life of his baby.

All he wanted was for Skylar to emerge from this whole and strong and stand by his side.

"Zack?"

He spun around at the sound of her sleepy voice. When she held out her hand and smiled that sweet smile, Zack Manning came as close to weeping as he'd ever come in his life. She took his hand, moved the sheet aside and placed it on her abdomen.

"Now can you feel her?"

He felt her. Baby Amanda moved under fingers that had never felt so sensitized. Her tiny insistent prods completely overwhelmed him. They reached for each other at the same time and he wrapped her up tightly and lay his cheek against her wet face.

At eight o'clock, they were told they could go home, provided she rest up for the next few days. The doctor looked sternly at Zack's relieved face. "She must have someone with her constantly. You need to be aware of the danger signs."

"Danger signs?"

"Bleeding. Leaking of amniotic fluid, the vaginal plug, fever, pain.

Zack nodded and gave Skylar a grim look. "I won't let her out of my sight, believe me," he said with feeling.

"The main danger is infection. The jolt Ms. Fortune suffered may have thrown up a blood clot which the placenta is hiding. And then there is the concussion. She may feel nauseous, dizzy, have a bit of double vision. Anything more serious or more prolonged than that, we want her back here pronto." The doctor smiled at the relief on their faces. "But all the signs are good."

Eight

Skylar threw the sheets back and sat on the edge of the bed. Today, she would not take no for an answer. She was getting up and the heck with it.

Zack's fussing had driven her to distraction, especially when she'd overheard him yesterday telling Maya on the phone that she wasn't up to visitors. He had not left the cottage, barely left her room, for three days. She wanted to see Roscoe, who apparently had made a full recovery, and make sure Bob and the team were coping with the extra workload, since Zack was now spending all his time watching her like a hawk.

She showered and dressed, surprised he hadn't come in to check on her yet, shove that damn thermometer in her mouth or take her blood pressure with the gadget he'd had delivered. How long would he keep this up? she wondered, buttoning her fire-engine red jacket.

Totally overprotective. Heaven help the unlucky lad who came to pick their daughter up for her first date.

That thought made her smile as she descended the stairs, but she checked at the sound of his voice.

"I'm sorry, Dad, I can't get away. It's unavoidable."

Zack's back was to her. She considered briefly escaping out the door before he noticed, but something in his tone made her pause.

"No, I don't blame you. Just do your best to keep a lid on it. I need a few more days."

Skylar burned with curiosity. She'd gotten the distinct impression he and his father were not close.

Zack sighed heavily and began to turn toward where she waited at the bottom of the stairs. "If this gets out right now, it will have major implications for me." He saw her standing there and his whole demeanor changed. "Right, gotta go. Good luck." He broke the connection and stared at her. "Where do you think you're going?"

"Out," she said promptly. "To get some fresh air."

He moved forward and put a hand on her forehead. "You're a bit flushed."

"It's the jacket," she replied tartly, "reflecting my perfectly pregnant glow."

As expected, he refused to let her out the door until she had eaten and had her temperature, blood pressure and pupils thoroughly checked. "No pain? Nausea…" He ran through the long list of symptoms the doctor had warned him to be on the lookout for. "Just a half hour then," he said, finally satisfied. "And I'm coming, too."

They set off for a leisurely stroll through the trees toward the stables. It was all Skylar could do not to skip in the early summer sun. She felt she'd been let out of prison and could finally breathe. Although Zack hadn't said or done anything to show he blamed her for the accident, her own guilt had her walking on eggshells around him. Her stupidity had given them both quite a scare.

"What's the problem with your father?"

Zack did not look at her.

"The phone call," she reminded him.

"No problem," he said shortly, frowning into the distance.

"What implications for you were you referring to?"

"Nothing I can't handle."

"Zack—" she expelled an impatient breath "—you say you want us to spend time together, get to know each other, yet every time I mention your family, you clam up. What are they, a bunch of axe murderers?"

Her attempt at humor elicited a cool gaze. "Very funny."

Skylar sniffed, her good mood evaporating in the sunlight. Okay, she may not be the most sophisticated conversationalist in the world, but she had a right to know more about him and his family. After all, his family was going to be her baby's family...

She opened her mouth to tell him so when his head snapped up and he pointed through the trees. "Someone's looking for you."

Roscoe nickered as they broke the line of trees and stepped out onto the driveway. After a few minutes being fussed over and petted, he trotted along the fence beside them as they walked. The vet had come straight out the night of the accident and administered mineral oil to clear the blockage in his intestines. He looked to be in no discomfort now.

All the boys crowded into her office, grinning and talking over each other to bring her up to date. Foaling was finished and it was just as well, Bob told her, as she'd need to get the alarms checked. He had tested the alarm before going to bed the night before but it hadn't activated. The last foal of the season had arrived unannounced during the night and, thankfully, none the worse for it.

One by one, they left to carry on with their chores. "Zack, if I promise not to leave the office, can I stay for an hour? Check the e-mails and pay some bills?"

Unexpectedly, he grinned down at her. "Writing checks is supposed to put your blood pressure up, isn't it?"

There were times when being around Zack Manning caused her blood pressure to go right through the roof and this was one of them. Her frustration about his overprotectiveness and reticence to discuss his family melted away. Awareness tickled along her spine, reminding her of his appeal. Lean-hipped, tightly defined muscles, long, strong legs. She grinned back, thinking if he was a stallion, she'd never get out of the receiving barn!

"What?" he asked when she snorted.

She waved him away, muttering that her blood pressure was just dandy, thanks. The moment the door closed behind him, she picked up her diary, flapping it in front of her burning face. Holy Toledo! When he smiled at her like that, with genuine affection and humor sparkling in his eyes, she wondered how she could deny him anything.

Her smile faded as silence descended. She wanted more than affection, much more. Because she was seriously considering his proposal.

Zack was the only man she had ever wanted, or slept with. He respected her as a breeder and was the one person apart from Patricia she felt she could rely on. They had much in common with their love of horses and the outdoors. Skylar thought his home was beautiful and a part of her had always regretted not traveling, seeing the world before setting herself up in a business that occupied all her time.

So what was she waiting for?

How could she? It was a ridiculous notion to run off with a virtual stranger, putting not only herself but her baby completely in his hands.

It was the attention, she supposed, scrolling disinterestedly through the mail. She enjoyed being the center of his attention. She had never felt that before. Robust good health and her disinterest in men meant her family barely noticed her existence.

Except Patricia. She missed her so much. Her father was right, Patricia would love to see her expecting, happy, in love. She was the one constant in Skylar's life, especially during the adolescent years when she felt the lack of a mother most keenly. Patricia had always built her up, noticed her, heaped praise on her head when no one else even knew if she was in the room.

Patricia would like Zack, and for no other reason than because Skylar did.

Pregnant women were supposed to want their mothers, she reflected. Yet she did not have the same burning desire to show Zack off, or show herself off, to Trina.

The phone rang, startling her. Talk about ESP! "I was just thinking about you," she told her mother.

"Blake told me what happened." Her mother had many voices and today's crackled with dry sarcasm. "I suppose it would have been too much to ask for a phone call from my baby doll's hospital bed."

"Sorry, Mother. I didn't want to worry you unnecessarily." She was surprised her mother could find time in her busy schedule to call.

"Sweetie, if you insist on making a grandmother of me, you could at least keep me up to date. Is everything all right?"

"Yes, I'm fine. A knock to the head, that's all."

"Well, darling, I have the perfect cure. I'm going on a cruise this weekend. Five days around the Caribbean. Why don't you join me? Good food. Sun and shopping and all the pampering you need at this time of your pregnancy. And," Trina's voice lowered conspiratorially "I'm sure we could find someone to make your Kiwi jealous enough to pop the question."

"Mother…" Skylar chided. You could count on Trina to manipulate a situation to her advantage. "Sorry. It's really not my scene."

There was silence. Quite a long and awkward silence. Skylar sat up a little straighter, slightly perturbed. Trina didn't do silence. "Mother?"

"Skylar, I know I haven't been much of a mother…"

Trina didn't do sentiment, either. "Is something wrong?" Amazingly, she felt concern, when exasperation was a more normal emotion toward her mother.

"Nothing. I'm being silly. Is everything really all right? How are your smelly horses?"

"Fine." If you didn't count all the little things going wrong lately, she mused, but it was strange that her mother would express an interest in the stud farm.

"And your father?"

Skylar chewed on her bottom lip, not sure how much,

if anything, Trina knew about Patricia's disappearance. As far as she knew, it hadn't hit the papers yet, but Skylar didn't bother much with the papers. "He's well. What is it, Mother? Why the sudden interest?"

"Can't a mother express an interest in her only daughter's life? Especially when she's expecting her first child?"

Skylar's distance from her mother originated from years of being let down. Birthdays forgotten, graduations not attended, weekend visits canceled because Trina had gotten a better offer…but despite all that, Skylar warmed at her mother's words. Maybe mothers and daughters did grow closer with the advent of children.

Surprising herself, she invited her mother to meet her for lunch in town before her vacation. It seemed Trina had something on her mind. The least Skylar could do was give her an hour of her time.

"Zack?"

Skylar's voice from the passenger seat jolted him back to reality, just as the car behind gave a sharp toot and he realized the lights had changed.

"I know what you were doing."

He accelerated smoothly, a small smile threatening to break loose. "Tell me you weren't," he challenged.

They were in town for Skylar's checkup and another ultrasound. Happily there were no bad effects from the accident and she had been given the green light to go back to work. Of course, his and her ideas about what constituted work were as wide as the Atlantic Ocean.

Sitting at the lights in Sioux Falls on the way home, a class full of kids—little ones, all with hands linked—had crossed the road in front of their car. They wore a maroon uniform with hats and shorts and cute little shoes. Some skipped in a clumsy sort of congo line. Some sang. One little girl with blond pigtails looked right in the window at him.

"I hope our girl looks just like her," he murmured. "A mini version of you."

"She's got no front teeth," Skylar protested.

Getting the all clear from the doctors was a relief. Watching the scan for the second time was just as magical. That was his baby, his flesh and blood in her belly, moving, sucking her thumb, yawning. It was over too soon. He wondered if he should invest in a home scanning machine so he could see it every day. He seemed to recall some big movie star or other had one.

Beside him, Skylar gave a little jerk and he glanced at her. "What is it?"

"Nothing," she reassured him. "She's squirming. At least, she's making me squirm."

"Man, that must feel…"

"It feels like—bubbles," she said happily, moving her hand over her belly.

"Like you've got wind?"

"No. Like exhilaration. When you've just had the best exciting news and you can't wait to tell someone because you know they're gonna be wowed." She gave him a sunny smile.

Something tugged at him, deep inside. Whatever the future held, he would not trade sharing this pregnancy with her for anything.

Later, she succumbed to an afternoon nap while Zack prepared dinner. Nagging her about marrying him wasn't an option while she recuperated, but the pressure was mounting. His father's phone call the day before reminded him that things he had no control over were threatening to blow the lid on the pleasant domestic situation he was currently engaged in.

His father, John Carter, was living rough in the South Island of New Zealand when Zack's private investigator had finally tracked him down. Bitter about the hand life had dealt him, he initially wanted nothing to do with his son. But when Zack heard his story, he persuaded him he had the means to help in his quest for reparation or revenge.

Together, father and son tracked down witnesses and hired lawyers to bring a civil case against the Thorne family, Zack's mother's family. But they hadn't bargained on the Thorne's political clout. One-by-one, the lawyers opted out, intimidated. The case floundered in February, when Zack was in South Dakota the first time, considering making a move on Skylar Fortune.

Zack spent a great deal of time and money hunting down offshore lawyers from firms he hoped would not be so easily put off. But a few weeks ago, frustrated by the lack of progress, John Carter took matters into his own hands. While Zack was in South Dakota, discovering Skylar's pregnancy, his father put into motion plans that could irreparably harm the likelihood of them sharing in the life of Skylar's baby. He'd contacted a reporter on a top current affairs TV show.

When Zack found out, he and his father persuaded the reporter not to air the show right away. He doubted he would ever get Skylar's, or her family's, agreement to marry him with the scandal that his father was intent on exposing.

Unfortunately, the government of New Zealand had called a snap election and the reporter was putting the acid on his father to air the show now. The scandal involved the leader of the opposition and there was a good chance the man could be the next prime minister of the country.

And that's why Zack had about a week to get his ring on Skylar's finger. Because when the news broke in Australia and New Zealand, the fallout would be huge. The Australian Fortunes would hear of it and as much as Max's father, Teddy, thought of Zack, he would feel it his duty to inform his American cousins of Zack's background.

Skylar came into the kitchen, her hair brushed out and still damp from her shower. She came up behind him and slipped her arms around his waist. Zack craned his neck around to peer at her. "Hungry?"

"Hungry for something," she murmured, pressing her face into his back.

He turned to face her, resting his hands on her shoulders. "You smell like apples." He bent his head to her hair, breathing in deeply. He'd noticed the apple-scented shampoos and lotions in her bathroom.

Skylar reached up and touched her lips to his tentatively. She pulled back, watching him. The kiss may have been uncertain but there was a candid and determined look in her eye.

Zack's mouth quirked. "You *are* hungry."

Her gaze dropped and she blushed. "I phoned the doctor when we got home. Asked him if it was safe to, you know…"

He waited, trying not to smile at her discomfort.

Skylar studied the buttons on his shirt. "If we could…"

"You rang the doctor to ask if we could have sex?"

She went even pinker. "'Resume sexual relations' was the phrase, I think."

"Why didn't you ask while we were there?"

Her shoulders raised in an embarrassed shrug.

Although they shared her bed, Zack heeded the hospital's warning that she take things easy for a few days. Just as well he was familiar with sheep, New Zealand's most populous livestock by far. Veritable flocks of them marched through his brain as he lay beside her, listening to her breathe, feeling her warmth, clasping his hands together to stop from touching her.

He nuzzled the base of her ear. "And what did the doctor say?"

"No swinging from the chandelier." She rubbed her cheek against his lips.

"Lucky." He nipped at her earlobe. "We don't have a chandelier." His fingers pressed in firmly up the length of her spine, a particularly sensitive spot, he'd discovered.

Sure enough, she arched into him. "You want to turn whatever's burning off?" Her fingers began undoing his shirt buttons. "I'm in rather a hurry."

Zack reached behind him and complied. Who was he to argue? "Hurry, huh? It's not good to keep a pregnant lady waiting."

"It's not," she affirmed, slipping her hands inside his open shirt and skimming his chest. "They get cranky."

Zack returned the compliment by making short work of the buttons on the front of her blouse, delighted to find she was not wearing a bra. She wore a sarong-type wraparound skirt that reached almost to her ankles. "You must be wearing a thong," he murmured, running his hands over her backside. "Can't for the life of me feel any panties under this very thin material."

Skylar rubbed against his groin, torturing him. "No panties."

He took her mouth and swallowed her gasps, his blood racing now. What had happened to his shy little virgin? Her tongue lashed his and he groaned into her mouth. "We're not going to make the bedroom if you keep this up."

"Good." She pulled back, her hands clutching both sides of his open shirt. She tugged him over to the dining table and used her toe to hook one of the chairs out to face them. Zack just had time to let the blind down and wonder if the door was locked before his impatient lover pushed him down into the chair.

"I can't wait." She leaned down and nipped at his mouth while deftly undoing the fastening of his jeans. "My hormones have gone sex mad."

Her breasts were right in front of his face, heavy, fragrant. Inviting. He leaned forward and took one large dark nipple into his mouth. She stopped what she was doing and arched closer.

"Oh, harder," she breathed, and tangled her fingers in his hair. "I can't bear it if you don't."

Zack obliged happily and transported her to a level of excitement he hadn't seen in her before. Busy as he was, he managed to push his pants down around his knees and started on the tie to her skirt, but she had other ideas. She stood over him and lifted the folds of material up until it bunched around her waist.

His body strained with excitement. She hadn't lied. No panties and no thong, either. He gripped her hips and she spread her legs and moved over him. Zack thought he'd died and gone to heaven when she dipped her knees and teased him over and over. He could barely contain his need to plunge deep, but this was about her. This was about her asking him, trusting him, blossoming in her newfound sensuality.

In the end, her greed won out and she resisted his firm grip on her hips and jerked down. They stilled, staring at each other and she looked unsure again, as if now that she had what she wanted, she didn't know what to do with it. Zack took the lead and lifted her arms above her head so she was stretched out above him.

Her breasts trembled in front of his mouth and she jerked again when he feasted on them. He felt her thighs bunch as she braced herself and began to slide up and down on him, her tight tummy brushing his chest.

It was hot and fast. Within seconds, her fingers gripped his hard and her breath came in rhythmic agonized moans. He suckled harder and fought to keep his control when she clenched hard around him, flooding him with her heat. Her lower body and legs stiffened, but her fingers slid limply from his and she slumped, gulping air, her damp face pressed against his neck.

Zack nudged her face around with his chin and took her unresisting lips in a long, carnal kiss. "I want you up again. Slower, this time." He burned with the need to climax but first he wanted to test the theory that pregnant women were prone to multiple orgasms, something to do with increased blood flow to the extremities.

After a long, slow loving, their mouths and eyes locked on each other the whole way, she succumbed to a shivering climax that seemed to go on and on. Only then did he firm his hands on her hips and thrust strongly up while she clung to his neck and rode him. Zack climaxed hard, digging his heels into the floor, every muscle rigid, yet boneless inside where the ecstasy swirled and licked and nibbled into every cell.

Bathed in sweat, he wrapped her up in his arms, swaying and rocking. Thank God for sturdy chairs.

After dinner, they lay in bed chatting idly. Zack raised up on his side and placed his hand on Skylar's sweetly rounded white belly. Their daughter obediently kicked on command. They lay for a long time, watching for the telltale little movements on her skin. A little bump appeared, then nothing for a minute, then again in a different place. Skylar directed his hand to different parts of her belly and he was enthralled by the activity under his fingers. "This isn't because we made love, is it?"

She smiled. "She's just letting us know she's there and she's great." She blinked at a particularly strong kick. "I'm going to be black-and-blue inside."

"It must feel amazing. For the first time, I feel like women are the lucky ones."

"You won't be saying that at the birth," she told him with a grimace.

Zack questioned her endlessly on how her body was changing, her moods, her tastes. Cheated out of the first few months of this pregnancy, he wanted to know every detail.

"I hope I'll be a good mother." Skylar sighed, nestling into his side. "I was just thinking yesterday how sad it would be if little Amanda thought about me the way I feel about my mother."

"No chance," Zack told her and then felt ungracious. He hardly knew the woman. But his own mother sacrificed everything for him and it was hard not to feel strongly about the type of woman who would leave her child feeling unwanted. It may not have been Trina's idea to leave her children with Nash, but she could have fought for them and involved herself a lot more in her daughter's life.

"Thing about mothers," Skylar continued lazily, "they're the people in the world most everyone has regrets about. My mother is selfish and shallow, but sometimes I think she has her regrets, just like everyone else."

"At least it's shown you how you don't want to be." Zack gave private thanks that Skylar recognized her mother's shortcomings and seemed determined not to repeat them. Her core values were much too wholesome to be impressed by beauty and wealth.

"What was your mother like?"

"Bossy." He was so relaxed and content, it didn't even occur to him to deflect her. He stroked her tight bulge, spreading his hand wide. "Strong."

Zack had loved and admired his mother, but there had been only the two of them. Close relationships were hard to forge when you moved every year. Gill Manning had been demanding and she had expected high standards of him but he had never once felt unloved or unwanted.

The only time she ever let him down was the day she sided with Rhianne's parents. Even so, he understood where she was coming from. She'd worked hard to provide for him. Watching him throw away the chance to go to university and make something of himself was intolerable for her.

Pressing his fingers down into Skylar's tummy gently, he sucked in a breath. "Feel that? She's really going for it."

A lump formed in his throat as he felt the tiny prodding against his fingers. "God, she's so... Can I listen?"

He shifted down and laid his ear on her stomach. There was that squishy heartbeat again and tiny, otherwordly thumps as his baby kicked. He was glad Skylar could not see his face. She couldn't begin to comprehend the emotion swamping him at this moment. His baby, inside her womb. His baby, feeding, beating a tattoo on her mother's insides. His baby breathing and sucking her thumb. Yawning and stretching. He closed his eyes tightly and the sounds intensified as his senses adapted to blindness.

Everything he had achieved, everything that made him the man he was came down to this, the tiny life inside the body of this surprising and warm woman he was sated with loving. The years of bitterness about what he had lost faded into nothing as Zack basked in contentment. He would give his life, gladly, for the tiny soul pressed against his ear and for the woman nurturing her. More than anything he wanted to keep them both safe.

"Can you hear her?" Skylar whispered.

Zack opened his eyes and nodded. He wouldn't give them up, he thought with a ruthless determination usually reserved for the boardroom. Either of them. He pressed his nose into her fragrant skin, surprised that she was fast becoming as vital to him as the baby she carried. He had not expected that.

Her hands moved on his head. "Zack? Why haven't you had babies before?"

He swallowed, toying with the idea of telling her about Rhianne. Toying with the idea of telling her everything. They were closer now and time was running out for him.

How much faith did he have that she would stand by him? Quite a bit, he conceded, but he didn't trust her family. He needed her agreement to marry him before his father's story hit the airwaves and her family stepped in and cut him out.

But if he told her about Rhianne, she might understand how much this baby meant to him.

And how much she meant to him.

There were similarities to his feelings for Rhianne and Skylar. Somehow they both pulled at him. Two girls from wealthy domineering families who'd had their lives mapped out and did not know where they stood in the world. Somehow that touched him, more than all the girls and women in between. Executives, stewardesses, professional women, fun-loving women... No one else had ever dragged out the tenderness and protectiveness from the brash boy who started off on the wrong side of the tracks and now ran his own empire.

Zack took a deep breath. "I got a girl pregnant once," he began.

Her hands, stroking idly through his hair, stilled.

Nine

This wasn't his first baby.

She lay perfectly still, frozen by a familiar disappointment, that of never quite making the grade. She wanted to be his first.

First baby, first love.

Zack moved back up the bed and onto his side, raised up on his elbow. "She was sixteen, still in school. I was a couple of years older and about to go to university."

The fist clutching her heart eased a little. It was a very long time ago.

"But I didn't fit the image of the man that her parents wanted for their precious, wealthy daughter."

Bitterness hardened his voice. Skylar turned onto her side also so she could watch his face.

"They offered us money to leave town. When my mother refused, they threatened to have my scholarship annulled and see to it that every university in the state would bar me." He cleared his throat. "They had the power to do that. We, my mother and I, had no power. It was as simple as that."

"What was her name?"

"Rhianne. Rhianne Miller."

"What happened?"

"They persuaded her to have an abortion."

"Oh, Zack." No wonder he was so overprotective, so determined not to let her out of his sight. Her eyes brimmed. To think she had withheld her pregnancy from him for so long. How could she make it up to him?

His eyes met hers briefly then he looked around the room, settling on each corner, as if he didn't want her to see his pain. "I didn't blame her for not sticking by me. I wasn't much of a catch back then. But all these years, I've wondered about my son or daughter, what he or she would have been like. How different my life might have been had he or she lived." The muscles worked in his jaw. "That was hard to swallow."

Skylar felt a little chill and her hands went involuntarily to her tummy. She knew, especially after her accident, she'd never get over losing a baby.

"It taught me one thing. I never wanted to be poor and at someone else's mercy again."

How appalled he must have been when history repeated and he found himself in the same situation. "Did you never meet anyone else you wanted to have a baby with?" Surely he must have had other lovers in the ensuing years, other relationships. She might wish she was the only one but that was unrealistic. The guy was in his midthirties.

He shook his head. "I nearly got engaged once but I

realized at the last minute I didn't feel enough for her. It wasn't like it was with Rhianne. It never was."

Do you feel it with me? How she wanted to ask but this was his story. His heartbreak. She wouldn't make it about her. "I'm so sorry I didn't tell you earlier, Zack. About the baby."

His face tensed up again. He leaned over her and reached out to cup her face with firm hands. "I won't lose this baby, Skylar," he grated. "I know what it's like to grow up in a one-parent family, to have the wealthy, the old money, look down their noses. I won't have—" his eyes slid down to her midriff "—Amanda suffer that, as well."

She didn't blame him but felt it was unfair to compare her family with Rhianne's. Anyway, Skylar had no intention of allowing her family or anyone else to dictate to her. "I'm not like that. Nobody here looks down on you."

"Prove it." He eyes glinted like steel. "Say you'll marry me."

She gazed at him for several moments, wavering, so close to saying yes. So close to trusting her inexperienced heart. But a slide in her belly cautioned her that it wasn't just her life she was impacting on. "I want to…" She squirmed out of his grasp and jammed herself into his side, so he couldn't see her face. Having heart-to-hearts, face-to-face made her cringe.

"I just—I'm not sure yet. But I promise, Zack, I am considering it very, very seriously."

He put his arms around her then, but the tension in the set of his jaw and the tightness of his chest as he appeared to sleep kept her awake for a long time. She closed her eyes and prayed for the courage to take that step.

Skylar felt she'd been largely ignored by her parents and siblings. She'd grown to be comfortable with it, but she could never accept that from Zack. He may be attentive and protective of her now but in two years or five or ten, would she be left sitting in his beautiful home alone while he was off having fun with his daughter and excluding her?

Or worse, off with another woman, one he could love like he loved Rhianne?

When she had given up everything she knew, would she still be left with nothing?

Late the next afternoon, Skylar was watching Zack's home movie when the phone rang.

"What are you up to?"

She sighed at the sound of Zack's voice.

"Same thing I was doing when you called the last time."

Three phone calls already and he had only been gone since lunchtime. He had driven over to Deadwood to meet with a breeder staying at Blake's casino.

"I'm on my way home now. Do you want to eat out?"

"I'll fix something. Maya's coming over for a visit after school." Maya taught at the grade school in the city. Skylar was looking forward to company.

She put the phone down and couldn't help smiling and patting her belly. "That's your daddy," she whispered. "Driving us nuts."

Even though it was exasperating, his constant checking up, insisting she rest and keeping her from her work, it still made her smile. She was the most pampered mother-to-be in the world. Zack would never let her down. She sensed he was the one person she could always rely on. A pretty great trait for a father, she thought. Her treacherous brain added *husband* to that.

She sat down and turned the DVD back on. This was the second time she had watched it today. Following his tour through the large modern house, she admired and considered the decor and layout of the rooms. Even imagined herself there moving about his kitchen, lying in his overmasculine bedroom or sitting on handsome wooden outdoor furniture by the pool.

She had it bad. Aside from his growing impatience with her dillydallying about marriage, they were closer in the days since the accident. He deserved an answer, some sort of definite commitment to their future.

His stud operation was impressive, much larger than hers, though he was still in the process of setting it up. She marveled at the state-of-the-art stables, more modern than anything she had seen.

That was another thing about Zack Manning Skylar admired. When he did something, he did it well. She'd had ample opportunity to see that in the way he tackled everything. From helping Bob run the stables in her stead, to cooking and looking after her—and don't get her started on the bedroom.

Skylar didn't know if she suffered from a surfeit of sex hormones or was just an overenthusiastic late starter. She was insatiable where sex with Zack was concerned. He was in danger of being attacked every time he walked into the cottage.

Not that she'd heard him complaining.

Maya, hidden behind a huge basket of goodies, interrupted the DVD. There was fruit and chocolate, baby clothes and creams and potions for stretch marks. "Have you been talking to Eliza?" Skylar asked. She had suffered several phone calls from her half sister about taking proper care of herself.

She poured glasses of iced tea and they opened some candy and watched the DVD. Maya was loud in her approval of Zack. It seemed every time Skylar turned around, someone was raving on about how great he was, how lucky *she* was.

Just once, it would be nice to hear it the other way around.

"It looks great," Maya enthused. "Can't wait to visit."

"Don't you start," she grumbled. "I wish everyone would stop pushing me to what they all see as a logical conclusion."

"You're crazy about him. It's obvious."

"Maybe so," she admitted. "But it'd be nice to know he was crazy about me, too."

"Would he ask you to marry him if he wasn't?"

Skylar cradled her tummy. "He's definitely in love with this little thing," she said softly. "You should have seen him last night, lying with his head on my tummy, listening to her move."

"Oh, wow!" Maya gave a loud sniff.

Skylar looked up in surprise. Her friend's beaming smile of a moment ago had vanished. She was on the verge of tears. "What is it?"

Maya wiped her eyes. "Mom would so love to see you like this. If only we could get word to her. She'd be home in a minute."

"I miss her heaps but it must be so much harder for you."

"I'm so scared," Maya whispered. "I just can't see why she'd go without a word. What can be so bad that she can't even tell me?"

Maya was Patricia's only child. It had always been just the two of them until they'd moved to the Fortune Estate. Patricia took on the job of looking after Nash's children after he kicked Trina out. Although the two younger girls quickly became friends, Maya wasn't so close to the other Fortune children. The boys and Eliza were old enough to remember Trina's manipulations and regarded Patricia and Maya with some suspicion.

"Dad will find her," Skylar reassured her. "All the boys have people working on it. In fact it's nice to see them and Blake all pulling together for Dad's sake. Whatever's gone on in the past, everyone wants Patricia home where she belongs."

Maya looked wistfully into her tea. "She was so happy when Nash retired and they took that trip to Australia. It was soon after they returned that everything changed. She seemed worried and distant. I wish I knew…"

"Skylar," a male voice called from the door.

"Oh, no," Maya groaned. "Creed."

Skylar made a face at her and went to open the door.

"What brings you here?" Her siblings rarely visited her at the cottage.

"Oh, you know," Creed hedged, looking guilty. "Just passing."

She stared at him. "Zack sent you, didn't he?"

Creed couldn't hide his grin. "Be thankful he's so—attentive."

She stood back to let him in, shaking her head. "I don't believe him."

Creed stopped, his grin fading fast when he saw Maya on the sofa. "Maya." He gave her a brisk nod.

She reciprocated coolly. Skylar always felt uncomfortable around these two. They seemed to spark off each other and often ended up arguing. It had been that way as long as she could remember.

"Want some iced tea or something?" She fetched another glass when Creed nodded. "We were just talking about Patricia. You haven't heard anything from Dad, have you?"

Creed shook his head somberly. "Nothing as far as I know."

Maya heaved a big sigh.

"You have to give these things time, Maya," he said, accepting Skylar's drink with a roll of his eyes.

"She's my mother," Maya retorted. "I can understand her not contacting you but why take it out on me?"

Creed sighed and turned to Skylar. "You don't suppose Trina would have anything to do with this, do you?"

She looked baffled. "How?"

"I don't know. She does seem to have the knack of getting under everybody's skin."

Skylar was well aware of her mother's shortcomings. Trina delighted in causing mischief since being banished from the estate. It wasn't enough that her prenup was generous and Nash cared for the children she would have found to be a burden. She was bitter at losing her social status. Just in the last few months, she'd sold several untrue stories to the Sioux Falls social pages, even lying about Blake, her own son. Trina thought only of herself.

"Patricia knows what she's like, and she's too sensible and too secure to let Trina upset her."

Maya sniffed. "Sky's right. Mom is more likely to be upset by you or Case than Trina."

Creed jutted his chin out. "What is that supposed to mean?"

Maya got smartly to her feet and faced him. Skylar blinked to see her friend's heated pout and clenched fists. Surely they weren't going to resort to fisticuffs, as they sometimes had as children.

"You know very well what I mean, Creed." Maya's voice was carefully controlled and cold. "Ever since Mom and I came to live here, you've never welcomed either of us. You and Case thought my mother was just another Trina."

Before Skylar could voice her protest, the two of them let fly, just like old times. Creed shouted and Maya dropped her aloof stance and shouted back.

Skylar sat back, openmouthed, amazed at how fast the argument got out of hand. This was totally over the top for the provocation. Maya's brown eyes flashed and snapped with temper, and Creed inflamed the situation by stepping forward with each forceful missive. They were soon face-to-face and only inches apart, both breathing heavily.

Zack walked in, an incredulous look on his face. "What the hell's going on?"

"Don't ask me," Skylar murmured, still overwhelmed by the passion of the argument.

Zack moved to her side quickly. "You all right?"

She nodded.

He turned back to glare at Creed. "I could hear you two from Deadwood."

"Maya's a little upset," Creed said smoothly, overriding Maya's muttered apology.

"*I'm* upset?" she snapped back. "Damn right. I wouldn't put it past you to have said something. I know you don't think she's good enough for your father."

"I think nothing of the sort."

"Just because Sasha dumped you for Blake, you can't stand to see anyone happy."

They were off again, voices rising like applause at a baseball game. Creed flung a heated barb about Maya's on-again, off-again boyfriend and then Zack pushed between them. "Out! Both of you."

"Zack," Skylar protested, more interested in seeing where Creed and Maya were going with their passionate argument.

He ignored her. "Out, now. You're upsetting Skylar."

"For Pete's sake—" She began to protest but he cut her off.

"I mean it."

Everybody stared at him, and then Maya bent and picked up her bag. "It's time I was going anyway."

"Maya, don't go," Skylar entreated, scowling at Zack's face.

Her friend stalked to the door.

Creed threw his arms in the air, sighing heavily. "Maya, I'm—sorry."

Maya tossed a look over her shoulder. "You're sorry. You're always sorry, until the next time."

She looked at Skylar and Zack. "I'll call you, Sky. Take care."

Creed stepped forward, wincing as the door banged behind her.

"Where do you get off," Skylar rounded on Zack, "ordering people out of my house?"

"I won't have you upset—" he began, but she cut him off.

"The only person upsetting me right now is you." She turned to the door. "I'm going after her."

But on the way to the door she threw a scathing look

in Creed's direction and caught a glimpse of such desolation in her half brother's face, she quickly forgot about being mad at Zack. Desolation and something else, the same thing she had glimpsed at the restaurant but wasn't sure of then. Longing. He had spoken of unrequited love.

Creed was in love with Maya.

She was sure of it. Did Maya know?

"Creed?"

He blinked and it was gone.

Skylar opened the door, calling out as Maya got into her car. "Maya. Wait up." She caught up with her friend. "What's going on with you and Creed?"

"He just...he brings out the worst in me." She inhaled deeply, still visibly agitated. "I'm sorry if we upset you."

Skylar waved her apology away. "Maya, I think if you just opened your eyes, you'd see that Creed cares for you. He's got his own investigator trying to find Patricia, too."

Her friend snorted. "He's only looking for something incriminating. Nothing would please him more if he found something to discredit us."

They halted their conversation when their subject came out of the door. Creed gave them a long cool look on the way to his car.

"I think you're wrong," Skylar murmured as they watched his car move off. "He's not as bad as you think he is. As *I* thought he was."

"I wish I could believe that," Maya grumbled.

Zack's cell phone bleeped at four-thirty in the morning, waking both of them. At the sound of Max Fortune's somber voice, he was wide-awake in seconds.

"Wassup?" Skylar mumbled groggily as he eased out of bed.

"Business." Zack dragged on his jeans and headed for the door. "Go back to sleep."

Max was watching the evening news in Australia and thought Zack should know, regardless of the time. It was as bad as it could get. The current affairs TV show had scooped everyone, reneging on its promise not to air his father's interview until the eve of the New Zealand elections.

The country's foremost political family, including the current leader of the opposition, Zack's uncle, was drowning in allegations of blackmail and corruption. The government was overjoyed and Zack's name was back in the limelight, big-time.

"I thought your old man was dead," Max said.

"So did I." Zack switched on the television and turned the volume down with the remote.

"It sounds like a bad soap opera. Framed for a murder he didn't commit..."

Zack grunted and flicked through the international news channels. "Oh, he did it, but it was self-defense. The family bribed the three witnesses, had the police plant evidence and prejudiced the judiciary. It should have been manslaughter."

"How long for murder in New Zealand?"

His eyes flicked over a headline: *Historical conviction sinks New Zealand opposition party.* "Thirteen years, give or take." He chuckled mirthlessly. "He learned a few bad habits inside and continued on his winning ways."

"So that's why you moved to the South Island? To keep an eye on him?"

"I wanted to support him, help him."

By throwing money at him when all the old man really wanted was revenge. But all of Zack's money and desire to help could not prevent the demise of the court case.

"Does Skylar know any of this?"

"Dad had already done the interview by the time I found out I was going to be a daddy. The snap election was out of the blue. I thought I had a few more days up my sleeve."

Max exhaled. "Zack, do you want to marry her?"

"Yes!"

"Why?"

Zack considered for a moment. "It started off just being about the baby." And because he hoped a grand-child might make up for the crap hand his father had been served.

"Zack?"

He quickly changed channels and twisted around to frown at Skylar. "Did I wake you?"

She shook her head, yawning. "Anything wrong?"

"No, baby. Just some stock market stuff."

"Oh." She yawned again. "'Kay." She shuffled off toward the stairs like a sleepwalker.

"You know, Zack, when I recognized that Sky was falling for you, I almost warned her off. Not because I've ever seen you treat a woman badly, but you charm a woman into thinking it's her idea to keep things casual." Max chuckled. "I had you pegged as the world's biggest commitmentphobe."

"I'm committed," Zack muttered. He stared at the stairs where Skylar's sleepy form had ascended a few seconds before. His word should be enough for Max.

Although they rarely discussed personal feelings, Max knew him better than anyone.

"This isn't going to look good on your CV as far as the Fortunes are concerned," Max told him.

"Any chance you can keep Teddy from telling Nash? At least until I get a commitment from her. I think once we're engaged, the family might close ranks and support me."

"A fait accompli," Max mused. "I'll try but he and Nash have grown close. They're in almost daily contact since Patricia left. Dad thinks the world of you, but…"

"But blood is thicker than water," Zack finished for him. Especially, he thought, in a family like the Fortunes. Hadn't he experienced that sort of snobbery before? Another girl, another pregnancy, another wealthy family who liked to run roughshod over everyone.

Zack couldn't take the chance of the family turning their backs, not when his baby was at stake.

"Regardless of whether I can persuade my father to keep quiet," Max continued, "there is another problem. A couple of people rang the offices today, looking for you. The girls didn't know your whereabouts was a secret. Since every reporter in Australia and New Zealand wants to talk to you, it could be one or two of them are winging their way to South Dakota right now."

Ten

Zack's mood worsened the next morning when Skylar arrived at the stables, wittering on about Maya and Creed. She'd called Eliza last night and cooked up some harebrained scheme to throw the unassuming couple together alone, with no escape. Zack told her she ought to keep her nose out of it.

He was tired of waiting. The phone call from Max reminded him he'd given her all the leeway he could afford. As soon as he could get away, he strode to the office, just as she yanked open the door and started out.

Slapping the grain and dust from his thighs he looked at her face and stilled, seeing her distress. "What's up?"

It started to rain. Skylar had the car keys in her hand but backed up into the office, motioning him inside. "Someone's bought the pasture I lease from next door."

He followed her in. "What does your contract say?"

She looked down, scuffing her boot. "No contract. It was an informal arrangement."

Zack rubbed his hand over his stubbled face; he didn't bother shaving here until the day's work was done. "If you don't mind my saying, that's a funny way to do business."

"Yes, thank you, Zack," she muttered. "At the time, it suited us both. He was well paid."

She jingled the car keys in her hand.

"Where are you going?"

"I'm meeting a land agent in town. He's going to show me some plots."

"Now?" He was all fired up to talk about a different kind of deal.

"I need to find somewhere for the sixty mares I have booked this summer. This will lose me clients by the truckload."

Suddenly his brain cleared. "If you think about it, this couldn't have come at a better time. Maybe it's a good opportunity to scale the operation down."

Her head rose sharply. "Scale it…" She sounded disbelieving. "Whatever I decide to do, Fortune Stud will not be downgraded to some sort of hobby farm."

Zack wasn't in the mood to hear about Fortune Stud. He'd cooled his heels enough the last two weeks. "You have—" his eyes dropped pointedly to the tight roundness of her belly "—different responsibilities now. Be realistic, Skylar. It's time you were making arrangements. Call your clients and tell them to arrange alternative accommodations for their mares."

Skylar squared off and planted her boots, eyes sparking.

"Or, since you clearly don't like that idea, give Bob the responsibility. Make him manager. You have bigger things to think about."

"I don't have time for this." She huffed out an impatient breath and turned to the door.

Zack took a step and nailed her arm in a firm grip. *Oh, no, lady, you don't walk away from this.* "I want an answer, Sky," he told her grimly. "And I want it tonight."

Skyar raised her chin and met his uncompromising gaze. She knew exactly what he was talking about and it had nothing to do with Fortune Stud. How did they go from discussing her problems with the land to his marriage proposal? So much for a sympathetic ear!

The driving rain did nothing to improve her mood on the way into town. She felt disconnected lately, as if she'd been picked up and dumped into someone else's life and it wasn't just the pregnancy. She was not used to work-related calamities. Everything usually ran like clockwork around here but in the last few weeks, so many weird things had occurred. Nuisance things, nothing of any real importance but things that made her look unprofessional and could impact on business.

Was it hormones stoking her imagination, or was someone trying to sabotage her operation?

She considered the other thoroughbred breeders in South Dakota but there were so few of them. The Fortunes were prominent in business—maybe someone had a beef. But they would be more likely to target Case and Creed than her.

Who could profit from her loss of business? As she drove, her mind veered away from a nasty little suspicion that whispered and nagged. All through her consultation with the land agent she forbade herself to think of it, but it taunted and distracted her.

Zack Manning had something to gain if her business suffered.

If someone had designed this campaign of mischief to discourage her, it was working. She had built up a strong business since leaving college. She and her father invested heavily in expanding and refurbishing the facilities and when her gamble on Black Power paid off, she'd earned as credible a name in this industry as any young female had, even if her surname did open a few doors.

The land agent opened a big black umbrella and led her out to his car. Zack was right. She had other responsibilities now. But maybe he was banking on her seeing it would be simpler to make a fresh start if things were going wrong here. A fresh start in a new country.

"Are you all right?" the land agent asked. "You're a little pale. Morning sickness?"

Skylar shook her head. "Past all that."

Who had bought the land? Her neighbor, John Burke, said the buyer wished to remain anonymous and had gone through an agent. He apologized but said he'd left two messages. She hadn't gotten back to him.

Because of the accident and then being wrapped in cotton wool by the father of her baby…but there hadn't been any messages.

Suddenly she recalled Zack's handwriting on her desk pad. Burke's name and the phone number. The man *had* called, only no one—certainly not Zack—had told her.

She was getting this out of context. Everyone was entitled to the benefit of the doubt.

They drove to a second property but already Skylar knew it was unsuitable due to its distance from the estate. How could she look after sixty mares and foals if she lost the land? They got out of the car for a minute but the umbrella promptly turned inside out by a gust of wind.

"Tornado weather," the man said pleasantly. Many around here worried about tornadoes at this time of year after a cluster of devastating storms a couple of years back.

Was Zack Manning a tornado, ripping through her carefully structured life, sucking up her options so that starting anew with him seemed like the obvious answer?

An icy dread lodged under her ribs and she hugged herself.

The cardinal sin for shy people was to believe that one day their peers would seek them out and see how animated and interesting they really were. Skylar learned early not to draw attention to herself.

Zack's attention and concern for the baby had deluded her into thinking it extended to her, too. It was easy to visualize how good it could be between them, how right. She'd allowed herself to hope they had a future together.

The land agent chattered on but she kept mostly silent on the way back to his office, wondering how she'd suddenly found herself in love. Skylar Fortune who never looked at a man twice, who actively avoided situations where romance might flourish.

And the man she had finally accepted into her heart was trying to ruin her.

"The weather sure has set in. You drive careful now."

She nodded, opening the door against the deluge. That was another thing about love, she thought, turning away from the man with a listless wave.

The rain streamed down her face as she unlocked her car and slid inside.

Love hurt.

* * *

Darkness chased her home, even though it was only late afternoon. Her thoughts were dark, too, as was Zack's face when she opened the door and found him on the phone, pacing her living room. He stopped when she entered, his eyes unreadable from across the room, and then he turned away. She peeled her wet jacket off and heard him mutter something about having no comment to make.

Was he cooking up something here in her own house?

"What's wrong?" she asked when he snapped his phone shut and faced her.

"Nothing." He crossed the room and took her jacket, hanging it up on the hook. "You're wet."

"A little." He was tense, his face drawn and pale. Concern and worry rose up.

Dammit! That's what made this love thing so sickening and—girlie. Here she stood, worried to death about him while he was likely trying to ruin her.

Skylar averted her face, afraid he'd see the foul suspicions in her eyes. "Who was on the phone?"

"No one. Where have you been?"

She walked over to the gas fire, warming her hands. "Told you. With the land agent."

He grunted and leaned against the edge of the sofa, his arms folded across his chest.

"Your mother called."

"Oh, heck!" Skylar clapped a hand lightly against her forehead. The lunch date with her mother… "Was she mad?"

A brief rise of his shoulders.

"I'll have a snack," she decided, "and then go."

His brows beetled. "It's pouring out there and nearly dark. Just call her."

Skylar stared into the fire and considered that option hopefully. She wasn't thrilled about going back out into the rain but... "She's going on vacation tomorrow. I need to see her."

Straightening, she walked into the kitchen and opened the fridge, looking for something quick and easy. The back of her neck prickled when Zack stood behind her, close enough to feel the anger emanating out of him.

"We have things to discuss tonight...."

"Creed thinks she may have something to do with Patricia's disappearance. I want to see her face." She paused and tossed him a meaningful look over her shoulder. "I can generally tell when someone's lying."

Zack's gaze narrowed. "Skylar, this is just one more reason, one more excuse to keep me at arm's length. If it's not work, it's your family or your friend to fix up. It's one step forward and two back with you."

She shrugged. "I'm sorry. I have a lot on my mind right now."

"What's it going to take to get a simple answer from you?"

She banged the fridge door shut, annoyance tickling her throat. How come he got to make all the demands? "Maybe I want some answers, too. Why are you pushing so hard, Zack? Because I don't buy the illegitimacy thing."

He raised his head imperiously. "Shall I remind you of your father's wishes on that subject? Your brothers, also, haven't been slow to point out to me the importance of the family reputation."

She knew all that but she'd bet her lucky horseshoe that

the Fortune reputation was not the main thing concerning him. "Those are bows to your arrow, Zack, but they're not what's driving you to be so insistent on a quick wedding."

He paused, measuring her up. "I told you about Rhianne. I won't let you or your family cut me out of this baby's life. Not twice in one lifetime."

"You must know I would never keep her from you."

"Then commit. Announce it to the world."

Skylar shook her head in exasperation. "You want to pick me up and dump me in some godforsaken place I never even heard of before I met you, and you expect me to be chafing at the bit?"

This was getting them nowhere. She took a glass down from the shelf and filled it with water.

Zack leaned against the counter, his eyes on her face. "I'm not happy about it but I've already decided you can stay here until after the baby's born. I don't want you flying that distance at this stage of your pregnancy."

"You're taking a bit much on yourself, aren't you?" she began, fighting to rein in her temper.

"It means I'll have to go back and forth," he interrupted. "But if that's what it takes to get a commitment out of you…" He stopped and looked at her. "Will that make it easier?"

Skylar thought she might just explode. "*You've* decided?" she seethed. "*You* don't want me to fly?"

His chin lifted. "But if I'm going to be in and out of the country, I want a public announcement of our engagement. That way, I'll know you won't disappear on me."

Skylar banged her glass down on the counter, imagining it was his head. He wasn't taking a bit of notice. She might as well have been in the next room!

She forced herself to take a couple of deep breaths and count to ten. Nothing would be gained by losing her temper. "It's more than that, Zack," she said, striving for a more reasonable tone. "My business is very important to me."

"Skylar, you made it a success here, you can do it again somewhere else."

He wasn't taking the bait. Wasn't giving her anything tangible to grasp on to. If only he'd say that he loved her or even really liked her. "There is so much I don't know about you. I need to be sure what sort of family I'm buying into. Your family is going to be your daughter's family. You won't speak of your father…"

His head rolled back in a gesture of impatience. "You said you hoped you were a better mother than yours. I could say the same about my father. What our parents did, how they managed, or mismanaged, their parental responsibilities has nothing to do with us."

He came to her and grasped her shoulders. "Who have you been living with the last couple weeks? We're good together, Skylar. It's more than most people start with."

He had an answer for everything, except the things she really needed to hear. "This isn't bringing us any closer to an agreement, Zack," she told him sadly. "You're not giving me anything different. Anything that gives me hope for our future together."

"You're doing it again," he snapped. "Grasping at straws. Every time I try to get close to you, you fire a different shot. What's next, I wonder?"

"Did you buy that land?"

The second the words were out of her mouth, she regretted them. And in the long seconds when her quiet words hung in the air between them, she thought wildly that she didn't want to know. She did not want to hear he could be so underhanded. It was bad enough being a girl in love without knowing that she'd fallen for a sly manipulator.

Zack looked stunned. "What are you on about now?"

She nearly wavered. *Take it back,* whispered through her mind. But to not know was burying her head in the sand. "You have to admit some weird things have happened since you arrived."

It was time she stopped backing down. Otherwise she'd continue to live her life unseen and unheard. "Bookings canceled. Foaling alarms turned off. And now, a person who doesn't want to be identified has bought my land."

Zack released her shoulders and took a step back. "Maybe I'm dense. Explain to me why I'd want that land when all I want is to marry you and take you home."

"Let's be hypothetical. Someone is causing mischief. Not much, just small niggling things that make my business seem badly run. Small things designed to discourage me." She paused and took a deep breath. "Perhaps to discourage me enough to consider a fresh start, somewhere else."

There. She'd said it. Please, God, it wasn't true but since he wanted a heart-to-heart, she would tell him what was in hers.

Not all of it, though. If he knew she loved him, he would exploit that.

"You are accusing me of sabotaging your business to get you to marry me?"

It sounded preposterous when he said it. But secret

phone calls, secrets period. Closeting her here in the cottage, keeping her away from the stables… Skylar looked him full in the face, her heartbeat thumping loudly in her ears. Had she made a terrible, life-altering mistake?

Yet he hadn't denied it….

"Is a marriage to me so unappealing, you'd think I would resort to ruining you to get it?" he asked softly.

"Zack, tell me you think more of me than that. That it's not just the baby you want."

"What I think of you isn't the issue." He shook his head as if to clear away a fog.

"If you did those things because you cared for me, about me, then I could—I will—forgive them." She was that desperate.

"*If* I did them…" An icy light leapt to life in his eyes but the rest of him was still.

"If you didn't," she said urgently, "*tell* me you didn't, and I'll believe you."

Please tell me, she begged silently. There had to be some explanation for the strange events. One that didn't involve this honorable man standing in front of her now.

"I'm beginning to get the picture here." Zack pushed away from her and began pacing the small room. "I'm not good enough. Is that what you're saying?" He stopped and stared at her. "An uppity commoner from the bottom of the world who got lucky enough to plant his seed in the hallowed Fortune turf."

"That's ridiculous." That he could think that of her astounded her. Her birthright had nothing to do with who she was and no one had ever called her a snob before.

"No old money or tradition here," he continued, resuming his pacing. "Just a lowly businessman. Can't have any old genes cluttering up the family breeding ground."

Disappointment made her voice raw. "That's not it at all." She'd practically begged him to say he cared for her and his response was to throw snobbery in her face. He didn't get it.

Hadn't denied it, either.

"I thought we had a connection, something I haven't felt for anyone since Rhianne." He stopped again and ran his hands through his hair. "What a priceless joke."

Skylar shook her head. "I'm not laughing." She made for the door, tired and hungry. Angry and sad.

His clipped tones halted her at the door. "Maybe you're as shallow as your mother, after all."

She stopped but did not turn. "What's my mother got to do with this?" Skylar was getting a little tired of everyone dissing her mother. As far as she was concerned, that job should be reserved for her and Blake, no one else.

"Maybe all you want is the baby. Not the man. Not a relationship." He gave a hard sort of grimace that was probably meant to be a smile. "A baby accessory."

It was like a cold water slap in the face. He was a good shot. "You are so wrong, Zack."

"And you're totally wrong about me, too, Skylar. Ha!" There was no mirth in his exclamation. "So we do have something in common after all."

Skylar stalked across the room and snagged her still-damp jacket off the hook. "Not enough to base a marriage on." She opened the door. "I'm going to see my mother."

Eleven

Zack prowled the room like a caged animal. The cottage sat in the midst of a copse of trees, intensifying the roar of the wind. He peered blindly out into the night as rain lashed the windows. The minutes crawled by.

He should never have let her go. The cheap shot he'd fired about her being like her mother was purely a knee-jerk reaction to her accusations. Swallowing his anger, he knew how unwarranted it was.

He had only met Trina once but Skylar was nothing like her. In fact, he suspected she lived her life as the polar opposite of her mother. The dressing down, no interest in attracting men—save for one memorable occasion—her dislike of her mother's shallow pursuit of beauty, money and men, in that order.

And the biggie: there was no way in hell Skylar would ever abandon her child. Zack guessed that her mother's abandonment and her frequently mentioned disappointment at her daughter's choice of occupation left Skylar feeling unwanted and unloved. She would never inflict those feelings on her own child.

After an hour, he called her, spinning around when he heard her ring tone coming from the tote she'd tossed on the kitchen table. Zack swore viciously. They had a deal. It was one of his conditions that she be contactable at all times.

And she would have been if he hadn't upset her so much; she'd rushed out with only a thin jacket and her car keys.

Two hours after she'd left, he called her mother. The woman was subdued, saying Skylar had left an hour ago and, no, she hadn't mentioned going any-where else.

That was a quick visit, he thought, calculating the distance from here to town. It was a thirty minute drive at the most, even in the terrible conditions.

The eaves of the cottage shuddered. He turned the evening news on, trying to distract himself from a grow-ing worry. The local station reported on the storm, say-ing severe weather patterns were in play and already some of the streets of Sioux Falls were awash.

Zack called the big house and ascertained she wasn't there. With one eye on the TV, he then called Maya.

"She's left her phone here. Which way would she drive home from her mother's?"

Maya outlined a possible route just as the reporter on television said that wind had knocked all the traffic lights in the city out and there were widespread power cuts all over the region. As if to underline the point, the lights in the cottage flickered briefly.

"Is Creed home?" Maya asked.

"No." Zack got up, thinking he'd better find some candles. "Nash said he's staying in town because of the storm."

"I'll call him—you call Case and Gina."

Zack found Skylar's stash of candles and laid them on the table. Deeply worried, he put some water on to boil and then picked up the phone again.

Case and Gina were huddled up at their apartment in town. "Sioux Falls is notorious for flooding. She'd have to cross Skunk Creek, which sometimes flash floods."

Thanks for putting my mind at rest, Zack thought. "I'm going to take the truck and go looking."

"You stay there," Case insisted. "The streetlights are out in town and you're not familiar with the area."

Case promised to go looking and hung up, leaving Zack his cell phone number in case Skylar turned up. Maya called to say Creed was on his way to pick her up and they would scour the streets. Zack felt useless but she persuaded him that they were more familiar with the routes she was likely to go if required to detour. "Besides, when she turns up wondering what all the fuss is about, you can call us."

He saw the logic but it was excruciating to sit there by himself while his woman and baby were out in the storm with no means of communication.

As another hour crawled by and the storm intensified, his self-recriminations were bitter. He had reacted to her accusations by attacking her. He let his pride prevent him from saying what he wanted to say, what she needed to hear. That he loved her. That it wasn't just the baby he wanted. That she was the most precious and important thing in his life.

Why hadn't he told her? Pride and his fear she would shun him once she knew the truth about his dysfunctional family.

She wouldn't. Skylar couldn't have cared less. Deep down, he knew she was begging him to love her, even if she couldn't say it. But he'd let ego and righteous indignation get in the way.

Dammit! He would lose her if he didn't come clean.

A blast of thunder rocked the house and the lights flickered off for a few seconds. He moved to the window. The trees outside thrashed and swayed. The weather report said this was tornado weather, mild humid air, winds chopping and changing direction, heavy rain and now thunder. A couple of years ago this region was smashed by around fifty storms and tornadoes in a matter of days. The locals would not sleep tonight.

When he saw her next he wouldn't let her go. Ever.

That was, after he'd throttled her for going out without her phone.

After he'd come clean about his past and warned her of the scandal heading their way. The eagle-eyed reporters in this town who delighted in bagging the Fortunes at every opportunity would have a field day.

After he'd told her he loved her.

Skylar's chest pressed against the steering wheel as she leaned forward to peer through the windshield. The wipers were barely coping with the deluge.

Damn her mother. She eased a hand from its iron grip on the steering wheel and swiped at her cheeks. Damn pregnancy for turning her into a blubbering idiot. The fight with Trina had been spectacular.

After suffering the usual inspection—"Lovely cheek-bones, darling. You get those from me. And your skin has improved with pregnancy…"—Skylar, still smarting from her fight with Zack, launched into her mother, demanding she swear she had nothing to do with Patricia leaving.

Stung, Trina denied it but then broke down in an uncharacteristic display of emotion and guilt. That's when Skylar discovered the ultimate betrayal.

Lightning flashed again, close, frightening her. It seemed like she'd been in the car for hours, fighting a growing panic. Why hadn't she gone to Maya's, or to the Fortune building or hotel? She imagined Zack's worry and anger at her for being without her phone.

That's if he was still there. After her disgusting accusations, he may well be on his way back to New Zealand. It was all so clear now. He may be overbearing and too protective at times, but manipulative? No way. Her stupid pregnancy hormones made her crazy. She wanted to hear that he loved her. He hadn't said that, but looking back, he had said he'd felt a connection, right from the start. Something he hadn't felt for another woman since Rhianne.

She wiped her eyes again and focused on that. He was still in his teens when he'd gotten Rhianne pregnant. That was a heck of a long time not to feel something for a woman.

Skylar's heart turned over. If that wasn't a declaration of love, it was pretty close to it. And he'd felt that when they met, not when he discovered the pregnancy.

Maybe everything wasn't about the baby after all.

But she'd gone and ruined it now, and all for nothing. Trina was the one responsible. The new stable hand, Ben, was her stooge, put there to cause trouble. He left Deme's stall unlatched and turned off the foaling alarms, as per Trina's instructions. She was responsible for the canceled mare and buying the land.

"I did it for your own good, darling," she'd pleaded. "You were wasting your life."

"Be honest, Mother. You did it to get back at Nash."

Skylar had long since accepted the shallowness and vanity of her mother. She only ever wanted anything to do with her children when doing so would strike at Nash. But to actively attempt to ruin her own daughter's business was unforgivable. "That's it. I want nothing to do with you ever again."

"You don't mean that." Trina's beauty-parlor-induced glow paled. "The baby…"

"I don't want my baby anywhere near your bitter poison."

She'd walked out with her head held high and a bruise on her heart. Whatever Trina's failings, she was still her mother. Now that Skylar was expecting, her own daughter cutting her off was something she could not imagine in a million years.

She shook off her pity. Her mother deserved no less. Because of her mischief, Skylar may have lost Zack for good.

Another mighty gust of wind rocked the car. The land agent had warned her about tornado weather. She peered into the blackness, aware that a twister would be on top of her before she'd see it. *Please, please get me home safely,* she prayed. *I need to tell him how sorry I am. I need to find the words to tell him that I love him.*

Finally, through the lightning and near-horizontal rain on her windshield, she saw the pillars of the estate up ahead. She'd made it.

Her relief faded when she pulled up to the cottage. The lights were out. He wasn't there.

She got out of the car and raced through a wall of water to her door, just as it opened. Skylar stopped with a jerk, peering through the murk at the broad shoulders crowding the doorway a foot in front of her. Her heart leapt with joy.

Short-lived joy. His hands gripped her shoulders and he shook her. "Dammit, are you *trying* to lose this baby?"

Skylar closed her eyes, too relieved to protest. Then his grip changed and he propelled her forward and into his arms.

"Thank God," he muttered, crushing her to his chest. Her arms were trapped and she couldn't hug him back. They stood on her porch, stinging rain whipping into every part of her, which meant he was getting soaked, too, but they stayed that way for long moments.

Finally he stepped back and pulled her inside.

Most of the storm noise was cut off abruptly when he closed the door. Zack led her to the fire and then left the room without a word. She stared around at the candles on the mantel and coffee tables. The power must have gone off, not unusual for a storm of this magnitude in these parts.

Zack returned with a couple of towels and a blanket. "Dry off," he ordered. While she mopped her face and hands, he pulled the sofa in front of the fire.

Skylar shook with cold and emotion but her most desperate need was the bathroom. Her bladder hadn't anticipated the long drive home. When she returned, mugs of steaming soup and a plate of sandwiches sat on the coffee table.

Zack picked up his phone. "Eat," he commanded, nodding at the snack.

"How did you…"

"I found a Thermos while I was hunting out candles." He punched some numbers into the phone. "I have everyone in the country out looking for you."

She wrapped her icy hands gratefully around a hot mug. Zack called Maya first, thanking her and Creed. Skylar hated that she'd worried everyone. Some people might find it gratifying that they'd caused such a fuss. Unaccustomed to attention, she just felt stupid.

Dialing again, he nudged the sandwiches closer, his eyes stern. She sighed, inhaling the steam off the cup of instant soup. Tomato. How did he always know just what she needed?

Zack finished talking to Case and stood looking at her. He looked more grim than angry.

Skylar gulped down a mouthful of soup and felt the too-hot liquid inch down her throat. "Those things I said earlier…" she stammered. "I just want to curl up and die."

He gave her an inscrutable look then sat down beside her and began unbraiding her plait. "What are you doing to me, woman?" His voice was gruff, his hands rough on her hair and she quickly put the soup mug down.

"Eat something, will you?" he said.

She picked up a sandwich and took a quick bite. Zack finished combing her wet hair out with his fingers and then picked up the towel and began rubbing her head briskly.

She sighed and put the sandwich down. "It was my mother." She closed her eyes while he rubbed her down like a horse. God knows what she looked like. "Ben's on her payroll. I hired him at her request. He's the son of a friend of hers. She paid him to cause trouble and she bought the land."

Zack ceased his rubbing and leaned back to peer into her face, his eyes questioning.

It hurt, saying it out loud. Her mother's complete disregard for her feelings astounded her—though she should be used to it by now. After all, this was the woman who had happily left her here with Nash when he kicked her out. Children were noisy, messy and a social no-no as far as Trina was concerned.

"To get back at my father mostly. I guess she thought hurting me, especially financially, would hurt him."

Zack stared at her. The last vestiges of anger drained away, and he looked more tired than she'd ever seen him, except for the long night at the hospital. Another night when he'd ministered to her, taken care of her, even though she'd brought it all on herself.

"I'm...sorry," he said simply.

Skylar shrugged again. "That's okay. I'm used to it."

"But you're her daughter, her own flesh and blood."

"So's Blake, yet she sold lies to the papers about him and Sasha breaking up." Zack nodded. "He told me."

"She's so bitter toward my father, she really doesn't think about anything except hurting him."

He stared at her face for a moment more and then tossed the towel down and laid a blanket around her shoulders. "You should get out of these wet clothes."

She pulled the blanket tightly around herself. "We won't have to worry about her anymore," she said heavily. "I've cut all ties, told her we're finished and that I don't want her to have anything to do with the baby."

Zack took her chin gently, bringing her face around to him. "Don't do that, Sky. You'll regret it."

His earnest tone surprised her.

"You can't turn your back on your parents, just like you and I will never turn our backs on little Amanda here." He swallowed. "No matter what she does."

She nodded, knowing it was the truth. "You're very forgiving after what I accused you of."

"I have to tell you something." He leaned back, his eyes serious. "It's going to come out any minute, anyway."

Skylar began to hope. Was he finally going to open up to her?

"My mother," he began, staring into the fire, "got pregnant at seventeen, with me. Her family was very wealthy, very powerful, politically. Back then, you couldn't get an abortion in New Zealand except on the street and they couldn't risk someone talking. So they had a family member fly her, against her will, to Australia for an abortion there."

Skylar closed her eyes in anguish. Not once, but twice. How could he bear it?

"But she got away, disappeared. I think she was genuinely afraid they would kill her, or me. She changed her name and never stopped running. I didn't find any of this out until after she died, but it fit. We never stayed in one place for more than a few months."

"Why didn't your father go?"

"They'd spirited her away in the middle of the night. He went to them, looking for her. There was an argument with one of her brothers, just a bit of pushing and shoving. The guy fell and hit his head but there were witnesses present who said he was bashed from behind with a poker as he left the room."

"There must have been evidence, fingerprints…"

"It was thirty-odd years ago. Forensics wasn't like it is now." Zack shrugged. "Anyway, the family had the police in their pockets."

"So he went to jail?"

"For quite a few years. When he got out, he had nothing. I suppose he thought he may as well live up to everyone's opinion of him. He spent most of his life in and out of prison, petty stuff, mostly, until I found him."

Skylar tried to conceal her shock. How long had he expected to keep it from her? "How do you get on with him?"

Zack laid his head back on the edge of the sofa, peering at the ceiling. "It's an uneasy relationship. It's hard for him to trust. He's straight now, but he wants his revenge and I can't blame him." He put his hands behind his head. "Especially when the son of one of the witnesses has backed Dad's story. A few months ago, I bankrolled a court case against my mother's family so he could have his day in court."

Skylar slid down off the sofa, still draped in the blanket, and leaned against his legs. "What happened?"

"We lost. Politics is their game and they're good at it. There have been two prime ministers in that family and my uncle still heads the main opposition party. There are elections coming up and it's entirely possible that he could be our next prime minister."

"Have you met them?"

Zack shook his head. "I don't exist, just like my mother ceased to exist for them when she ran away." He looked down at her seriously. "The reason I've been anxious to marry you so quickly is because my father has gone to the media. He tried it my way with the lawyers and it didn't work. The story broke over there last night."

"And your name is mentioned?" She frowned. "What *is* your real name?"

"My mother changed her name legally so I'm sticking with Manning. Her name was Greta Thorne. My dad is John Carter."

It was so much to take in. "Why didn't you tell me this, Zack? It would have explained so much."

He inhaled slowly. "I couldn't take the chance that you or your family would cut me out of the baby's life."

Oh, heck, of course he would think that. Her throat closed with sympathy and her eyes filled up again. "Just like your mother and then Rhianne," she whispered. "It's like history repeating."

"For the third time."

She rested her chin on his knee, not even caring that she was blubbering again. "Did you really think I would turn my back on you?"

He pursed his lips and let out a tense breath. "Not you, no. But I thought your father and brothers might. And if history *was* going to repeat, they would persuade you, or force you, into cutting me out."

A smile flickered across her lips and she shook her head. "They wouldn't succeed."

Zack dropped his hand, stroking her hair, and she slipped her arms around his leg.

"You would have me then?" he asked softly.

She sighed and rubbed her face against the still damp denims he wore. "In a Midwest minute."

Gently, he fisted his fingers and tugged her face up so she had to look at him. "What do you think your family is going to think of their Fortune princess hooking up with the son of a convicted murderer?"

"They'll back me, if I ask them to."

"It could get ugly," he warned. "Lots of headlines, especially once the papers here realize my connection to you."

"It'll be nice to be noticed for once," she told him with a wry smile. "I haven't exactly set the gossip pages alight with my nonexistent love life."

He gazed at her for a few intense moments. "I know I'm asking a lot, expecting you to give up everything and move halfway across the world. But I've been thinking. If you promoted Bob and I hired some extra help to run my businesses, we could split our living arrangements between here and New Zealand, depending on whose breeding season it is."

Skylar stared at him, overwhelmed. "I...don't know what to say." His concern and thoughtfulness reinforced her belief that Zack would make an exceptional father. She also realized that where they lived wasn't important, but the fact that he had offered the compromise was everything. "You don't know what it means to me that you said that," she told him haltingly. "Zack, I don't care where we live, as long as..." She closed her eyes, felt the old shy stammering Skylar Fortune flow back into her.

"It makes sense, Skylar. That way, Amanda gets to grow up with both her families."

"Both her grandpappies," Skylar agreed. "How does he, your father, feel about the baby?"

Zack looked thoughtful. "I'm hoping this will bring

us closer and also make up a bit for what he's missed out on all these years."

"I can't wait to meet him."

Zack leaned down and laced his fingers through hers. "It's taken me," he exhaled noisily, "eighteen years to find the woman I want to be with forever."

Her eyes brimmed and she ducked her head. Maybe if she wasn't looking at him, the constriction in her throat might ease a little. "Do you, Zack? Want to be with me forever?"

He squeezed her fingers. "If you don't know that by now, Skylar, then I don't know how else to show you."

His voice was warm but discussions about personal feelings crucified her. She was too shy to see if his dimples were showing.

"It's not just about the baby?" she mumbled into his knees.

"It didn't start with the baby—it started in January, when we met."

That was unexpected.

"There was something about you, even then, even before the night of the wedding," he continued. "Because you were so shy I didn't want to push it, but I'd already decided I was coming back in September. If I still felt the same zap, I *would* have pushed it, lady. Making love with you the night of the wedding just made me more determined." He tilted her head up so she had to look at him. "I kept in touch, remember? Every two weeks."

She wrenched her gaze away, staring into the fire. "I had this major-league crush but I sure as heck didn't know what to do about it."

"Until the wedding." Zack cleared his throat. "When I found out about the baby, well, I knew I couldn't lose this chance." He shook her fingers gently. "I haven't been celibate all these years, Skylar. But if I had gotten any one of those women pregnant, I'd have wanted to be involved with the baby but I sure as hell wouldn't have married them."

Her breath caught in her throat. Really?

"You were my special one," Zack murmured, "the one woman who made me want to consider forever."

Oh, she liked the sound of that very much. The baby rolled over. There was no other explanation for the fluttery exhilaration shivering through her. This was a lot to process and she had to respond but she was so lousy with words. "Zack, I…" She had to try. "You were the one for me, too. Only I never expected you to feel the same way. Things like this don't happen to me."

"Things like what?" he asked gently, stroking her hair.

She shrugged self-consciously. Someone get her a bag to put over her head. "You know. Feelings. Thinking about forever. Stuff like that."

He sighed. "Max reckons I'm good with the ladies but I'm sure making a mess of this." He lifted her hands off his knees and slid down until he was sitting on the floor beside her. "Look at me," he commanded, gripping her wrists tightly. "Help me out here. I'm in love with you, Skylar. Tell me you feel the same way."

Her eyes flew to his face and her mouth dropped open. He loved her, no, he was *in* love with her. "Oh," she said, wondering which was better. Love or in love.

They both sounded pretty darn good.

"Oh?" he asked, his brows almost meeting in the middle.

"I'm sorry, I'm not…" Her brain still wasn't functioning but her heart was rattling away at a gallop. She felt the smile start and was unable to stop it. And it got bigger and bigger, till her jaw ached and then Zack was smiling, too, right back at her. The two of them sat on the floor in front of the fire, holding hands and grinning at each other like idiots.

Finally, he shook his head and wiped his eyes. "Well, I'm not sure where that leaves us exactly but they do say a smile is worth a thousand words."

"I'm not very good at…" Her heart tripped again. She took a deep breath. "What *you* said. I love you, too." What a relief to finally get it out, even though her words *had* come out in a garbled rush.

Zack rubbed a hand over his eyes. "Perhaps you'll do better with a simple yes or no." He took one of her hands and brought it to his mouth, kissing each and every finger. "Skylar Fortune, will you marry me?"

Her heart was still jumping around like popcorn in the pan. The baby was squirming and the intense light in his eyes brought all the fine hairs on her neck and shoulders up. But at least her tongue seemed to escape from the knot it had tied itself into.

Skylar tugged his hand toward her and laid it on her cheek, still wearing that idiot grin on her face. "Yes, Zack Manning, I'd be honored."

* * * * *

FORTUNE'S FORBIDDEN WOMAN

WOMAN

by
Heidi Betts

HEIDI BETTS

An avid romance reader since school, Heidi knew early on that she wanted to write these wonderful stories of love and adventure. It wasn't until her first year of college, however, when she spent the entire night reading a romance novel instead of studying for exams, that she decided to take the road less travelled and follow her dream. In addition to reading and writing romance, she is the founder of her local Romance Writers of America chapter and has a tendency to take injured and homeless animals of every species into her Central Pennsylvania home.

Heidi loves to hear from readers. You can write to her at PO Box 99, Kylertown, PA 16847, USA (an SAE with return postage is appreciated, but not necessary) or e-mail heidi@heidibetts.com. And be sure to visit www.heidibetts.com for news and information about upcoming books.

For Mom – because it's been a while.
I love you!

One

"Thank you for dinner," Maya Blackstone said as she fitted her key into the lock of her downtown Sioux Falls town house. She twisted the key and then the knob, opening the door a crack before turning back to Brad McKenzie.

It was dark outside, but the yellow glow of the porch light reflected his tall frame, chestnut hair and handsome face.

"You're welcome," he said, offering a small smile as his hand stroked down her arm, left bare by the sleeveless knit top she was wearing. "Aren't you going to invite me in?"

Gooseflesh broke out along her skin, making her shiver. She shouldn't have been surprised by his suggestion. They'd been dating for almost a year now, and Brad was one of the nicest guys she'd ever met. It was only natural that their relationship would begin to move in a more physical, intimate direction. Lord knew he'd been pushing for it for months now.

Not aggressively, and not in any way that would make her feel pressured, but she wasn't stupid. She knew what all the little touches and caresses meant. She also knew that most couples who'd been seeing each other as long as she and Brad had would already be sleeping together.

And there was no reason she *shouldn't* go to bed with him. He was kind, good-looking, successful and treated her like a princess. She was even attracted to him.

So what was her problem? What was she waiting for?

Taking a deep breath, she steeled her nerves and made her decision.

"Of course." Pushing open the front door, she stepped inside and flipped on the light that illuminated the small entryway. She set her purse on the decorative bench she kept against the wall and headed for the kitchen, leaving Brad to close the door and follow along. He'd been inside her house often enough to know his way around and make himself at home.

"Would you like something to drink?" she asked, going to the refrigerator to see what she had to offer. "Iced tea or a glass of wine. I could make some coffee."

He came up behind her, standing so close she could feel the heat of his body at her back.

"Wine would be good," he murmured in a low voice, taking the opportunity to rub her shoulders.

Fighting the urge to shrug away from his hold, she grabbed the open bottle of chardonnay from the top shelf of the refrigerator, then opened a nearby cupboard to retrieve two glasses. She walked around the corner into the living room, breaking Brad's hold on her but knowing he was close on her heels.

They lowered themselves onto the overstuffed, floral-patterned sofa. Maya sat forward, setting the glasses on the coffee table while she popped the cork and poured a generous amount of the fragrant liquid for each of them.

She turned to hand one of the glasses to Brad, taking a deep breath to keep from shifting farther away. He was sitting close, his thigh pressing along hers, his shoulder brushing her own as he took the wine.

This was ridiculous, she chastised herself. What was she afraid of? What was she waiting for?

Brad sipped his wine while she drank hers a bit more forcefully, then set her empty glass on the table in front of them. Turning, she smiled and settled against his side, both of them leaning into the soft back of the sofa.

His brows lifted, and it took a second for his arm to tighten around her.

She didn't blame him for being surprised, since she wasn't usually the one to make the first move.

Usually? Try never. She had never made the first move with Brad. A part of her couldn't believe she was doing it now.

But a year was long enough. She *wanted* to be with Brad. She wanted to be normal, have a normal relationship. And if things were ever going to move forward with them, become more serious, she needed to get over these intimacy issues she seemed to have.

Tipping her head back, she silently invited him to kiss her. An invitation he wasted no time accepting.

Despite her reservations, she had to admit he was a good kisser. Even she had no trouble recognizing that aspect of his personality.

His mouth moved over hers smoothly, his lips warm and firm. He caressed her shoulders, then her arms, his hands sliding around to her back.

It felt good, enjoyable, and she thought they really might make it this time.

With a moan he pulled her closer, deepening the kiss and pressing their bodies together so that she could feel the clear sign of his arousal.

Her stomach clenched, but not with desire. Nerves flared to life in her bloodstream, her muscles growing tense, her breathing growing labored as panic set in.

Dammit. She stiffened, whimpering partly in fear and partly in aggravation as she put out her arms and shoved away.

Brad blinked, his chest heaving, stunned by her sudden retreat.

"I'm sorry," she said, shaking her head and shifting back as far as she could against the arm of the couch.

Why, *why* did she keep doing this? Why couldn't she

act like a regular twenty-five-year-old woman and sleep with her boyfriend without being plagued by so many doubts? Without seeing *his* face when she closed her eyes, and hearing *his* voice thundering in her ears.

Damn, damn, damn.

Brad blew out a breath and ran his fingers through his hair, frustration rolling off of him in waves. "I know. You're sorry, but you can't."

The words held no accusation or anger whatsoever, which only made her feel worse.

When he got to his feet, she jumped up and followed him across the room toward the front door.

"I really am sorry," she told him, feeling guilty and miserable, but not knowing what else to say.

What else *could* she say? She *was* sorry, even though she couldn't offer him any more of an explanation than that.

At the door he paused with his hand on the knob and turned to meet her gaze. She thought he must surely be entertaining thoughts of chewing her out at this point, but his hazel eyes remained soft and gentle.

"I know you are. So am I." He lifted a hand to tuck a loose strand of hair behind her ear. "I told you I wouldn't push you, Maya, and I meant it. I'm becoming a pro at cold showers," he added with a tiny lift to his lips, "but no pressure."

Stepping onto the front stoop, he turned back to kiss her cheek before walking slowly back to his car.

She watched him drive away, then closed the door

and banged her head lightly on the cool wood a few times. Even she was getting tired of this, so she could just imagine how poor Brad was feeling. She only wished there was something she could do about the anxieties that were turning memories from the past into a full-blown phobia.

It was all *his* fault. She hadn't seen her step-brother in months, but still Creed Fortune somehow managed to be the plague of her existence.

Ever since she was a little girl, when she and her mother had moved into the Fortune Estate so Patricia could act as nanny to Nash Fortune's four young children, Creed had been nothing but cold to her. Even after Nash and her mother had fallen in love and married, making Nash's kids Maya's new stepsiblings, she had still gotten along with the others better than she had with Creed.

It was easy to be friends with Skylar, who was only a year older than Maya. They'd had a lot in common and had played together from the time they were little.

Eliza had been six years older and not much interested in playing role model to another girl other than her own half sister, though she'd always been nice to Maya. And Blake—Skylar's brother and Nash's son from his second marriage to Trina Watters—had thankfully been kind to her.

But Case and Creed Fortune—sons from Nash's first marriage to his now deceased college sweetheart, Elizabeth—were several years older than Maya and had always treated her like an outsider. They'd ignored her and made her feel unwelcome in what was supposed to be her own home.

She'd never really been comfortable living in that big house with so many people who were technically her family but felt more like strangers.

In addition, Maya had always been the ugly stepsister. She was plain and quiet, and not a true Fortune. She was simply the shy, unremarkable girl who'd shown up one day with the new, live-in nanny and ended up a sister when their parents fell in love. But that didn't mean any of the *real* Fortune children had to like her.

Pushing away from the door, she dragged herself back to the living room to collect the wineglasses and nearly empty bottle. When she reached the kitchen, she put Brad's glass upside down over one of the spokes of the dishwasher basket, then poured the end of the wine into her own glass, watching the last few drops *drip, drip, drip* as her head began to pound.

And after all of the insecurities and loneliness, she'd still been crazy enough to develop a childhood crush on Creed almost from the moment she met him. He'd been handsome, older…and so sophisticated.

He was still handsome, older and sophisticated…but she'd long ago given up on winning his heart.

Honestly, she'd have had better luck attracting the attention of a fence post. No matter how often she followed him around or how many cow-eyed glances she'd sent him, he'd never given her the time of day. If anything, he'd only grown colder and more distant the longer her crush had lingered on.

It was highly humiliating. And what made matters even worse was the fact that she apparently *still* wasn't over him.

Was she in love with him?

She didn't think so. She certainly didn't want to be.

But she also couldn't seem to get him out of her brain. He swirled in there, making her neurotic and half-insane.

She was mature enough to realize that the case of puppy love she'd entertained as a kid had been nothing more than a sick case of hero worship. Unfortunately, that hero worship had since worked itself into a maddening and unhealthy obsession with Creed Fortune.

Which was hopeless and futile, considering he'd never shown the least bit of interest in her as a woman. He'd never shown the least bit of interest in her, period.

Yet he still managed to intrude on her self-confidence, her sexuality and her relationship with Brad.

With a growl Maya threw back the last of the wine, added her own glass to the dishwasher basket, then slammed the appliance door closed. She swore, if Creed were standing in front of her right this minute, she'd be sorely tempted to slap him.

Taking a deep breath, she turned on her heel and headed for the stairs. What she needed was a hot shower and a solid eight hours of sleep.

What she *didn't* need was this flood of doubts and frustrations. For God's sake, her life was already com-

GET FREE BOOKS and a FREE MYSTERY GIFT WHEN YOU PLAY THE...

Just scratch off the silver box with a coin. Then check below to see the gifts you get!

SLOT MACHINE GAME!

YES! I have scratched off the silver box. Please send me the 2 FREE books and mystery gift for which I qualify. I understand I am under no obligation to purchase any books, as explained on the back of this card. I am over 18 years of age.

D8CI

Mrs/Miss/Ms/Mr _____ Initials _____

BLOCK CAPITALS PLEASE

Surname _____

Address _____

_____

Postcode _____

7	7	7	**Worth TWO FREE BOOKS plus a BONUS Mystery Gift!**
🍒	🍒	🍒	**Worth TWO FREE BOOKS!**
♣	♣	♣	**Worth ONE FREE BOOK!**
🔔	🔔	🍒	**TRY AGAIN!**

Visit us online at www.millsandboon.co.uk

NO STAMP NEEDED!

THE READER SERVICE™
FREE BOOK OFFER
FREEPOST CN81
CROYDON
CR9 3WZ

NO STAMP
NECESSARY
IF POSTED IN
THE U.K. OR N.I.

plicated enough without adding a lukewarm romance and painful memories to the mix.

Instead of worrying about her love life, she ought to be concerned about her mother.

Patricia had been missing for six weeks now. No one had a clue where she was or what had caused her to leave. All they knew was that one day she was there and the next she wasn't.

Poor Nash was beside himself, frantic and confused, not knowing what had driven Patricia away, but desperate to find her.

Maya was equally upset, and couldn't imagine why her mother would have taken off the way she did. True, Patricia had seemed somewhat distracted over the past few months, but Maya had never expected it to lead to anything like this.

Her mother's disappearance was the main reason she'd been out with Brad tonight. Nash had immediately hired private detectives to try to track down Patricia, so there was very little Maya could do except wait and worry. Thoughts of her mother had her completely preoccupied, even during work days, when she should be concentrating on educating the young minds of her grade-school students.

And because Brad was kind and considerate and thoughtful, he understood what she was going through and wanted to help however he could—mainly by keeping her busy with dinners out, long drives, even the occasional cultural events.

It was one more reason she cared for Brad and was so angry with herself for not being able to take their relationship to the next level.

She was halfway up the stairs and still steaming when the phone rang. With a grumble she turned around and moved to answer the kitchen extension rather than race the rest of the way up the steps to her bedroom.

"Hello?" she all but snapped.

"Maya?" a deep male voice replied, as though the caller wasn't sure she was the one who'd answered the phone. "It's Creed."

She knew who it was. If there was one voice she could identify over all others on the planet, it was Creed Fortune's.

"What do you want, Creed?" she asked none too politely.

Of course she already knew. He'd been calling on a regular basis to check on her ever since her mother went missing.

Why he bothered, Maya couldn't fathom. He certainly hadn't given a fig about her the past thirteen years he'd known her.

"I just wanted to see how you're holding up. The detectives Nash hired haven't turned up anything on your mom yet, but I'm sure they will soon."

"How am I holding up?" she repeated, her annoyance with both him and herself flaring to life again and coming out in the razor sharpness of her tone. "How am I holding up? Oh, I'm fine. Just peachy. Damn you, Creed."

Her fingers tightened on the handset and she began to pace back and forth across the kitchen, as far as the spiral cord would allow.

"This is all your fault. You've ruined my chances of ever having a normal relationship with a man, ever *sleeping* with a man. You blamed a seventeen-year-old girl for being attacked by her boyfriend and called me a slut. You're the reason I can't have a normal relationship, and I hate you for that!"

Her tirade ended with her voice at least one octave higher than usual. Without giving him a chance to respond, she slammed the phone down, muttered a low curse, and marched off to bed.

It was almost midnight and the windows were dark, but Creed Fortune couldn't have cared less. He stomped up the steps to Maya's town house and pounded on the door with the side of his fist.

To hell with the doorbell. To hell with the fact that she was probably sound asleep. He wanted to talk to her, and he wanted to do it *now*.

Where did she get off telling *him* he'd ruined her for ever going to bed with a man?

She sure hadn't had any trouble attracting the opposite sex in high school, not once she'd begun to fill out with those soft, feminine curves and grown into her striking half-Yankton-Sioux features. The long, black hair, chocolate-brown doe eyes and ripe little body had had boys panting after her like a mare in heat.

He pounded again, louder and longer this time. Across the street a dog barked, and inside he thought he heard movement. A second later a light flicked on and the door swung open.

He took a moment to hope she'd checked the peephole first, then rational thought spun away as he took in her tousled hair, drowsy eyes and the short, faded nightshirt that seemed to cling in all the right places.

With a tired sigh, she leaned against the edge of the door and let her lashes flutter to half-mast. "Now what do you want, Creed? In case you hadn't noticed, it's the middle of the night and *some people* are trying to sleep."

"At least we know you're sleeping alone, don't we?"

A spark flashed in her narrowed eyes. "Go to hell," she said, and made a move to slam the door in his face.

He stuck out his booted foot, blocking the motion. It didn't keep her from pressing forward and throwing her body against the heavy wood.

"Get your foot out of the door, Creed. Go bother someone else and let me go back to bed."

He added his knee and upper body to the battle, causing her to grunt as he pushed her back and forced his way into the house. Kicking the door closed behind him, he leaned against it and crossed his arms over his chest. Maya did the same, retreating several steps until she'd put what he was sure she felt was a safe distance between them.

"Adding forced entry to your résumé these days?" she asked belligerently.

He shrugged, keeping his face blank even as heat started to pump through his blood and pool near the region of his groin. Dammit, why did she have to be so beautiful?

She was his stepsister, for God's sake. Not related by blood in any way, but related through the marriage of his father to her mother.

No matter how you cut it, she was forbidden fruit, and he had no business lusting after her. No business at all.

Never mind that he'd secretly been doing just that since she'd hit puberty. He was ten years too old for her, and supposed to play the part of big brother, but still he'd wanted her.

Why did she have to grow up in so many interesting places? Why couldn't she have remained a plain and gawky child forever?

Tamping down his errant thoughts, he kicked away from the door and headed toward her. "If I have to," he said in answer to her question.

"What are you doing, Creed?" She continued her backward shuffle, occasionally bumping into the wall or glancing behind her to make sure the path was clear. "Why are you here?"

"Do I need a reason?" he asked, never breaking eye contact.

"Yes. You do. Have you found out something about

my mother? If so, tell me and then get out. Otherwise, just get out."

They both stopped moving. One corner of his mouth lifted in a humorless half grin. Since when had she become so good at telling him off and ordering him around? It certainly was a change from the quiet, meek girl she'd been when they were kids.

"No, nothing about your mother. The private investigators are still working on it. I'm here because of what you said on the phone."

Her expression flickered, the hard, angry glint in her eyes being replaced by wary uncertainty. He even thought he saw a touch of pink color her high cheekbones.

"*I* ruined you for other men?" he pressed. "Just what the hell is that supposed to mean?"

She flinched. A small, almost imperceptible motion, and the only sign that she was uncomfortable with the topic of conversation. But he caught it, and some part of him reveled in his ability to shake her.

"Nothing." Her voice was low and she gave one quick, jerky shake of her head. "It doesn't mean anything. I was tired and worried about my mom. I didn't know what I was saying."

Valiant effort, but he didn't buy it.

He took another step forward. "Guess that means Brad isn't getting any, huh? Nearly a year of sniffing around your skirts, and he gets nothing for his trouble. Poor, pathetic loser."

Her chin went up at that, her shoulders squaring as

she straightened her spine. "Look who's talking. I may not be sleeping with Brad, he may not be 'getting any,' but at least he's a gentleman. He would never barge into my house and corner me like this. He would never accuse me of being a tramp, or make me feel like one the way you did just because a boy sweet-talked me into his car when I was seventeen and then *attacked me.*"

It was his turn to flinch, but only on the inside. He remembered that night as though it were yesterday. Stumbling upon Maya and her current boyfriend—or at least one of the boys she'd been hanging out with quite a bit that summer, ever since the opposite sex had begun to take notice of her fine feminine form... Taking notice of the tell-tale rocking of the shiny Trans Am and the noises that were emanating from inside...and then realizing Maya's cries weren't of the pleasurable variety.

He remembered the fury he'd felt as he'd opened the driver's side door and yanked the boy out by the scruff of his neck. The kid—some varsity football jock with a letterman jacket—had been lucky to get away with only a few scrapes and bruises, because Creed had sincerely considered killing the little bastard.

As it was, he'd given the jerk a beating he wouldn't soon forget. Then he'd dragged Maya home, filling her ears with lectures and invectives the whole way.

"That's why you won't sleep with Brad McKenzie?" He made a scoffing sound, his mouth twisting into a wry smirk. "He must not be very persuasive. I could have you begging for it in two seconds flat."

Any intimidation or discomfort Maya might have been feeling flew out the window at his cocky remark. Her brown eyes glittered dangerously and every muscle in her body went rigid. She'd been backed up until her calves hit the edge of the sofa, but now she took a single, confident step forward.

"Oh, really. And just how would you manage that? Twist my arm until I told you what you wanted to hear, whether it was true or not?"

Her words were like gasoline thrown on an already raging brush fire. The low-level desire humming through his system suddenly ratcheted up several notches to full, mind-numbing throttle.

He reached out, taking her by the wrist and tugging her against his chest.

"No," he breathed. "Like this."

And then he took her mouth with his.

Two

For a moment Maya froze, so stunned her mind went blank and her body refused to move. But Creed's lips were firm, his body hot, his arms like steel bands where he held her tight against him.

Her eyes slid closed and her fingers curled into his shoulders, kneading like a kitten. She moaned.

How long had she dreamed of this? Of having him kiss her, hold her, *want* her.

Forever, that's how long. Since she and her mother had moved into the Fortune Estate and she'd first been introduced to the brooding, much older young man who towered over and intimidated her. Even as a shy, somewhat awkward girl, she'd known her own heart, and her heart had wanted Creed Fortune.

But she'd never truly believed she could have him.
Not when he took every opportunity to make it clear she
was nothing but a thorn in his side. An uninvited sibling,
forced upon him by an unexpected romance between
his father and her mother.

Now, though…now she knew she'd been wrong.
He'd done a good job of hiding it, but apparently he
shared her feelings and wanted her as much as she'd
always wanted him.

His kiss was sweltering, raising her temperature and
causing her to break out in beads of perspiration. He
worked her mouth as if she was a decadent dessert and
he couldn't get enough.

Tongues tangled, teeth nipped and clashed. She
pressed herself close to his tall frame, letting her breasts
brush the solid wall of his chest, the insistent bulge of
his arousal nudge the space between her legs.

This was better than anything she'd ever experienced. Better than any other kiss she'd shared with any
other man. Better even than all the times over the past
year that she'd tried to relax enough to make love with
Brad, but ended up pulling back at the last minute.

It was better, she knew, because it was Creed. And
with him she wasn't afraid, she wasn't shy, she wasn't
self-conscious.

With him she didn't recall his long-ago accusation
that she acted like a slut, but instead remembered all
the times she'd wanted him, lusted after him, dreamed
about him.

And now, finally, she could have him.

Her arms tightened around his neck, her fingers playing in the ends of his short, dark brown hair. She whimpered and wiggled in his hold, striving desperately for something she couldn't name.

He pulled away, chest heaving, breathing ragged. His blue eyes glittered as he held her gaze.

Muttering a heartfelt curse, he shook his head, then swooped in to take her mouth again.

This time he didn't settle for just kissing. His hands clasped her waist and swung her around, manipulating her as easily as a tailor's mannequin. Without breaking the contact of their lips and tongues, he walked her backward through the living room and hall, up the staircase and into her bedroom.

She didn't stop to wonder how he knew his way through her house or which bedroom was hers; she was simply relieved by his focus and excellent navigational skills. And she clung to him, wrapping her legs around his waist halfway up the stairs to aid his progress.

He carried her into the room and straight to the bed, laying her on top of the covers, rumpled from where she'd thrown them off when he'd woken her with his pounding.

Her nightshirt bunched to her waist, the rough denim of his jeans rubbing against the soft skin of her inner thighs. His hands sneaked over her hips and waist, beneath the hem of the shirt, pushing it higher as his fingers moved toward the swells of her breasts.

His lips caressed her chin and jawline, brushing the lobe of her ear before trailing down her throat in a series of nips and licks. When she felt a gentle pressure beneath her arms, she lifted them willingly above her head and let him pull the nightshirt off entirely.

The cool evening air blew across her naked breasts and torso, and she quickly lowered her hands to cover herself.

"Don't."

Creed's fingers circled her wrists like manacles, slowly tugging her hands away to reveal her nudity to his hungry gaze.

"Don't hide," he said again, his voice low and strained. "I want to see you, all of you."

He ran the side of his thumb over the tip of one breast, grinning when it puckered and swelled beneath his ministrations.

She sucked in a breath of air, her back arching into his touch. Her face felt flushed, her entire body a wriggling mass of fever-hot nerve endings, even as she fought not to let her natural tendency toward embarrassment take over.

He had her hands pinned above her head, the rest of her pinned by his weight and bulk. And the look in his eyes was that of a hungry wolf—fierce, predatory, determined.

"Lovely," he murmured, then swooped in to lick a tight, budded nipple.

She gasped, her fingers clenching into fists above where he held her arms down. He licked the other nipple, just a quick, light swipe, before settling in with more thorough, undivided attention.

His tongue rasped like sandpaper along her sensitive nerve endings. He turned her flesh hot with his mouth, then cool with the soft hush of his breath. After creating a world of sensual devastation at one breast, he moved to the other and did it all over again.

When he lifted his head, he was grinning. "Like I said, lovely."

His fingers loosened from her wrists, but she didn't bother attempting to lower her arms. She didn't have the strength, even if she'd wanted to. She simply lay there like a rag doll, depleted of energy or the will to move.

Still smiling, he skimmed the underside of her arms, the sides of her breasts, her waist, until he reached the top of her high-cut bikini panties. They were nothing special, just plain lavender cotton. But then, she hadn't known anyone would be seeing them when she'd dressed for bed a few hours ago.

Her choice of undergarments didn't seem to bother Creed, though. He brushed his lips around her navel and along the waistband of the panties, then slowly began to drag them off.

A flutter of self-consciousness rippled in her belly, and she had to curl her fingers into the sheets to keep from covering herself again or trying to wiggle away.

If Creed noticed her sudden bout of discomfort, he didn't acknowledge it. Instead, he kept his gaze locked on the dark triangle at the apex of her thighs that he was revealing inch by agonizing inch. He pushed the panties down her legs, slipping them over her feet and letting them fall to the floor beside the bed.

A moment later he pushed to his feet and straightened, all six feet, two inches looming above her.

For a second Maya thought he meant to leave…leave her there, naked and flushed, and walk away. But then his arms lifted and his fingers began to deftly release the line of buttons at the front of his shirt.

One by one, he slipped them through their holes, and little by little his chest became exposed. The bronzed skin. The firm muscles. The light sprinkling of dark hair.

Maya's mouth went dry and she had trouble breathing. He was so beautiful. Tall, athletic, sculpted like some sort of Greek god, or the epitome of the perfect man every woman fantasized about.

He was certainly her idea of the perfect man.

Tugging the tails of his shirt out of the waistband of his jeans, he released the last couple buttons before shrugging out of the shirt and letting it drop to the floor. He started to kick off his boots, at the same time unzipping his trousers.

He pushed everything, jeans and underwear, down his legs and off. But instead of leaving them in a pile on the floor, he withdrew a rear pocket, pulled out his wallet, then dug out a small plastic square. Dropping the clothes, he stepped intently back to the bed in all his naked glory.

He was the first man she'd ever seen completely nude, but for once, she wasn't flushed with embarrassment. She was…awed.

Amazing didn't quite cover it. Neither did *fabulous, marvelous,* or any of the other two hundred adjectives that flitted through her mind. A few of her more precocious students might say *hubba-hubba,* and that came close.

His shoulders were broad, his waist flat and tapering down to narrow hips, his legs long and well-muscled. But it was what hung between those legs that held her rapt attention.

Admittedly, her experience of such things was limited. Limited, ha! Verging on nonexistent, was more like it. But even so, she was familiar with the basics of the male anatomy, and in her somewhat biased opinion, Creed was a most impressive specimen.

Before she had a chance to look her fill, he was stretching out above her, covering her from head to toe. The hair on his legs and chest tickled, but she didn't laugh. She was too distracted by the rigid length of his erection rubbing her in all the right places.

His fingers drifted over her temples, threading through her hair to hold her steady while he planted light, butterfly kisses on either side of her mouth. First one corner, then the other before he took her mouth for a slow, luxurious exploration. He made her feel like a particularly decadent sweet he wanted to take his time with and really enjoy.

While he continued to kiss her deeply, his hands

traveled down her body, one pausing to toy with the tip of her breast, the other sliding lower. Past her waist, over the curve of her buttock, and down her thigh until he reached the bend of her knee.

He lifted her leg, bringing it up to hook around his hip so he could settle more fully against her. His arousal, already sheathed in the condom he'd retrieved from his wallet, prodded her feminine opening.

Cocking her hips, she opened herself even wider, doing everything she could to ease his entry. He slipped inside, just the tip, but she was already wet and ready for him. She'd been waiting for this moment all her life, and her body was primed and more than eager for him to finally claim her.

A low groan rolled up from his diaphragm as he pressed deeper. Inch by inch, he filled her, stretching her slick inner folds until she thought she could die from the sheer pleasure of it all.

Just when she figured he couldn't go any farther, he pushed forward again. This time, instead of pleasure, a sharp, lightning flash of pain made her stiffen and bite her bottom lip to keep from crying out.

Thankfully, the discomfort passed quickly, and she was once again able to breathe. Above her, Creed held himself perfectly still, staring down at her. His brows knit in consternation.

"Are you all right?"

The words were strained, his chest heaving as he struggled to get enough air into his lungs. The muscles in his biceps quivered with the effort to hold his weight off her.

She nodded, offering a small smile to let him know she was telling the truth. A beat passed while he considered her answer, then seemed to take her at her word.

He returned his mouth to hers, kissing her softly but thoroughly while lower, he began a slow in and out motion that washed away any lingering tenderness. Instead, there was only pleasure.

It started as just a trickle, the temporary replacement of something not-so-nice with something not-so-bad. But soon enough the sensation grew, building in ever-increasing waves.

She lifted her legs to lock more tightly around his waist, urging him closer. Her hands smoothed up and down his back, the nails alternately digging in and clawing long lines across the sweat-slickened flesh.

His own fingers clasped her bottom, kneading and stroking as his thrusts picked up speed. He moved deeper, harder, faster, until she was gasping against his mouth and reaching for…she didn't know what. She only knew she wanted it, needed it, might die without it.

Still holding her hip and buttock, Creed's other hand slipped between them and stole into her damp folds, finding the tiny bud of desire hidden within. He rubbed the spot, first lightly, then with more pressure, making her cry out and writhe beneath him.

"Come with me," he whispered raggedly. The rough

line of his cheek abraded hers, his lips mere inches from her ear. "Come with me *now*."

He pounded into her again, at the same time his fingers worked their magic, sending her off like a rocket. Her mouth opened on a soundless scream, her back arched and her vision went hazy.

From somewhere outside her body, she felt him thrust once, twice more and then stiffen above her. Oxygen left his lungs in a loud sigh as he collapsed, his weight pressing her down into the mattress.

She lay there, her legs still wrapped around his waist, her arms still linked about his shoulders and a smile as wide as the Big Sioux River curving her lips.

Making love with Creed Fortune was everything she'd ever imagined and more. It had fulfilled every one of her adolescent fantasies, not to mention more than a few of the hopes and dreams she'd envisioned since becoming an adult.

For the first time, she was glad she hadn't slept with another man, even Brad. She hadn't realized what she was really doing all those years, but she'd inadvertently been saving herself for Creed, and for that she could never be sorry.

She knew better than to think everything would be perfect from this moment on. Creed wasn't going to ask her to marry him in the next five minutes, or declare his undying love.

This was a start, though. They may have put the cart before the horse in their personal relationship by sleeping together before they'd ever even been out on a date, but there was time for all of that.

Time to get to know each other better—really get to know each other. Time to go out, have fun and get the family used to the idea that they were going to be together.

It would come as quite a surprise to the Fortunes, she imagined, including her mother. But they all loved her and Creed, and as long as they were happy, she knew they would offer their support wholeheartedly. She hoped so, anyway.

The important thing was that this was the beginning. The beginning of everything she'd ever wanted, and for the first time, she realized she could have it.

Delight coursed through her veins and her grin widened. It was all she could do to keep from giggling aloud.

She couldn't remember ever being so happy. And she would make Creed happy, too, she swore she would.

Above her, he shifted slightly, slipping out of her and rolling to his side. Cool air brushed the perspiration dotting her skin, and she immediately missed his weight, his warmth.

With a groan, he sat up, rubbed his fingers through his hair, then stood and headed for the adjoining bathroom. She heard the water running for a second, then he was back, in all his naked glory. He stalked across the room, and she took the opportunity to admire him every step of the way.

Expecting him to rejoin her, she shimmied toward the head of the bed, rearranging the pillows and crawling under the covers, leaving plenty of room for him to crawl in beside her. They would probably cuddle a bit first, maybe take a nap, then hopefully make love all over again. She couldn't wait.

Instead he bypassed the bed altogether, bending to retrieve his jeans from the floor. Without a word he stepped into them, adding his shirt and boots in short order.

Her brows met in a frown. "What are you doing?"

He didn't bother to meet her gaze as he finished buttoning the pine-green shirt, tucking it into the waistband of his pants.

"I'm leaving."

"Leaving?" Clutching the sheet to her breasts, she scrambled forward, climbing to her knees. "What do you mean you're leaving? I thought…" She'd thought so many things, but she settled for, "I thought you'd at least stay the night."

"Why would I stay? Now that I've gotten you out of my system, I can leave you alone. Get on with my life."

He finished rolling the sleeves of his shirt to just below the elbows, finally glancing in her direction. "Good night, Maya."

Then he turned and walked out of the bedroom.

She could hear his footsteps in the hall, pounding down the steps and through the rest of the house. A second later the front door slammed, sending a shiver down her spine.

She sat frozen, unable to believe what had just happened. He'd made love to her, made her believe he cared, that they had a future together, and then walked out. He'd gotten dressed and walked out as if she meant nothing to him.

She felt stunned, her heart squeezing painfully inside her chest.

Drawing her knees up, she buried her face in the wrinkled sheet and wept.

Chase stood on Maya's front porch, leaning against the closed door with his eyes tightly closed.

He hoped she didn't chase after him. He didn't want to see her again, not right now.

For one thing, there was nothing left to say. It might have sounded harsh, but what he'd told her back in her bedroom was the absolute truth: succumbing to his baser instincts meant he could move past the almost obsessive longing he'd always felt when he was near her.

Now that he'd been with her, the mystery was solved. Any questions he might have been harboring about what she would look like naked, how her skin would feel beneath his hands and mouth, what sounds she would make when he was inside her, had been answered.

For another, he wasn't entirely sure he could look at her right now and not be sorely tempted to make love to her again. He was a man, after all, and the last he'd seen Maya, she hadn't been wearing anything more than a thin white sheet, which would be easy enough to dispense with.

Shaking off erotic images that were beginning to reheat his blood, he pushed away from the door and headed for his car.

What the hell had gotten into him, to touch her at all? How could he have let things get so out of control?

He'd wanted her for a decade, lusted after her in a way no stepbrother had any business lusting. But he'd never, ever intended to act on those desires, and he thought he'd done a pretty good job of hiding them from Maya and everyone else.

Starting the engine, he flipped on the headlights and pulled away from the curb, heading home. He needed a good night's sleep, and maybe a nice, stiff drink to clear his head and make sense of what he'd done not twenty minutes before.

She was off-limits. Forbidden. She always had been. If they'd ever crossed the lines of impropriety, the scandal would have been huge.

He took a hand off the wheel, scrubbing it roughly over his face. Dammit, it would *be* huge, if anyone ever found out what had taken place tonight.

Which meant it couldn't happen. No one could find out.

He would never intentionally do anything to bring shame or undue attention to his family, so he certainly wasn't going to tell anyone. And he doubted Maya would, either.

So all he had to do now was keep his hands to himself.

Using his pass key, he opened the electronic gate of the underground garage at the Dakota Fortune office building and pulled his dark-blue Mercedes S-class into his personal parking spot near the elevators. His brother Case had a reserved space right beside his own, but except during business hours, it mostly stood empty these days.

The same could be said of Case's apartment, across the hall from Creed's. The top floor of Dakota Fortune had been split into two separate living areas, which the brothers had occupied after moving out of the Fortune Estate and taking over as copresidents for the family company.

Of course, Case was now happily set up in a house just outside Sioux Falls with his wife, Gina. She'd inherited her childhood home when her father died, and after living in an apartment in town for a while, they'd moved onto the larger estate and begun a few renovations. They were also expecting their first child at the end of the year.

Creed was happy for them, truly he was, but he had to admit he missed running into his brother in the hall between their two front doors. Or only having to cross that small space in order to talk to him.

His brother's willing ear and sage advice would certainly come in handy at the moment, though he imagined Case's response to Creed's dilemma would be much the same as he'd already concluded on his own.

Stay away from Maya. Chalk up tonight's activities to scratching a long-standing itch, then put it behind him and move on.

Not a problem. He'd pretty much made that decision even before he'd rolled off the bed at Maya's house and made his hasty exit.

And a few shots of scotch could only bolster his determination, he thought, as he let himself into his apartment and headed straight for the liquor cabinet.

Three

The Fortune Estate was about the last place Maya wanted to be right now. But it was Nash's birthday, and even though he'd insisted he didn't want to celebrate—in fact, that he was in no mood to celebrate while his beloved Patricia's whereabouts were still unknown—the Fortune children had been adamant about getting together.

They were keeping the so-called party low-key. No decorations and no guests other than immediate family, just a relaxed cookout and a few understated gifts for the man of the hour.

Maya parked along the side of the wide circular drive at the front of the mammoth, gothic-style stone mansion. The trim light gray with wrought iron accents and a black roof. It sat on a hundred and seventy-five acres about twenty miles west of Sioux Falls, just outside the plush suburb of Colonial Pine Hills.

The main house consisted of seven bedrooms and nine bathrooms, but there was also a pool, guest house, stable and the cottage where Skylar and her new husband, Zack Manning, were living until their baby was born. After that, they planned to move back to New Zealand, where they would work together on the horse breeding venture they both had dreamed of.

The property also boasted a small lake and numerous trails that Maya and the Fortune children had all made great use of when they were younger.

Her shoes crunched on crushed stone as she made her way over the drive, beneath the porte cochere and across the wide verandah to the front door, her gift for Nash clutched in her hands. She was wearing a simple yellow sundress and her hair was pulled back in a French braid.

If it weren't for Nash, she wouldn't be here at all. Being around the Fortune siblings made her uncomfortable enough under normal circumstances, but it had been only a week since her ill-fated decision to give herself to Creed, and she had no desire to see him again so soon. Or ever, if she could have managed it.

But the only thing worse than seeing him again was letting him think her a coward, and that's exactly what would happen if she begged off attending Nash's party.

Taking a deep breath, she squeezed the latch on the front door and let herself into the large marble foyer with its grand, double staircase and giant chandelier twinkling overhead.

Everything about the Fortune Estate was both comforting and daunting. She'd grown up in this house, so she felt a certain connection and warmth, yet she'd also always felt out of place within the family, and suffered a sense of detachment whenever she found herself once again inside the vast, artfully decorated walls.

That was part of the reason she didn't return home very often, and hadn't since she'd left for college.

The other part was her deep-seated reluctance to run into Creed.

She laughed silently to herself, the mocking sound reverberating through her brain. How ironic that she'd spent years avoiding the man as often as she could, only to find herself even more desperate to do so now that they'd slept together.

The front of the house was empty, but she heard voices coming from the back and knew everyone was already gathered out on the west verandah, overlooking the pool.

She moved to the right through the cavernous foyer and west gallery area to the hallway leading past the dining and gathering rooms.

Most of the house was decorated in shades of pale gold and deep red—her mother's choice when she'd redone the interior of the estate soon after marrying Nash. The kids, including Maya, had of course been allowed to decorate their own private living quarters when they'd gotten old enough.

The Fortunes also boasted an impressive collection of modern art and sculpture, some of it lovely, some slightly obscure. For the most part, Nash and Patricia added pieces that caught their fancy, and for no other reason.

Above all, the one thing that could be said for the house—which could have easily come across as showy and pretentious—was that regardless of the extravagant decor, it was comfortably livable.

The closer she got to the verandah, the louder the voices grew. There was laughter and merriment, but it was more subdued than usual. No matter what they were doing or what the conversation might be, there was no denying that Patricia's absence was foremost on everyone's mind, weighing down their hearts.

Maya wished, not for the first time, that there was something she could share, some snippet of information she knew or remembered that would help to find her mother. But no matter how hard she concentrated, nothing came to mind.

Standing in the doorway leading outside, she observed the entire Fortune clan in action.

Nash and the women of the family were seated at a large round patio table. The two Fortune daughters, Eliza and Skylar, sat closest to their father. Case's wife, Gina, Blake's fiancée, Sasha, and Max's wife, Diana— the two were back in town—made up the rest of the circle, with empty chairs in between for the missing men. They sipped lemonade from tall, hand-painted glasses and munched on potato chips and an assortment of vegetables surrounding a large bowl of dip.

A couple of servants bustled around them unobtrusively, topping off drinks, making sure the platters of food never emptied and providing anything else the family might need.

Across the verandah, at a shiny silver gas grill the size of a small car, Case, Blake, the Australian cousin, Max, Eliza's husband, Reese, and Skylar's New Zealander husband, Zack, stood together. The men were holding frosted mugs of frothy, imported beer and arguing good-naturedly about how well-done the steaks sizzling on the hot rack should be.

And, of course, there was Creed. He stood out from the rest, seeming taller, darker, more handsome. He was also the one manning the grill, holding the others at bay with a long metal spatula that he wielded like a sword before turning to flip the big chunks of browning meat.

Maya's stomach tightened at the sight and at the memories that flooded her of their single night together.

Creed, she was sure, would be plagued by no such thoughts or memories. He was over her, remember? Now that he'd had her, she was out of his system.

That's what he'd said, his parting shot as he'd turned and walked out of her bedroom, out of her house.

Too bad he hadn't also walked out of her life. She wouldn't be standing here, struggling for breath and feeling like she might throw up, if he had.

She didn't know which was worse—having to attend a Fortune family gathering when she wasn't a part of the family…or having to face Creed so soon after her intimate humiliation at his hands.

Without her mother there to make her feel more at ease, she almost wanted to turn around and leave before anyone noticed her, especially Creed. But she knew how much Patricia loved Nash, and that she wouldn't want him to be unhappy. Maya also knew that her mother would want her to do whatever she could to try to ease Nash's burden.

That meant attending this party, in spite of her personal reservations.

Taking a deep breath, she stepped out onto the verandah with a smile on her face, hoping no one would notice how forced it was.

Nash spotted her first and rose from his place at the table to greet her.

"Maya, sweetheart! You're here."

He hugged her and kissed her cheek, and at least a portion of her grin turned genuine.

"Happy birthday," she told him, handing him the be-ribboned gift, a gold money clip engraved with his initials.

"You didn't have to do that," he said, but the corners of his eyes crinkled with pleasure. He took the present and set it with a pile of other brightly wrapped boxes of varying sizes on a low cedar bench along the outer wall of the house.

"Come sit down," he invited, taking her hand and leading her over to the table. The women smiled in greeting, the men waving and calling out from the other side of the verandah.

Only one person failed to say hello and looked less than pleased by her arrival. From the corner of her eye, she saw Creed's expression tighten, his hard gaze on her as he lifted the mug of beer to his lips and took a long swallow.

He certainly wasn't looking at her like a man who'd recently shared her bed…or wanted to repeat the experience. In fact, she couldn't say he was looking at her any differently than he ever had.

The realization shouldn't have wounded her, but it did, sending an arrow straight through her heart.

Before she could dwell much longer on his indifference toward her, Gina handed her a glass of lemonade and patted the seat of the chair to her left. The sleeveless denim shirt she wore over white shorts completely hid any signs of her pregnancy. Of course, she was only a few months along, still in the first trimester, and they had only just recently shared the news with the family.

Skylar, however, looked ready to pop, even though she still had a couple of months to go before her due date. Once the baby was born and it was safe for them to travel, she and Zach would be going back to New Zealand. They would return to the States to visit, but that's where they planned to make their home.

Maya felt a tiny stab of envy at the picture-perfect lives of the people surrounding her. They were all so happy together, and now positively ecstatic about the impending births of the next generation of Fortunes.

And they deserved it. No doubt about it. But Maya couldn't help the longing and regret that welled up within her when she compared their level of happiness with her own.

She and Nash, it seemed, were the only ones whose lives were in shambles. And at least her stepfather's misery was reasonable and already public, so he didn't have to hide his emotions from everyone. Maya, however, spent the majority of her time pretending to be happier than she was, while inside she felt like weeping.

Sparing a quick glance at Creed, who was busy flipping the steaks again, she decided he didn't belong in the same category as Nash and her. He didn't look miserable in the least, and she was pretty sure he had no interest in settling down anytime soon. Certainly not with her, at any rate.

"Sit down and join us," Gina said with an inviting smile. "I'm so glad you could make it."

"Thank you." Maya took a seat between Nash and Skylar, reaching for a chip and holding on to her glass so she would have something to do with her hands.

"The guys keep saying the steaks will be done soon," Eliza said, her lips twisted wryly. "If you ask me, though, I don't think they know what they're doing. It's been about two hours now, and this rabbit food just isn't cutting it anymore."

Eliza rolled her eyes and flicked a hand over the vegetable tray. "We should have insisted on bringing in caterers or whipping up something a little more civilized, the way we girls wanted, instead of letting the men devise the menu."

"Oh, let them go," Diana said with a light chuckle. "They're enjoying themselves over there, drinking and flexing their muscles. And we can pay them back later when we start talking about babies and nurseries and wedding plans." She cast her gaze around the table at the two expectant mothers and one soon-to-be newlywed.

Skylar waved a hand to hush the discussion. "Shh, shh, here they come."

Maya made a point of not looking at Creed as he set a giant platter of charred meat on the table.

"Steaks are done," he announced. "You can stop your whispering and complaining now."

"We weren't complaining," Eliza responded innocently. "We were just saying how nice it is of you to grill these delicious-looking steaks for us."

Creed shot his sister a pointed look while he took another sip of beer. "Uh-huh."

"I'll get the plates," Sasha announced, jumping up and heading into the house.

"I'll get the potato salad and mixed fruit," Skylar said, starting to rise.

Laying a hand on her arm, Maya signaled for her to stay where she was. "You sit. I'll get them."

The next few minutes buzzed with chatter and movement as items were gathered and the table was set.

When Maya returned to the verandah with a large bowl of mixed seasonal fruit in her hands, she stopped in her tracks to find that the only chair left vacant after everyone had shifted and reorganized the seating to make room for the men was directly beside Creed. She swallowed hard, wishing she could slip back into the house and hide.

Sitting right beside him, so close that their arms and legs would likely brush, was more than she could tolerate.

Unfortunately, it didn't look as though she had much choice.

Forcing her feet to move, she carried the fruit to the table and set it down before circling around to the one lone empty chair and reluctantly taking a seat. She still refused to look at Creed, to even acknowledge his presence, but her skin hummed at his proximity, the hair on her arms standing at attention as if they'd been struck with static electricity.

He flipped a juicy steak onto her plate, but she ignored him. He passed her the bowl of potato salad and refilled her glass of lemonade, but she refused to offer him a word of thanks.

Under the table, his knee bumped into hers, and she went stiff waiting for the contact to end and her lungs to once again resume functioning.

Did he know he'd touched her? Had he done it on purpose, or was it simply a result of the cramped situation? She couldn't be sure.

The conversation through dinner was upbeat, but with an underlying note of gravity, especially any time Patricia's name happened to come up, causing a veil of sadness to fall over Nash's eyes. Whenever that occurred, they all rushed to change the subject and get Nash's mind off the very real concern of his missing wife.

It surprised Maya to see just how much all of the Fortune children cared for their father. What they were willing to do and how far they were willing to go to put a smile on his face and help keep him from wallowing in the sorrow of his wife's absence.

For so long, she'd thought them cold and aloof, but now she realized she may have been mistaken. Maybe her view of them had been skewed by her own internalized feelings of desolation and not fitting in.

Maybe if she hadn't felt so out of place all her life and had opened up a bit more, let the Fortunes truly become her family, she would have seen their warmth and compassion sooner.

She found herself swamped with guilt for that, for not being more open-minded in the past. But she was also glad she was finally beginning to see another side to the people she'd lived with for half her life. It was comforting, lifting her spirits at least for a moment.

She only wished she could identify and alter her feelings for Creed as easily as her feelings for the rest of the Fortunes seemed to be changing. But where he was concerned, her insides were knotted with disillusionment and uncertainty.

He'd come over to her house and made love to her, taken her virginity and then walked out like it meant nothing. She hadn't seen or heard from him since, and now that they were forced to be near each other, he hadn't made a single gesture or remark that even acknowledged what they'd shared.

While her body flushed with heat every time he glanced in her direction or got too close, he was treating her no differently than ever before. Like a sister, not a lover.

She swallowed hard, the last bite of birthday cake she'd just eaten sitting like a lead weight at the bottom of her stomach.

She'd gone from thinking all of her dreams concerning Creed were finally coming true, to having them dashed just as quickly. It was enough to make her want to give up on men altogether.

Glancing surreptitiously at her watch, she decided she'd been at the party long enough that she could make her excuses and slip away.

The meal dishes had already been cleared, Nash had opened his gifts, and everyone had enjoyed at least one slice of cake. And as much fun as she'd had, as glad as she'd been that she could be there for Nash, she didn't know how much longer she could be near Creed without either screaming or bursting into tears.

Using the excuse that she had lessons to correct for school the next day, she quietly made her way around the verandah to say good-night. They all hugged her and kissed her cheek, some asking if she was sure she couldn't stay longer, others inviting her to their respective homes anytime she had a mind to visit.

Maya was touched, and found herself promising she would, even though she had no idea when she would find the time to drive to Deadwood, which was more than three hundred and fifty miles away, let alone fly all the way to Australia.

The only person she didn't bother saying goodbye to was Creed. Although she hadn't done it on purpose, she was able to leave the verandah and head back through the house to her car before he returned from a trip to the kitchen to refill the ice chest with sodas and beer.

That one thing, at least, had fallen in her favor.

Creed caught sight of Maya's retreating form the minute he set foot back out on the verandah with an armful of assorted cans and bottles. It was just like her to sneak away, slink off quietly the same as she had so many times when she was a kid.

He paused for a second until she'd disappeared from view, then strode to the open cooler a few feet away. Dropping the drinks into the pool of melting ice, he slammed the lid closed and turned on his heel.

His brother Case stood nearby, watching his actions with a raised eyebrow.

"Be right back," he said without further explanation, stalking across the verandah and into the house after Maya.

He caught up with her as she was getting into her car. The driver's-side window was down, a soft breeze ruffling the wisps of dark hair that had come loose from her braid to fall around her cheeks and temples.

"Maya, wait up."

For a minute he thought she was going to ignore him and drive away, even though he was sure she'd heard him. Then her shoulders seemed to slump and her hand fell from where it had been ready to turn the key in the ignition.

Slowly she lifted her head to meet his gaze. Her brown eyes, usually so soft, were cold. She didn't say anything, simply stared at him and waited for him to speak.

He wondered if she realized what a beautiful woman she was, then could have kicked himself for letting the thought slide through his mind. She was off-limits, that's all there was to it, and he had no intention of lowering his defenses enough for a repeat of the mistake he'd made last week.

It was true, though. The half-Sioux blood running through her veins made her features striking. High cheekbones, brown eyes and dark, sultry skin all came together to create a stunningly sensual package.

If she stopped wearing the shapeless dresses and oversize tops and slacks she was so fond of, she'd be a real knockout. Of course, then she would have even more men sniffing around her skirts than she already did.

A flash of anger poured through him and his jaw clenched. Whatever he'd planned to say when he'd first followed her out here was suddenly replaced by the image of her with other men, including that Brad McKenzie she'd been seeing for the past year.

His teeth ground together even harder. Creed was the first man she'd been with; he knew that because he'd been the one to take her virginity. And up to now, he'd felt a little guilty about that.

But if her first time hadn't been with him, it probably would have been with McKenzie, and that was somehow an even more bitter pill to swallow.

"Where are you going?" he asked, his voice sharp, with an accusing edge he hadn't intended when he'd approached her.

She bristled visibly, her knuckles going white where she gripped the steering wheel. "Not that it's any of your business, but I have papers to grade before school tomorrow."

At her response, the tension in his muscles began to ease. He didn't know what he'd expected her to say, but he was unaccountably relieved the answer didn't have anything to do with another man. Especially McKenzie.

He leaned down, resting an arm on the roof of the car while his other hand rested on the open window frame of the driver's-side door.

In a tone more relaxed than before, he said, "Just so you know, I hired a couple of extra private detectives to look into your mother's disappearance. Some guys

I've worked with on and off over the years. They're good, so hopefully we'll have some information soon."

Seconds ticked by in silence with her gaze locked on his. Her tongue darted out to lick her dry lips and she nodded. "Thank you."

Pushing away from the car, he straightened and shoved his hands into the front pockets of his jeans. "I did it as much for Dad as for you. The P.I.s he hired don't seem to be making much progress, and I figured a few more men on the job couldn't hurt."

He took a step back and then another, the soles of his boots crunching on the stone drive as he put a safe distance between them. If he didn't, he was afraid he'd be tempted to do something stupid.

Like kiss her again.

And that was a definite no-no, so the sooner he went back inside and let her be on her way, the better.

"Thanks for coming. It meant a lot to Dad. Drive carefully," he added, then spun on his heel and put her promptly out of his mind.

Four

Maya was in the middle of a math lesson when the office buzzed that she had a phone call. Butterflies fluttered wildly in her stomach while she went next door to ask Mrs. Kurschbaum to watch her class for a few minutes. Then she walked down the hall to the teachers' lounge where she could use the phone.

She hoped it wasn't Brad again. He didn't make a habit of calling her at work unless it was important, but lately he'd been more dogged than usual in his attempts to get ahold of her.

Not that she could blame him, since she'd been avoiding him as assiduously as he'd been trying to get in touch with her. She'd spoken to him a few times, but so far managed to circumvent seeing him in person.

She knew he was getting suspicious, that he knew something was wrong or going on behind his back. And he was right, because she simply didn't know how to face him after sleeping with Creed.

She'd been dating Brad for nearly a year, growing closer by the week. She even thought they might have eventually ended up walking down the aisle. Even so, when it came to moving past first or second base, she'd kept him at arm's length.

But the minute Creed looked at her with so much as a hint of passion in his shadowy blue eyes, she'd fallen into bed with him faster than he could say "pretty please."

A rush of shame washed over her at the memory. She'd thought that night was the beginning of happily-ever-after for her, but Creed's behavior immediately after they'd made love had disabused her of that notion quickly enough.

Now she almost felt like an adulteress, as though she'd cheated on Brad with a much less desirable man.

Well, not less desirable. Creed could never be described as that.

Oh, no, he was still infinitely desirable. No matter how hard she tried to deny it or to block him from her heart and mind, she couldn't seem to *stop* being attracted to him.

She wished to heaven she could. It would make her life so much easier.

Finally reaching the teachers' lounge and phone, she lifted the handset and punched the blinking button for line three.

"Hello?"

"Maya?"

It wasn't Brad, and the butterflies in her stomach didn't know whether to settle down or speed up. She swallowed hard and lowered herself into a nearby chair.

"I'm in the middle of a class, Creed. What do you want?"

Was there nowhere she could be safe from of this man? Bad enough she ran into him at the Fortune Estate every time she went to visit. Even those times she did her best to avoid being there when she thought he might be around. But now he was showing up at her house and calling her at work.

She wished she knew where her mother was. Wished Patricia had said something before she'd disappeared, and that Maya might have had the chance to go with her. Anything to gain a little peace from Creed Fortune's overwhelming, overbearing and increasingly painful presence.

"We need to talk," he said without apology for making her abandon her students in the middle of a lesson. "When school lets out, don't leave. I'm going to pick you up."

Her brow creased. "Why?" And then her heart skipped a beat. "Has something happened? Is it my mother? Did you find—"

"I have some information, but we can't discuss it now. I'll pick you up in a couple hours."

Before she could protest or demand he tell her what was going on, the line went dead. She sat in stunned silence for another minute the dial tone ringing in her ears as loudly as Creed's words.

When she thought she could function without feeling as if she'd just run face-first into a lamppost, she returned the phone to its cradle and walked slowly to her classroom. She thanked Mrs. Kurschbaum for watching her students and somehow managed to stumble her way through the rest of the day.

Her mind raced the entire time, her pulse not far behind. She wondered what Creed had found out. Did he know where her mother was? Was she all right?

The end of the day couldn't come quickly enough, and as soon as the kids had gathered their things and raced out of the building, Maya grabbed her purse and followed. Normally she would have stuck around for a while, straightening the room, dealing with paperwork, even gathering a few things to take home with her. Today, though, she left everything behind in her mad dash for the parking lot.

Buses loaded with rambunctious children were pulling away from the curb. She smiled and waved several times as students who weren't used to seeing her again before they went home called her name, but her eyes were scanning the area for Creed's car.

As the last bus lumbered off, she spotted his midnight-blue Mercedes-Benz turning into the school's main drive. He coasted to a stop directly in front of her, the tinted windows hiding everything inside the vehicle from view.

Reaching for the latch, she yanked the door open and jumped inside. She twisted in her seat to face him, slightly out of breath, not from exertion but anxiety.

"All right, what's going on? Did you find Mom?"

He shook his head, keeping his gaze trained straight ahead as the car rolled forward. "Not yet. Let me get you home first."

"Home? Why call me in the middle of the day and pick me up at all when you could have just waited until I got home and met me there? Tell me what's going on, Creed."

He slowed to check traffic, then pulled away from the school and onto the main road.

"Soon. Now buckle up." Reaching across her, he grabbed the seat belt and stretched it toward him, fumbling blindly for the snap while he kept his eyes on the road.

With a frustrated sigh, she took the buckle out of his hand and clicked it into place herself. Although she wanted to argue, she knew better than to think she could get him to say anything before he was darn good and ready.

Thankfully, her town house wasn't far from the school, so it wouldn't take them long to get there. Still, she spent the ten-minute drive tapping her foot, fisting and unfisting her fingers, drumming her nails on the armrest.

She was surprised Creed didn't tell her to cut it out. But then, he seemed preoccupied himself, his jaw set in a tight line, his knuckles white on the steering wheel, more intent on his driving than usual.

When they reached her house, he found a place to park and cut the engine. Throwing open his door, he came around to hers, but she was already out, digging in her purse for her keys.

She unlocked the front door and let them both in, then tossed her purse aside and turned on him.

"Okay," she said, her arms folded beneath her breasts. "We're home. Now tell me what's going on."

He nodded, shrugging out of his jacket and loosening the tie knotted around his neck. He tossed both over the back of a kitchen chair, then headed for the living room.

Rolling her eyes, she clamped down on the urge to scream and followed him. She found him taking a seat on her sofa, his fingers undoing the buttons at his collar and wrists, rolling the stark white material of the dress shirt to his elbows.

"Have a seat," he told her, patting the cushion on his right.

"If I do, I want you to tell me what you found out," she demanded. "No more stalling."

Meeting her gaze for the first time since he'd picked her up at school, his mouth lifted in a half-hearted grin. "Sit down, Maya."

As much as she didn't want to, she stepped forward and lowered herself onto the sofa beside him. She jerked slightly when he laid one of his large hands over hers where it rested on her knee.

"One of the private investigators I hired contacted me this morning with some information about your mother. And I want you to know that I haven't said anything to anyone else yet. Not even Dad. I wanted to talk to you first and thought you should be the first to know."

She frowned, her concern growing by leaps and bounds at his soft tone and kind attitude toward her. He wasn't usually this nice, which meant something terrible must be going on.

"Just tell me," she forced herself to say past a throat growing tight with dread.

Lifting her hand from her knee, he turned it over and linked his fingers with hers. At another time the action would have warmed her, made her think that maybe he had feelings for her after all. Now it only made her realize how ominous the news he had to share must be.

"It turns out Patricia isn't actually a widow, as she's always claimed. Her first husband—your father—Wilton Blackstone, is alive. The investigators tracked him down and had a little talk with him. Leaned on him a bit," he said, the slight lift of one dark brow telling her exactly what he meant by "leaned on."

"It turns out he's been blackmailing Patricia for months, threatening to tell Dad that their marriage isn't valid because she's still legally married to him. We think that's why she disappeared, that she ran off to get away from your father—and to keep mine from finding out the truth."

Maya sat in stunned silence, her mind trying desperately to make sense of everything Creed had just told her.

Her father was still alive? Her mother had been lying to her all these years? Lying to Nash and the entire Fortune family?

Tears prickled behind her eyes, and her heart felt as though it would pound out of her chest.

"I don't understand," she said in a watery voice. "How can that be? If my father is still alive, where has he been all these years? Why didn't Mom tell me? And why didn't any of Nash's private investigators discover this earlier?"

"I don't know why Dad's guys didn't find out about this," he answered softly, "but my guys *are* good. That's why I hired them. I only wish I'd done it sooner. And I don't know why your mother didn't tell you any of this, but according to my sources, for the past almost twenty years, Wilton Blackstone has been living in Texas. I have to tell you, too, that from the sound of it, he's *not* a nice man, Maya."

His free hand moved to her back to rub reassuringly up and down her spine. "What, if anything, did your mother tell you about your father?"

She shook her head, as much to dispel the confusing thoughts and memories swimming around in her brain as to answer his question.

"She told me he was dead, the same as she told everyone else. I was only five years old when…well, when Mom told me he'd died, so I don't remember much about him. And what I do remember isn't good. He was very violent and abusive. Like you said, *not* a nice man."

"I'm sorry."

Overwhelming emotion threatened again, and she sniffed to hold back tears. "It doesn't matter. I don't even know him, and he obviously never cared much about finding or getting to know me if he's been alive all these years. I'm worried about my mother. Where could she be if she's hiding from him? She must be so frightened, and she's all alone."

Creed leaned in and pressed a kiss to her temple. His lips were warm, even through her hair, and she felt an unreasonable degree of comfort despite the common sense telling her it was merely a brotherly gesture and meant nothing otherwise.

"Do you have any idea where she might have gone?" he asked.

Pulling back, she glared at him through narrowed, damp eyes. "If I did, don't you think I would have said something by now? I'm just as worried about her as everyone else and want to find her just as much. Maybe more."

"I know." His fingers trailed up the line of her back and beneath the fall of her hair. Reaching her neck, he began to gently knead her nape. "But now that you understand why she disappeared, I thought something might come to mind, something you wouldn't have thought to consider before. Did your mother ever talk about Wilton, about her habits or behavior when she was with him? What she did when he—" he cringed "—beat her?"

She considered for a moment, but couldn't recall anything that might be helpful. "No, I'm sorry."

He tugged her close, his arm wrapping around her waist and holding her tight against his side. "It's all right. We're going to find her. The investigators are still on the job, and after turning up this information, I'm sure they'll be able to track her down."

"I'm so worried about her," Maya said in a small voice, leaning into him and letting his soothing disposition seep into her bones.

"So am I. But everything's going to be okay. I promise."

Raising her head, she offered him a tremulous smile. He couldn't promise any such thing, and they both knew it, but the words brought a modicum of solace all the same.

"Thank you, Creed. Thank you for being here and for doing so much to try to find my Mom."

His mouth curved slightly, his hands cupping her face as he wiped the tears from her cheeks with his thumbs. "We're all concerned about Patricia. Besides, you're family."

When she met his gaze, she noticed his smile slipping at the edges, and the look in his eyes was anything but familiar.

A spark of awareness flared low in her belly, spreading quickly outward, even as her mind warned her not to be drawn in by his kind words or the heat in his eyes. She'd wandered down that path once before and gotten nothing but heartache for her troubles.

But the heat of his palms caressed her skin, and his blue eyes were as deep and fathomless as the ocean during a storm. Pulling her in, making her feel safe.

For months now, she'd felt so isolated and alone. Even with all of the Fortunes rallying around Nash—and thereby remaining in close proximity to her—she'd still felt as though she was all by herself in this situation. No one could truly understand what she was going through.

Nash loved Patricia. She knew that. And in their own way, the Fortune children did, too.

But Patricia was *her* mother, giving them a bond unlike any other. Nobody knew what they'd been through together or what Maya had been going through since her mother had gone missing. The fear, the uncertainty, the insecurity of belonging nowhere and with no one, since Patricia was her only real link to the Fortunes, her so-called family.

She knew it was crazy, foolish and possibly even sheer desperation on her part, but Creed made her feel less alone, more like she belonged, and more as though everything really would work out in the end.

His fingers slid through her hair to cup the back of her skull and tilt her face up to his. She closed her eyes and surrendered to what she was beginning to consider the inevitable.

He was her Achilles' heel, her weakness. When he was around, her insides turned to mush and her brain ceased to function.

They'd done this before. She'd capitulated before.

Capitulated? More like thrown herself into his arms wholeheartedly and had practically been planning the wedding before the sheets were cold.

And immediately afterward, he'd gotten dressed and walked away.

That's why she was crazy to be letting this happen again. She knew better. She knew he would only hurt her—again.

The minute his mouth touched hers, the insanity seemed more than worth the price of admission. His lips were warm and firm, tasting of coffee and something else she couldn't quite identify. Maybe it was simply Creed, his unique essence invading her every pore.

His arms snaked around her back, holding her, cradling her against his hard chest. Her own arms felt leaden as she lifted them to his shoulders and neck, moaning as he deepened the kiss.

He'd said she was out of his system, that once he'd had her, he could move on. But this was far from moving on. He was just as involved in the kiss as she was, just as eager for more, and that gave her a sense of power she'd never experienced before.

Despite his claims to the contrary, he wanted her as much as she wanted him. Maybe not forever, or for more than this very moment, but it was enough.

She threaded her fingers through his hair, holding him closer and urging him on. His own hands began to tug at the tail of her shirt, tucked into the waistband of charcoal-gray slacks.

When he had the material free, he spanned her bare waist with his warm, broad hands. His fingertips were like conductors, sending tiny shockwaves through her, everywhere they touched.

Her limbs felt heavy, almost immovable. Heat pooled low in her belly, making her squirm with wanting, with need, with eagerness. The emotions rolled up her throat and came out her mouth, where it was still clamped tight to his. He groaned back and delved even more deeply with his tongue.

His hands beneath her blouse slid higher, skimming the edges of her modest white bra, then the undersides of her breasts and her quickly beading nipples within the cotton and lace. At the clear signs of her physical response to his caresses, he grew bolder, reaching around to release the hooks at the center of her back.

With the garment hanging loose around her, he was able to slide his hands up and under. He cupped her firmly in both palms, his thumbs alternately flicking and then drawing circles around the puckered centers.

She was writhing now, desperate for everything he could give her. One of her pumps slipped off her foot and fell to the floor with a clunk as she tried to crawl farther onto his lap. He grabbed her thigh and pulled her closer, brushing stray wisps of hair away from her neck so he could brush his lips over the rapidly beating pulse point.

Her fingers fumbled between them, working to release the row of buttons at the front of his dress shirt. With her head tipped back and her eyes closed in ecstasy, it was a simple task turned almost impossible.

But Creed took mercy on her, undoing the even smaller buttons on her blouse before finishing his own.

As soon as the two sides of the soft cotton separated, she drove her fingers under the collar and into the arm holes, pushing it down his strong, well-muscled arms. The cuffs caught at his wrists and she gave a small cry of frustration.

He chuckled and yanked back while she still held the edges of material in her clenched hands. Fabric tore and she heard buttons ping across the room.

His broad chest was gloriously bare as he sat back, studying her through heavy-lidded, desire-darkened eyes.

"Your turn," he whispered.

Not waiting for her to protest or comply, he reached out to strip both blouse and bra from her upper body.

The cool air of the room washed over her heated skin, making her shiver, and she suddenly felt self-conscious of her nudity.

They'd done this once before. She'd already been naked in front of him, but she wasn't quite ready to sit on her couch, in broad daylight, with her breasts hanging out.

She lifted her arms to cover herself, but Creed

stopped her, wrapping his fingers around her wrists and holding them away.

"Don't," he warned in a low voice. "You're beautiful. You should be proud of your body instead of hiding inside those oversize dresses and loose pantsuits you like so much."

His hands slid from her wrists to her elbows, then back, making the little hairs on her arms stand on end. She shivered again, even though she was far from cold this time.

And she squirmed, because his words made her uncomfortable. She wasn't beautiful; she knew that. She was plain and rather average looking.

But for this one moment in time, he made her *feel* beautiful. Sexy and sensual, even. His gaze, glittering with barely restrained passion, skimmed over her, singeing her from head to toe as thoroughly as an open flame.

He brought her hands to his mouth, one after the other. Pressed his lips to each of her knuckles in turn, then the center of her palms and the tiny, bluish veins on the insides of her wrists.

Any vestiges of shyness disappeared beneath his tender assault and reignited her yearning a thousand percent. Physiologically impossible or not, she felt ready to melt like an ice cube left too long in the sun.

He placed her hands, with their now-tingling digits, on his bare shoulders before leaning in to press a soft kiss to the corner of her mouth. He followed that up with a kiss to the other corner, then her cheeks, temples, eyelids.

While his lips drifted softly over her face, his hands toyed briefly at her breasts on their way to her waist, where he made quick work of loosening her slacks and pushing them down her hips. She moved in whatever ways he needed to get the pants, pantyhose and her underwear all the way off.

As soon as that was done, he shed his own shoes and expensively tailored dress pants, leaving everything in a wrinkled pile on the living room floor. All she could do while this was going on was knead his shoulders and squirm with the longing pumping through her veins.

Reality prodded the outer edges of her mind, threatening to ruin the cloud of euphoria that had formed around them, but she wouldn't let it. Tomorrow would be soon enough to deal with the fact that this wasn't real and wouldn't last. Soon enough to go back to the near-hostile stepsibling relationship that kept them walking on eggshells around each other.

Today, this very moment, she had a second chance at living out a lifelong fantasy, and she had every intention of taking full advantage of the opportunity.

Five

Grasping Maya under the arms, Creed scooped her up and redeposited her on the couch. He wanted her under him, open to him and arranged in such a way that he didn't have to worry about dropping her or bouncing her off the sofa at some highly inopportune moment.

Reaching blindly toward the floor, he groped for his pants and fumbled around until he found a condom tucked safely in the folds of his wallet. He kept one there at all times, just in case, and thanked God he'd remembered to add another packet after the first night he'd spent with Maya.

Keeping his gaze locked on her—her flushed face,

the rapid rise and fall of her bare, lovely breasts—he tore open the plastic square and safely covered himself.

Then, with her back against the arm at one end of the sofa and the soft, wide cushions supporting her lithe, blessedly naked form, he spread her legs and settled himself firmly between them. If he had a choice, he would keep her like this forever and never move out of the cradle of her smooth, welcoming thighs.

He should have left twenty minutes ago. Should have called her at school, or even waited until she'd gotten home, to tell her what the private investigator had found out about her mother and not-dead-after-all father. It would have been the safer route to take.

But he hadn't been able to bring himself to break news like that over the phone. And the twenty-minutes-ago ship had clearly sailed. Hell, the vessel was halfway around the world by now. He couldn't leave her now if someone held a gun to his head.

Lapse in judgment or not, he'd started this and he was damn well going to finish it.

Not that making love to her again was going to be any great trial. He was already so hard for her, he was ready to burst.

Their bodies melded together from chest to pelvis, his erection straining toward her warm, damp center. But he wasn't ready to end this encounter quite so quickly. He wanted to make it last, wanted the swirling, ragged sensations building inside them both to linger a while longer.

He kissed her, brushing her lips and teasing her tongue with only a fraction of the passion burning in his gut. His fingers sifted through her long, silky hair, spreading it out around her head, like a dark cloud in a thunder-riddled sky.

Abandoning her mouth, he trailed a line of nips and licks down her throat to her breasts. She was clawing at his shoulders, upper arms, and whatever part of his back she could reach. Driving him crazy and straining his already tenuous control.

He thought about grabbing her wrists again to keep her from sending him straight over the edge, but what she was doing felt too damn good. So he started counting from one to ten and back again—slowly, in three languages. Mentally reciting a few statistics for local sporting teams that came readily to mind. Rehashing the details of a recent business deal he and Case had made for Dakota Fortune. Anything to keep the top of his head from shooting off before he'd even gotten to the best part of being naked with Maya Blackstone.

And if she was going to take him to the brink, almost without trying, then he fully intended to do the same to her.

He began to feast at her breasts as he'd always dreamed, taking his time and being thorough. He circled one of the swollen peaks with the tip of his tongue, then scraped the rough surface across the pointed nipple. At the same time, he teased the other breast, squeezing, rubbing, tweaking with thumb and index finger. She squirmed beneath him, arching her back and offering herself to him more fully.

"Creed, please."

Her voice was a whimper, and a streak of power rushed through him. She was his for the taking. At his mercy. He could do just about anything to her and she wouldn't try to stop him.

But he didn't want to do anything *to* her, he wanted to do it *with* her. Now.

Without abandoning her breasts completely, he slid a palm down the plane of her stomach, into the triangle of springy curls between her legs to test her readiness. She was hot and wet against his fingers, and he groaned, clamping his jaw to keep even more desperate, pathetic sounds from working their way up his throat.

"I'm going to take you now," he all but growled.

A warning or a promise, he wasn't sure. He worked two fingers gently into her channel and was rewarded by the jerk of her hips and a high mewling rolling past her lips.

"Yes, please," she panted when she was capable of speech. "You're taking too long as it is."

He started to chuckle but ended with a low moan as she brought her legs around his waist and locked them at the ankles.

"Hey," he grated, surprised his brain was still functioning well enough to send sensible signals to his vocal chords. "Who's the more experienced person here? How would you know I'm taking too long?"

"I just do. Now get to it already," she demanded.

To emphasize her point, she moved a hand from his bicep to the narrow space between their sweat-slick bodies and wrapped her slim fingers around his burgeoning length.

The action was so shocking, and so pleasurable, he nearly came.

His muscles tensed, his entire frame going rigid as he fought to pull himself back from the point of no return. Inhaling and exhaling carefully, breathing through his nose as though he'd just run a thousand-yard dash, he covered her hand and pried open her surprisingly strong grip.

"Don't do that," he said, moving her hand a safe distance from what he now considered the danger zone.

At his firm reprimand, her chocolate-brown eyes turned cloudy and she seemed to pull back. Not physically, but emotionally. At her side, her fingers curled into a loose fist.

Dammit. Creed cursed himself and then Maya's innocence. She was too inexperienced to know just how close he was to losing it. To not only embarrassing himself, but robbing them both of the ultimate pleasure their joining could bring.

He wasn't used to dealing with virgins. Even if Maya was no longer a technical virgin, she had been only a week ago—before he'd taken her the first time. For all the more she knew about men and sex, she might as well still be one.

"Not because I don't like it," he told her, quickly trying to repair any damage he might have caused. "Believe me, I do. Too much. But if you keep touching me that way, I won't last long enough to get inside you. And I very much want to be inside you."

He watched the tendons of her throat tighten and release as she swallowed.

"So...I can touch you later?" she asked, her tone tentative.

He gritted his teeth even harder to stifle a groan, his fingers flexing on her hips. "Yes, you can touch me later. Touch me, kiss me, do whatever you like to me." He shuddered as his mind filled with visions of her taking him into his mouth. "Later."

She nodded, her expression solemn. "All right."

A second later she wiggled beneath him, her legs squeezing around his waist, her hands curling over his shoulders and drawing him closer.

"Hurry up and come inside me, then, so I can hurry up and touch you however I want." She smiled wickedly, her tongue darting out to lick her lips like a practiced courtesan. "I have ideas, and things I've been fantasizing about for years."

His body bucked at her blatant carnal promise, and he marveled that he hadn't burst into flames already.

"Heaven help me," he muttered raggedly. "You'll be the death of me. I won't make it through the hour."

She canted her hips, bringing her feminine center flush with his throbbing groin. "You never know unless you try."

His breath hissed out in a gust. "Devil woman." And then he took her mouth in a passionate kiss, guiding himself into her warm sheath.

Maya gasped as he entered her completely, filling her to the hilt.

She might not be as experienced as Creed, but a girl could definitely get used to this sort of thing: being in the arms of the man she'd had a crush on the majority of her life; having him touch her, kiss her, work her into a frenzy of lust so strong she wanted to weep.

He pounded against her, being less than gentle, but she didn't care. She raised her legs even higher around his waist, allowing him to enter her just a fraction more, until she swore he touched her womb.

Her arms clutched his back, her belly quivering with every stroke of his velvet hardness inside her. She panted for more and whispered in his ear for him to go deeper, faster.

He complied, a muscle in his jaw ticking rhythmically as he gripped her thighs, held her in place, brought her roughly into contact with him on each downward slide.

"Yes." Her lungs burned as she struggled for air. "Please, yes."

"Yes," he agreed, the word slipping from between clenched teeth.

A second later she was flying. Creed's hands and mouth and body worked as a single unit to drive her over the edge, gasping as wave after wave of orgasm shook her to her core.

Following her into the abyss, he ground against her one last time before shouting his release. He sank down on top of her, his heavy weight pinning her in place as their chests rose and fell in a synchronized bid for oxygen.

By the time either of them had the strength to move, the sky outside the town house windows was starting to grow dim with the first pale streaks of dusk. Creed rolled to his side, still holding her as best he could on the narrow sofa. The side of one thumb drew nonsensical designs on her upper arm while the fingers of his other hand drifted through the ends of her hair.

Her eyes were growing heavy, and she thought that if she let them close, she could probably sleep for a week. But he'd promised her something, and she didn't intend to drift off until she was sure he would follow through on their agreement.

She turned slightly, snuggling closer, rubbing her cheek against the smooth skin at the hollow of his shoulder.

"Now that that's done," she said, struggling to keep her tone level and detached, "it's my turn, right?"

Her fingers wandered over his left pectoral, lightly covered with a dusting of dark hair, then lower, down the center of his flat stomach. She felt his abdominal muscles tense as he sucked in his breath.

"Your turn for what?" he asked.

With her head tipped away from him, he couldn't see

her smile. He wasn't fooling her, though. Regardless of his words, his body knew exactly what she was talking about.

She lifted her face to his, leaning in to catch his bottom lip gently between her teeth and give it a little tug. "To touch you. Anywhere I like. Any way I like. Remember?"

He opened his mouth to deny it, even started to shake his head. But when she took hold of his reviving member and gave it a little squeeze, he could only groan in surrender.

"All right, all right. Yes, I remember. But are you sure…?"

She pumped him again, just once, but with enough pressure to let him know she meant business. He moaned again, a low, ragged sound, and closed his eyes as his head fell back against the arm of the couch.

Grinning at his acquiescence and the sudden rush of power bubbling through her bloodstream, she shifted around to straddle his legs and hover above him.

It was going to be a long night, and she intended to enjoy every minute of it to the absolute fullest.

And if she had her way, she would make sure Creed did, too.

Creed lay in the dark of Maya's quiet bedroom, wide awake and kicking himself for what he'd done. He'd let down his guard and touched her a second time when he never should have touched her the first time.

Second time, hell. Try third, fourth and maybe fifth times; he'd lost count somewhere around midnight.

For only recently losing her virginity, she'd been insatiable. Not that he'd tried very hard to put her off or keep himself from turning to her over and over again.

He never should have touched her to begin with. He knew that. But now that he had, he couldn't seem to stop. She was a fire in his blood, and he seemed powerless to stay away from her.

He sighed, then went rigid when she burrowed closer to his side. They'd already made love multiple times. So often and with such enthusiasm that Maya had finally fallen into an exhausted sleep.

But try telling that to his libido. The feel of her soft curves nestled against him like a second skin brought his arousal flaring back to life.

Her head on his shoulder…her silky hair falling across his arm…her dainty hand curled on his chest… one leg drawn up and twined with his own. How could any man resist such an enticing temptation, regardless of the risks involved?

It didn't sit well with Creed to concede that he was as weak as any other male of his species when it came to Maya Blackstone. But part of that weakness, he admitted, stemmed from the fact that she needed him right now.

She had been stunned by the news that her biological father was still alive, and terrified for her mother's safety, especially being aware that Wilton Blackstone was likely the reason for Patricia's disappearance. He'd seen the shock and despair etched clearly on her face as he'd broken the news.

That's why she'd turned to him, and why he'd allowed himself to move past the invisible barriers he'd erected to keep her at arm's length.

She'd needed him. Needed comfort and human contact, the distraction of physical intimacy to get her mind off the situation with her mother. And, God help him, he hadn't been able to walk away from her, even if he'd wanted to.

He tipped his head to stare down at her, doing his best not to notice the generous swell of her breasts or the way they spilled so attractively across his chest.

She still needed him, and would until her mother was found and brought home where she belonged. As soon as that happened, all of their lives would go back to normal and he would be able to leave her alone, focus his mind—and hormones—on other things.

Stress and uncertainty, that's all this was. They were both acting completely out of character, and he felt the tightness in his lungs and diaphragm ease at that crystal-clear realization.

As long as what was going on between them at the moment remained private, and no one—especially the media—found out, they would be okay.

He swallowed, relaxing more fully into the pillows at his back. Beside him, Maya stirred. Her soft brown eyes blinked open and she stretched like a contented cat, her rosy, well-kissed lips curving in a smile when she found him awake and watching her.

"Hi," she said, her voice a sensual purr.

"Hi," he returned with a suggestive grin of his own, welcoming the hot, heavy flush of arousal beginning to pump once again through every cell of his being.

"What time is it?"

He cast his gaze over her shoulder, in the direction of the digital clock on the bedside table. "About 4:00 a.m."

She groaned, closing her eyes and burying her face in his chest. But just as quickly, she came back up, shaking her hair out of the way and starting to press light kisses along the line of his jaw, which he was sure needed a shave by now.

"I have to start getting ready for work in a couple hours," she told him.

"Me, too," he said, bringing his hands up to skim her waist and the small of her back.

"I'll be so tired tomorrow I'll probably fall asleep at my desk."

He gave a rueful chuckle, picturing that very situation and how much ribbing he would get from everyone in the Dakota Fortune offices if they found out about it. "Me, too."

"But that gives us two hours to enjoy ourselves again."

He glanced at the clock, did the math, weighed the pros and cons of missing out on a full night of sleep.

There was no contest—making love to Maya would win every time.

Capturing her mouth, he kissed her breathless, then rolled until he loomed over her, and made sure neither of them got a wink of sleep before the sun broke over the horizon.

Maya had expected to be exhausted all day, but instead she was brimming with energy and couldn't seem to wipe the smile from her face. Not even when Mikey Roth put gum in Sally Mattea's hair, and the little girl screamed bloody murder for almost an hour.

She'd punished Mikey by putting him on animal-clean-up duty for the rest of the week, which basically meant he would be helping her care for the guinea pig and small aquarium of fish she kept as unofficial class-room mascots. Then she'd sent to the cafeteria for some butter and ice cubes, and spent all of recess sitting cross-legged at the edge of the playground, working a giant hunk of watermelon-flavored bubblegum out of Sally's blond, baby-fine hair.

There was no doubt what had put her in such a good mood—a night of mind-blowing sex with the man she'd dreamed of as Mr. Right for half her life.

She knew it was dangerous to let herself get too swept away by what was happening between them. There was no way it would last. No happily-ever-after for her where Creed was concerned.

Frankly, she was surprised he'd stayed with her all

night instead of running for the door as soon as they'd finished their impromptu lovemaking session on the living room sofa.

But he hadn't. He'd stuck around until morning, and they'd definitely made good use of the time.

She couldn't let it go to her head, though. She had to keep her feet firmly on the ground and her heart deeply rooted in reality.

Whatever was going on between the two of them right now was only temporary. Explosive, earth-shattering, beyond her wildest fantasies…but temporary.

Still, they weren't hurting anyone. As long as she kept her wits about her and didn't start imagining that things could develop into more than was possible, she would be all right.

She'd spent the morning carefully considering every angle of the situation, playing out every probable scenario. The result was that she'd decided to move cautiously forward with…whatever this was.

Before Creed had dropped her off at school on his own way back home and to work—because her car was still in the school parking lot from when he'd picked her up the afternoon before—he'd run a hand through her loose hair and leaned across the seats to press a light kiss to her lips. He'd asked her to give him a couple of days to put out more feelers about her mother, see what else his investigators could turn up, and promised that they *would* find her.

She'd nodded, swallowing hard as her fears for

Patricia's safety and emotional well-being came flooding back.

With all the tension and animosity that had passed between Creed and herself over the years, she was amazed at how easy it was to put her faith in him. Their relationship might be shaky, as wispy thin as morning dew, but where her mother's disappearance was concerned, she trusted him implicitly.

Then he'd done something that had shocked her even more than his spending the night with her. He'd told her he was coming over with dinner for both of them after work.

She'd been too flustered and—yes, she admitted it—delighted to question why he didn't want to eat out at a restaurant, in public with her, or why he didn't invite her to his place. That he wanted to see her again was enough. See her, spend time with her, and if the look in his eyes at that moment was any indication, likely spend the night with her again, too.

For as long as it lasted, she would take him however she could get him.

Just the thought made her stomach do somersaults. She put a hand low on her belly in an attempt to still the internal acrobatics while she finished saying goodbye to her students as they gathered their books, jackets and lunchboxes, and raced for the buses outside the building waiting to take them home.

After seeing them off and straightening her desk, she grabbed her own purse and a few papers she *should* look over for the next day's lessons, even though she suspected she wouldn't, and headed for her car.

Only a few more hours before she would see Creed again. Before he walked into her house with an armful of take-out and settled in for a quiet dinner.

He hadn't asked her what she wanted to eat, and she hadn't volunteered the information. But being forced to endure a meal she didn't care for would be a small price to pay for the satisfaction of being with Creed again. Even for just a short time.

Six

For the tenth time in an hour, Creed checked his watch, cursing at how slowly the minutes seemed to tick by. He hadn't done a lick of Dakota Fortune business all day, concentrating instead on uncovering anything else he could about Patricia's whereabouts. Making phone calls, putting a couple more investigators on the case, following a few of his own leads and researching some of the information he already had.

But through it all, in the back of his mind he'd been thinking about Maya and anticipating the hour when he could leave the office without arousing suspicion and head over to see her. Of course, he had a few errands to run on the way.

Dinner. He'd offered to bring dinner over to her place.

He shook his head, confused and uncomfortable with how he found himself continually responding to her.

The plain truth was he wanted to be with her. Their time together was limited, and deep in his gut he felt this urgency to store up as much of her as he could. When he had to walk away—and it would happen sooner rather than later—he wanted to have part of her deep under his skin to get him through the many long, lonely nights ahead.

That's why he'd suggested dinner at her house. He couldn't very well take her out to a fancy restaurant, where anyone might see them together. Especially since he knew he was likely to be looking at her half the night as though he wanted to rip her clothes off.

Ninety percent of the restaurant's patrons might not think anything of it, but it would only take the remaining ten percent—one person familiar with the Fortune family, one reporter, one gossip columnist—to create the very scandal he was trying so desperately to avoid.

He didn't want her to be seen going in or out of his apartment, either, for the very same reasons. Even though he lived on the top floor of the Dakota Fortune building, and her presence there might be accepted during business hours, after hours was a whole different story.

Going to her place seemed the obvious choice. From there it had been a short jump to offering to bring dinner.

Another glance at his watch showed only thirty more minutes until he could safely sneak out and get on with what had been consuming his thoughts all day.

Pushing back from his desk, he stood, scooped up a couple of files he needed to drop off at his brother's office, and headed for the door. He informed his assistant that he probably wouldn't be back before morning, then walked a short distance down the hall.

"Mr. Fortune." Case's assistant greeted him with a smile.

He inclined his head in reply. "Debra. Is it all right if I go in, or is he busy?"

"He just got off the phone, so it should be all right, but let me announce you."

Creed let her, preferring to give Case fair warning of his arrival. The last time he'd walked into his brother's office unannounced, it had been to find Case and Gina entwined like weeds on top of the desk, doing something Creed would have preferred never to witness. He loved his brother and new sister-in-law as much as anyone, but there were some things about their relationship he just didn't need to know firsthand.

He'd backed silently out of the office and never mentioned the incident to Case, but from that point on, he'd made sure to let Debra announce him or knock himself and wait for his brother to give him the all-clear.

Rising from her chair, Debra crossed to a door identical to Creed's own, with a brass name plate labeling it the office of one of the copresidents of Dakota

Fortune, and tapped softly, waiting for Case's muffled response. That she didn't simply open the door and walk right in made Creed wonder if she'd stumbled into an intimate moment or two between Case and Gina herself.

"Your brother is here to see you," she informed Case in a bright, casual tone, leaning around the now-open door.

"Good," Creed heard his brother say, punctuated by what sounded like a pen being tossed down. "I could use an excuse not to deal with this report until tomorrow."

Grinning, Creed strolled into his brother's office and took a seat in front of his desk, tossing the files in his hand on top of Case's already cluttered blotter. Behind him, he heard the click of the door as Debra closed it, ensuring the two brothers' privacy.

"I hate to break it to you, brother, but you're going to have more than one report to deal with in the morning."

Case groaned. "Thanks a lot."

"Look," Creed said, getting down to business, "I'm taking off for the night, but I wanted to fill you in on some information I found out about Patricia, and why I think she ran off."

His expression turning serious, Case listened as Creed told him about the extra private investigators he'd hired to look into their stepmother's disappearance and what they'd discovered about Wilton Blackstone still being alive.

When he finished, Case shook his head and swore

beneath his breath. "Dad won't be happy to hear any of that."

"I didn't tell him. And I'd appreciate it if you wouldn't, either. Not yet, anyway. I don't want to get his—or anyone else's—hopes up in case we're wrong about what we think is going on, and Patricia disappeared for some other reason."

Case nodded in understanding.

Creed shifted in his seat, crossing one ankle on the opposite knee and loosening the knot of his tie. "I've still got my guys looking into it, and looking for her."

"Good," Case murmured, his lips pressed into a solemn line. "Let's pray they find her."

Silence filled the room, the minutes ticking by while Creed focused on a spot outside the tall plate glass windows at his brother's back. He felt Case's gaze on him, and knew his brother was waiting to hear what else he had to say.

The problem was, Creed wasn't sure he should reveal the other problem weighing so heavily on his mind. Case was his brother, probably the person he was closest to in the world, but some things weren't meant to be shared with anyone.

"You might as well spit it out," Case said, reading Creed's mind—or maybe just the tight lines he knew marked his face. "Get it off your chest so you can stop sulking about it."

He wasn't sulking, but it sure did seem to occupy a fair chunk of his time these days.

With a sigh, he let his foot fall to the floor and ran splayed hands through his hair, giving the ends a tug for good measure.

"It's about Maya," he said finally.

"Yeah? What about her?"

"I'm sleeping with her."

He blurted it out quickly, like ripping off a bandage, before he could change his mind, then waited for Case's stunned response. He expected wide eyes, a dropped jaw, maybe a few choice expletives as his brother kicked back his chair and stormed around the room.

Instead Case remained perfectly still for one long minute. Then, very slowly, he said, "Okay. How serious is it?"

"Not...serious." Creed shook his head. "It can't be, not with the way things are."

"What things?" Case wanted to know.

Creed gave him a look hot enough to peel paint from the walls. "She's our sister, for God's sake."

"Stepsister," Case corrected, leaning back in his chair and adopting a less poised, more comfortable position. "Stepsister from Dad's third marriage. She's not *technically* related to us. We—*you*—don't share a single drop of blood with her, or a single strand of DNA."

"Does it matter?" Creed snapped, his brows knitting with annoyance. "She's still family. We grew up with her. Hell, she's ten years younger than I am. For that reason alone, I never should have touched her."

"So why did you?"

Leave it to his brother to cut right to the heart of the matter.

He thought about it for a second. No way was he going to tell Case that he'd been watching Maya for years, thinking decidedly *un*brotherly thoughts about her ever since she'd hit puberty.

"I couldn't seem to help myself," he said instead, his insides twisting at the admission.

Case considered that for a minute, rocking back and forth in the soft leather of his executive desk chair.

"So what's the problem?" he asked. "Maya may be younger, but she's a grown woman. If she's as interested as you are, I don't understand why you'd be concerned."

Muttering a low curse, Creed pushed to his feet and began to pace. "Do you know what would happen if word got out that a Fortune son was sleeping with his own stepsister? The press would have a field day. It could ruin the company, not to mention the humiliation it would cause for Dad and Patricia. And the rest of you…no one in the Fortune family would be safe from the gossip and disgrace."

"Do you really think that would happen? You and Maya *aren't* related, no matter how the media might want to spin things. And even if they did their worst, if you're in love with her and the two of you want to be together, you have to know that this family would support you. We've weathered storms before and come out on top. We can do it again."

Creed stopped a few steps from his brother's desk and absorbed what he was saying. It sounded good, exactly what he needed to hear. Exactly what he probably would have told Case if their situations were reversed.

But that didn't make it any easier for him to believe.

"The only thing I would warn you against," his brother went on in a grim tone, "is not to toy with Maya's affections. If you're not serious about her, then you should probably let her go and keep your distance. But if you are…"

Case took a deep breath, his lips quirking slightly. "If you *are* serious about her, and she's the woman you want to spend the rest of your life with, then don't let anything stand in your way."

Creed scowled, not the least bit comforted by his brother's advice. If anything, it set him more on edge, making his stomach clench with the acidic mix of conflicting emotions.

"Trust me on this, little brother," Case continued. "When a man finds the right woman, he has to hang on to her with both hands."

"Are you speaking from experience?" Creed asked, already knowing the answer.

His brother had been almost annoyingly chipper since his marriage to Gina, and it had only gotten worse since he found out he was going to be a father. And while Creed was happy for him, for them both, Case's good mood at the moment only made his own darker.

"Damn right I am," Case said proudly, grinning from ear to ear as he leaned back in his chair, then sent it rocking silently on its springs.

"And if Maya makes you half as happy as Gina makes me, then you'd be an idiot to let her get away. But if you're just using her as a temporary amusement…" He let the words hang in the air for a second, increasing their impact. "Well, I don't need to tell you how hot it will be when you get to Hell."

One of Case's brows lifted pointedly, and he held Creed's gaze until Creed scrubbed a hand over his face and dropped back into one of the chairs in front of his brother's desk.

After a tension-filled pause, Case sat forward in his own chair, leaning his arms on the edge of his desk. "Whatever you decide, Creed, I'll back you one hundred percent. You can count on that."

Blowing out a breath, Creed nodded and pushed to his feet. "Thanks. I don't know if I feel any better about what's going on, but…thanks."

A quick glance at his watch showed it was past time that he could get away with leaving the office and head over to Maya's to start dinner. His talk with Case tempted him to skip the visit altogether, but since the "date" had been his idea, he didn't feel right backing out at the last minute.

"I have to get going," he explained on the way to the door. "Remember not to say anything to Dad or the others about what the investigators turned up. Hopefully we'll find out something more in a few days, but until then I want to keep it all under wraps."

"You've got it. See you tomorrow."

Creed left his brother shuffling papers, muttering about the likelihood of drowning under the pile of reports now flooding his in-box, and made his way to the underground garage of the Dakota Fortune building where his car was parked.

He would stop at the store and pick up what he needed for the evening meal, then he'd head for Maya's house. The very thought made his muscles tense right down to the soles of his feet.

All day he'd been looking forward to seeing her again, *being* with her again. But after talking with his brother, he wasn't sure that was the smartest move on his part.

Case was right—he shouldn't string Maya along. If he wasn't serious about her, he should walk away, leave her alone, put the distance between them again that had been there the past twenty years.

And he wasn't serious about her. Couldn't be. The risks were too great.

Which meant he had to put an end to this…affair, relationship, lapse of judgment and giant mistake. He had to break it off, the sooner the better.

Sliding behind the wheel of his Mercedes, he started the engine and pretended not to feel the ball of dread that slid down his throat and twisted his gut.

* * *

The minute she heard Creed at the front door, Maya's heart skipped a beat.

She'd spent the past couple of hours lecturing herself to act normal, nonchalant, to not read more into his offer of dinner than there really was. After all, he could merely be feeling sorry for her, given her mother's continued absence and the news he'd delivered yesterday about her father not being deceased as she'd been led to believe.

She didn't want to think that was the case, but had to admit it was a distinct possibility.

He knocked again, and she rushed to let him in, not wanting him to think even for a second that he wasn't entirely welcome.

"Hi," she said, smiling and a little breathless from her race through the house.

He stepped inside, a large paper sack in one arm, but didn't return her smile. Instead his dark eyes barely met hers and lines bracketed his flattened lips. An aura of tension radiated from him in waves.

Her senses immediately went on red alert, her spine going rigid as she braced herself for the worst.

"What is it?" she asked in a hoarse whisper. "Mom… is she…?"

His expression indicated confusion and then just as quickly cleared. "No. God, no. I'm sorry," he said with a shake of his head, "my mind was on something else, something from work. I haven't heard anything else about Patricia yet. I'm sorry if I scared you."

Stale oxygen poured from her lungs in one long exhalation. "Thank goodness."

Creed still looked distracted as he moved ahead of her and walked to the kitchen. She was so relieved that nothing had happened to her mother—that they knew about, anyway—that she ignored his apparent bad mood and simply followed him.

He set the bag on the counter, then shrugged out of his suit jacket and tie. Laying them over the back of one of the four chairs surrounding the small round table, he loosened his collar and rolled up the sleeves of his pale-blue dress shirt before beginning to remove items from the sack.

"What are we having?" she asked. It was hard to tell from the nondescript cartons and containers stamped with the name of an upscale downtown eatery or from the mingled scents wafting from them. All she knew was that it smelled *good*.

"I'm not sure. I told them to throw together a full-course meal with a little of everything."

Instead of a separate container for each dish, the plates the restaurant provided came already arranged, the way they would if they were dining in.

"Want to grab some forks and glasses?" Creed suggested while he popped the lids off, then reached into the bag for a bottle of wine before setting everything else aside.

"Sure." Glad to have something to keep her busy, she turned for the cupboards, returning a moment later with everything they would need.

Handing him a corkscrew for the wine, she folded cloth napkins for each place setting, adding silverware to both. He filled their glasses, then took a seat at the head of the table.

She swallowed, fighting a return of the nerves that had plagued her even before he'd arrived. Having him look at her like that…so intense, so focused…made her feel on display. As though she'd just had one of those dreams where she showed up at work stark naked.

It surprised her that the skittishness hadn't lessened, now that she and Creed were sleeping together. She'd always thought that when two people became intimate with each other they started to feel *more* comfortable together, not less.

But for her the opposite seemed to be true. Making love with him had opened her to a whole new set of insecurities.

She worried that she would do or say the wrong thing and somehow send their relationship back to the way it had been before—with him treating her as either invisible or a nuisance, and her avoiding him as much as possible.

Most of all, though, she found herself on constant alert for the moment when everything would come crashing down around her. It was inevitable, she knew that, but waiting for it to happen, never knowing when the blow might come, made her jittery.

"Have you found out anything more about Mom?" she asked, taking a seat beside him.

He shook his head. "I was on the phone all day, but so far, nothing. They understand the importance of the situation, though, so I do believe they'll find something soon."

"I hope so."

"It smells delicious," she murmured, turning her attention to the meal in front of her.

They ate for a few minutes in silence, then, without warning, he put his utensils down and fixed his gaze on her. Startled by his sudden, intense focus, she froze, sitting back a little as she raised her eyes to his.

"What?" she asked, feeling like the proverbial bug under a microscope.

"Maya."

His voice was low, gentle, and the bottom dropped out of her stomach. Whatever he was about to say, it couldn't be good if he was using that tone on her.

"Oh, God," she said, her chest growing too tight for anything else.

He winced at her response, his hands balling into fists where they rested on the table, on either side of his plate.

"Maya," he said again. "We need to talk."

Seven

This was it, she thought. The shoe she'd been waiting to have fall, the rug she'd been expecting to have yanked out from under her.

He was going to break up with her. Tell her that it had been fun, a temporary diversion, but now it was time for things to return to normal, for them to go back to being nothing more than stepsiblings.

She tried to regulate her breathing, slowly in and out through her nose, but her lungs refused to function properly. Her vision blurred, her mind spinning a mile a minute. He opened his mouth to speak, and she braced for the impact his words would have.

A second later, though, his lips met…parted…met again, as though he was rethinking what he'd been about to say, or trying to come up with the best way to say it.

Shaking his head, he muttered something beneath his breath, too low for her to hear, then picked up his fork and started to eat.

Maya sat in stunned silence. He ate several bites of his dinner, his concentration focused entirely on chewing.

"I've been thinking," he said finally, resting his forearms on the edge of the table and tipping his head slightly in her direction.

Sucking in another breath, she waited, wishing he would just get it over with.

"Maybe we should try looking for Patricia ourselves."

Dammit, that wasn't what he'd meant to say. He'd meant to tell her that going to bed together had been a mistake. That it couldn't happen again and they needed to stay away from each other as much as possible.

"Excuse me?"

His grip on his fork tightened as she stared blankly at him. He couldn't blame her. Tonight wasn't going at all as he'd planned.

He never should have come over, but now that he'd started down this road, he didn't have much choice but to follow through.

Doing his best to act naturally, he resumed eating, but at a slower pace this time.

"You know your mother better than anyone. I'll

keep my investigators on the case, looking into every lead, working to track her down however they can. But maybe it's not such a bad idea for the two of us to take some of their information and go looking ourselves. Two more people out there, pounding the pavement, can't hurt. And if we manage to find her, I can't imagine that your mother would want to see anyone more than she'd want to see you."

It took a full minute for her to digest his words. "All right," she finally responded. "Whatever I can do to help. But…if that was all you were going to suggest, why did you make it sound so dire?"

Without meeting her gaze, he shrugged a shoulder, reaching for his wineglass and taking a long, fortifying sip. "I wasn't sure how you'd feel about taking a few days off work."

It wasn't true, but it sounded good. And what choice did he have now that he'd brought up the idea of trying to track down her mother themselves?

"If you think it will help, and that we actually stand a chance of finding her, of course I'll take a few days. I can call tonight and get tomorrow off, or even the rest of the week if we need it."

He nodded. "I'll call the private investigators in the morning and find out where they think we should start looking first. Wear something comfortable," he added, his lips quirking upward in a small smile. "We could be in for a very long day."

They passed the rest of the meal making only light,

casual conversation. Nothing too deep, nothing too personal. It felt awkward to Maya, but that was a state she was rapidly becoming used to whenever Creed was around.

After they finished eating, he helped her clear the table and put the leftovers in the refrigerator for later. Then he moved to retrieve the wine, holding her glass out to her as he lifted his own to his lips.

"Thank you," she murmured. She took the glass but didn't drink. She'd had two full glasses of the rich pinot noir already. Any more and she was likely to get tipsy.

Tipsy around Creed wasn't good. He already put her too much off balance as it was. Drunk, she'd be lucky if she could string two words together without sounding like a bumbling idiot.

"Dinner was delicious," she said while she still had the capacity to function within normal ranges. "Thank you again for bringing it over."

Rather than answer, he inclined his head. Tossing back the last of his wine, he set the glass onto the counter with a soft clink, then crossed the kitchen to gather his tie and jacket.

"I should get going," he said, slipping the silk tie around his neck but leaving it hanging on either side of his collar, and draping the jacket over his arm.

She placed her own half-full glass beside his, smoothing the palms of her hands down the sides of her skirt as she followed him to the front door.

"I'll swing by around nine o'clock tomorrow to pick

you up. That should give me time to talk to my contacts, get some leads and make arrangements to be out of the office for a couple of days."

"I'll be ready," she said with confidence.

Creed opened the door and took one step out, pausing on the darkened stoop. Only a sliver of moonlight and the occasional porch or streetlamp punctuated the blanket of black that surrounded the neighborhood.

Moving a few inches to the side, she flipped the wall switch for her own porch light so he wouldn't have to walk to the car in total darkness.

"Thank you again." She tucked a strand of hair behind her ear, glancing down at the ground before meeting his eyes once again. "For dinner and hiring the extra private investigators and…everything. It's made this whole situation a little less awful for a while."

In the dim lighting, she couldn't be sure, but she thought he offered a small smile.

"You're welcome."

Stepping forward, he wrapped a hand gently around her arm, just above the elbow, and leaned in. His warm breath danced over her face, and she could smell the musky, attractive scent of his cologne.

"Good night, Maya. Sleep well."

Her lips parted, and she tried to respond. But the minute his mouth brushed her cheek in a soft good-night kiss, every thought in her head dried up like a single drop of water in the midday heat of the Sahara Desert.

Creed straightened, and this time, even in the dark, she could see the blaze in his eyes, the stern set of his jaw.

Her heart lurched, and she felt it all the way to her toes. She licked her suddenly dry lips, her fingers going wide at her sides, as though bracing herself. For what, exactly, she wasn't sure.

His grip on her arm tightened, and then he shook his head, sharply.

"Dammit," he grated, a second before grabbing her other arm, dragging her forward and covering her mouth with his own.

The kiss stole her breath, seared her soul. She could have sworn her lips were burned away, leaving a path of ashes down through the center of her body.

Everywhere he touched, she tingled. From her elbows to her fingertips, where she grasped the sleeves of his jacket. The tips of her breasts that pressed to his chest. The front of her thighs brushing the front of his.

He readjusted the slant of his mouth, giving himself better access and allowing him to deepen the kiss. Their tongues tangled, working them both into a lather of un-repressed need.

Striding forward, he moved into the house again, forcing her to shuffle backward. He kicked the door closed with his foot, the slam reverberating through the room and through her.

But he didn't stop there. Instead he continued

stalking forward, one long, slow step at a time, until she hit the opposite wall.

Spreading his feet on the outside of hers, he pressed his body flush against her own. Flares of heat burst again in her bloodstream, and she wrapped her arms around his neck, bringing them closer.

His hands moved from her arms to her waist, then slid around to cup her buttocks. When he urged her hips up, she went willingly, reveling in the hard ridge of his erection, pressed sharply between her legs.

She was gasping, groaning, and she knew he was with her because he was doing the same. Fisting the hem of her skirt in both hands, he drew the material up, bunching it at her waist. Then he delved beneath and tore her pantyhose and underwear down to her knees.

While he fumbled with his own belt and zipper, she wiggled until she could shed the stockings entirely. As soon as his pants dropped and he reached for her, she was ready, lifting her legs to wrap around his waist.

He slid into her in one slick, smooth glide, making them both gasp at the friction and intense pleasure of finally being linked the way she suspected they'd both been wanting and anticipating all day.

Tugging at the back of his head, she pulled him down for a kiss. Lower, he was moving, stroking, thrusting, pounding into her. She slammed into the wall again and again, but she couldn't have cared less. The wall could take it, and so could she.

Strengthening her grip at both his neck and waist,

she joined him in the powerful, rocking give and take. Only seconds later, she stiffened in climax. Pleasure ripped through her, making her cry out. Her nails dug like talons into his shoulders as she fought desperately to keep her balance and her consciousness.

Inside her, Creed pulsed and thrust one last time before joining her with a shout of completion. Long minutes later she felt his muscles go as lax as her own and let her legs slide weightlessly to the floor.

Clearing her throat, she did her best to get her voice working again. "I'll cook next time," she said just above his ear in barely a whisper. "I was thinking breakfast…if you want to stay the night."

A shudder rolled through him, and he lifted his head to stare down at her. For a beat, his face remained impassive. Then his blue eyes began to sparkle, one corner of his mouth tugging upward in a grin.

"Sounds good to me."

She smiled as he dragged his pants up and fastened the top button, then broke into a full-out laugh when he scooped her up in his arms and headed for the stairs.

"I'm going to want bacon," he told her, the words rumbling through her as she bumped against his chest with each step. "And eggs. Maybe pancakes."

He carried her into the bedroom, tossed her to the middle of the wide mattress and followed her down.

"I can do that," she murmured just as his lips captured hers and he got the blood pumping heavily through her veins all over again.

* * *

Creed lay awake long into the night, chastising himself seven ways from Sunday, while Maya slept at his side, curled so snugly against him they might have shared skin.

He tried to be annoyed, tried to convince himself that she was clinging, that he'd rather be in his own apartment, in his own bed—*alone*—than here with her.

But the truth was, this had all been more his doing than hers. *He'd* been the one unable to resist her soft eyes or the pale, kissable bow of her lips. He'd been the one who couldn't walk away, crossing back over the threshold into her house to take her none too gently against the kitchen wall.

It was everything he shouldn't have done, but he couldn't seem to work up a shred of apology.

Damn, damn, damn. He cursed silently, using a few other, more-creative four-letter words as they came to mind.

This definitely hadn't been part of the plan when he'd knocked on her door this evening. After talking with Case before leaving the Dakota Fortune offices, he'd fully intended to tell her that what had happened between them before couldn't happen again. It had been a lapse, a mistake, the result of a moment—two moments—of weakness, and they had to go back to being only stepbrother and stepsister.

All that and more had been on the tip of his tongue when they sat down to eat. His gut had clenched, but he'd been determined to go through with it, to charge ahead and just get it over with.

And then…he couldn't do it. He'd taken one look in her eyes—at her stricken curious, wary expression, and his throat had gone stone dry.

He was going to burn for it—his brother was right about that—but damned if he could keep his hands off her. The minute his lips had brushed her cheek in what was supposed to be an innocent, brotherly, goodbye peck, he'd known it wasn't enough and had to have more.

Now look where he was. In her bed—*again.* Spending the night—*again.* Making love with her— again and again and again.

He could almost feel the flames of damnation licking at his heels.

But then, it was a hell of a way to go.

Maya shifted at his side in her sleep, and he glanced down, admiring her simple beauty. Her glossy black hair fell over her shoulder and down her back, framing a face any artist would kill to paint, with its high cheekbones and smooth, bronze complexion.

Her body was another work of art, one he'd explored and memorized every inch of it with his eyes, his hands, his mouth…

He didn't want to give that up anytime soon, that was for sure, no matter what his punishment might be later, either in this world or the next.

So maybe it was for the best that he was sticking

around. He wouldn't exactly get an award for Man of the Year, but judging by some of her behavior tonight, she was still very vulnerable where Patricia's disappearance was concerned.

Her panic when he'd first arrived and she'd misread his mood had been enough to convince him she wasn't handling the situation quite as well as she wanted everyone to believe. She was obviously very concerned—as they all were—and petrified that something had happened, or would happen, to her mother before they could find her.

She needed someone right now, and it looked like he was destined to be that person.

He hadn't planned it, he didn't even want it, but that's the way things appeared to be playing out.

For now, he would stick around. He would let things carry on as they had been and hope that nothing hit the fan because of it. If they were careful, no one—Fortune family and the press alike—ever needed to know. And he would deal with the rest later.

After they found Patricia, which he strongly believed they would, he and Maya would go their separate ways, resume their normal lives, never letting anyone so much as suspect that things between them had ventured down a forbidden path.

Hopefully, he wouldn't have any trouble convincing her that it was best for both of them.

Having made that decision, and what peace he could with it for the time being, he pulled the sheet a little higher over them both and closed his eyes, finally sinking into the deep sleep that had eluded him the past few hours.

Maya awoke to kisses being feathered down the side of her neck and over her breasts. It was the most delightful transition into wakefulness she could ever remember experiencing.

Moments later Creed rolled her to her back and wished her good morning in a most improper manner.

Not that she minded. In fact, from the noises she made while he pleasured her from head to toe, it appeared she approved very, very much.

After that, she showered and dressed, then went downstairs to start breakfast while he did the same.

With her hair still damp and left to air dry, she moved around the kitchen, lining an iron skillet with strips of bacon, cracking eggs and mixing batter for pancakes.

She couldn't remember the last time she'd cooked such a large meal. Certainly not for herself. A bowl of cereal or slice of toast and glass of orange juice usually sufficed on her way out the door to work.

But she liked the smells wafting from her stove, enjoyed the task of stirring, beating, turning and making sure that everything cooked properly without burning. By the time Creed came downstairs, dressed in the same suit he'd worn the day before, she was humming and piling two plates with what looked like enough food for an army.

He stopped in the entryway to the kitchen, tightening his tie and smoothing the wrinkles from the sleeves of his suit jacket. She was tempted to offer to iron it for him, but thought that might be a little *too* domestic for whatever was going on between them and wasn't sure he would appreciate the gesture.

"Something smells good," he remarked.

Smiling, she carried the plates to the table and set them down, then proceeded to fill two tall glasses with orange juice.

"Bacon, eggs and pancakes, as requested," she said. When he didn't move, she waved her hand. "Come over here and eat before it gets cold. You did say you wanted to get an early start looking for Patricia, right?"

He nodded, taking a seat in the same spot as he had for dinner the night before. After a few bites he murmured his approval and offered her a small smile.

"This is really good," he told her. "I didn't know you could cook."

She shot him a cockeyed glance, chuckling. "I do have to eat, you know. And I don't enjoy take-out enough to eat it every day."

"Wish I could say the same, but sometimes eating out or ordering in is just easier."

They both cleaned their plates, and this time when Creed helped her clear the table, he let her slip the dishes into the dishwasher for later rather than insisting on doing them by hand.

She knew it was because he wanted to get on the

road and start the search for her mother. He needed to make a few phone calls first, though, to the private investigators he had on her mother's case.

While he used the phone in the kitchen, she wandered around the house, hardly listening to his side of the conversation as she gathered some items she thought they might need. A sweater and her purse, a six-pack of bottled water, fresh fruit and some nutrition bars. She didn't know how long they would be gone or how often they'd be able to stop, and wanted to have at least something on hand to eat and drink.

She'd taken care of the issue of a substitute to cover her classes last night. It had meant calling the woman in charge of those things from her bedside phone, trying to sound sick enough to require time off work while Creed had done his best to make her moan in ecstasy, but she'd gotten her authorization.

If need be, she thought she could even get the whole rest of the week off. She just hoped it wouldn't come to that. She would much rather find her mother right away and be able to bring her home, where she belonged.

Several minutes later he hung up the phone and met her at the front door.

"How did it go?" she asked.

"Good. I have at least a few leads we can follow up on. Places your mother might have used her credit cards and such."

A thrill of anticipation and hope swept through her.

She said a quick prayer that they might actually find her mother today, even though she knew the chances were fairly slim. If Patricia was out there, able to be easily located, then the investigators Nash and Creed had both hired surely would have tracked her down by now.

But there *was* a chance, and she felt better simply taking a more active role in discovering her mother's whereabouts.

Eight

Twelve hours later Maya was exhausted and her optimism was definitely waning.

They'd driven what seemed like thousands of miles, and she was pretty sure they'd crossed the state of South Dakota at least·twice in their effort to track down Patricia Fortune.

It was possible her mother had left the state, but since none of Creed's leads specifically led them to believe that was the case, they'd stuck to exploring areas that Patricia could be linked to: the town where Patricia had been born and raised; the reservation where she'd lived with Wilton Blackstone when they were first married, before Patricia had taken a young Maya and run away;

and any number of tiny, out-of-the-way places in between.

Stopping only briefly for lunch and the occasional bathroom break, she and Creed had both gone on almost until they dropped.

She was glad he was driving, because she could barely keep her eyes open. As it was, she found herself raising a hand to cover her yawns every few minutes.

The sun had long since set, and the city of Sioux Falls was lit up with colorful neon signs and the intermittent lights of tall office buildings where some people were obviously working overtime. Traffic was thankfully thin, and except for a few red lights, they were able to skirt the deepest parts of downtown on the way to her town house.

Creed pulled up to the curb, leaving the engine running as he turned to face her. He looked just as tired as she felt, his eyes heavy, the lines of his face deeper than when they'd started out that morning.

"I think it would be best if I spent the night at my place," he said, his voice gritty with fatigue. "I need a long, hot shower and change of clothes before we start out again tomorrow. Will you be all right by yourself?"

She unlatched her safety belt and unlocked the passenger-side door. "Of course. We could both use a good night's sleep."

He glanced down, grimacing at the expensive Italian suit that was now more wrinkled than a Shar-Pei puppy. "Yeah, I'll wear something a bit more comfortable tomorrow."

"What time will you be picking me up in the morning?" she wanted to know.

"Is six too early?"

She stifled a groan at what sounded like an ungodly hour, but said, "No. I'll be ready."

Stepping out of the car, she turned back and leaned down to meet his gaze. "Thank you for today. I really do appreciate it, and I know Mom would, too."

He gave a rough nod, remaining silent.

"Good night."

"'Night," he said softly.

She closed the car door and made her way up the steps to the front of the house. She hadn't left the porch light on when they left that morning, so she moved slowly up the steps and used the tiny pen light attached to her key ring to unlock the door.

Creed remained at the curb, his Mercedes idling softly, until she'd gotten inside, locked the door behind her and waved from the kitchen window to let him know she was all right. She couldn't tell for sure, but she thought he raised a hand to wave back before pulling away.

The old Creed, the one she'd known half her life, wouldn't have been as considerate. Oh, he'd have made sure she got home safely, but once he'd dropped her off, she'd have likely been on her own.

This Creed, the new one, as she was coming to think of him ever since they'd begun this strange, tentative new relationship, seemed more considerate, more compassionate.

With her, at least. With his family, he'd always been happy and outgoing, but with her he'd always acted more gruff and closed off.

She didn't know what had changed, exactly, except for her mother's sudden disappearance. But even then, her mother had been missing for months now, whereas he had only started coming around and being more courteous with her recently.

It was probably just the sex, she thought, making her way through the house. She left her purse and jacket in the kitchen, knowing she would need them again first thing in the morning, then headed upstairs. With each step, she loosened another item of clothing, making it easier for her to strip and fall straight into bed.

The minute she hit the mattress, she sighed with relief. She would have no trouble falling asleep tonight, as tired as she was.

Since Creed was her first lover, she couldn't claim to be an expert in the field of sex and how it affected people's personalities. But it was the only thing she could put her finger on that might explain why Creed's attitude toward her had changed. Not suddenly, but enough to be noticeable.

And truth be told, she didn't care. Even if he was only being nice to her and doing all of this to help find her mother because he either felt guilty for sleeping with her at all, or because he acted this way with all the women he slept with, she was simply grateful. And if it didn't last…well, she would deal with that when the time came, she supposed.

For now, though, she found great strength in his presence and support. Her life had been so strained and stressful lately, it felt good to be able to lean on him a bit. It felt good to not be quite so alone.

She had never *really* been alone, she knew that. The rest of the Fortunes, especially Nash, were as upset and concerned about Patricia as she was. But since she'd always felt like an outsider thrown into the middle of the close-knit Fortune clan, and because she and her mother were so close, she'd felt especially isolated since Patricia had gone missing.

Creed made her feel as though someone understood what she was going through, and that there might be a light at the end of the tunnel.

It was difficult not to let her heart and imagination read more into his behavior than there was. Already she could feel herself slipping, feel herself *wanting* to believe she was in love with him—really in love with him, not merely suffering the residual effects of her childhood crush—and that he might come to love her, too.

But each time her mind started to flit off into those flights of fancy, she tried her best to rein it in and once again plant both feet firmly in reality.

No matter what happened, she decided, as she began to drift off, she could never be sorry for giving him her virginity…and her heart.

Even if he wasn't willing to give her his in return.

* * *

Bright and early the next day they set out again in search of her mother. This time they had a list of some of Patricia's acquaintances, both past and present, and also decided to stop at every hotel and motel they came across in their travels, on the off chance a woman fitting Patricia's description had checked in or out or been seen in the area.

By noon, Maya was once again wiped out and didn't know how she could possibly go another six or eight hours. She was also beginning to feel as though the search for her mother was a lost cause and they would all have to just sit back and wait for Patricia to return on her own.

The only thing that kept her going was the fear that her mother might really be in trouble and *need* help. Until Maya knew for sure what was going on, she couldn't stop looking.

"How about some lunch?" Creed cut into her thoughts to ask.

He was dressed more casually today, in a pair of tan chinos and a light blue cotton button-down shirt. From her side of the car, though, he looked just as weary and frustrated as she felt.

"Sounds good," she said, thinking that a bite to eat and a gallon or two of caffeine were exactly what they needed to get through the rest of the day.

They found a nice sit-down restaurant that seemed to cater to families, and parked near the front entrance.

Creed laid a hand at the small of her back, sending shivers of awareness up and down her spine as they walked inside. He kept it there until the hostess had seen them to their seats, only letting his arm drop when they slid into opposite sides of the low booth. A waitress brought menus and took their drink orders, leaving them alone again.

"I was hoping we'd have found something by now," he said as they studied the list of lunch specials.

"Me, too. I just can't believe that no one has seen or heard from Mom at all. She's not the type of person I would have expected to be able to disappear without a trace."

Creed's mouth turned down in a frown. "Yeah. It's not like she's a ninja or ghost for the CIA or something."

Even though the situation was far from amusing, that made her chuckle. "No, she's definitely neither of those things, but she sure is doing a good job of staying hidden."

The waitress reappeared then to deliver two tall glasses of iced tea and finish jotting down their orders.

"Are you sure there isn't anything you can remember that might give us a better idea of where to look?" he asked as soon as the woman left.

Her brows knit, every muscle in her body tensing. Taking a breath, she forced herself to relax, knowing he didn't mean the question to sound like an accusation. They were both frustrated and worried and grabbing at any straw they could find that might lead them to Patricia.

"No, I'm sorry," she said with a shake of her head. Reaching for her tea, she took a sip before continuing. "She never said anything to me about leaving. Nothing that would have made me think going away was in her plans or that might hint at her whereabouts. Honestly, Creed, I'm as confused about all this as you are."

Their sandwiches arrived, and they ate in silence for a while. Then Maya set down her sandwich and said, "You have to understand that all of this has come as a huge shock for me. Mom's running off was bad enough, but then you drop the bomb on me that my father is still alive. I had no idea, and if my mother could keep that information a secret all these years, then she certainly could have refrained from letting anything slip about her plans to leave town."

Creed nodded, chewing thoughtfully. "It definitely came as a shock."

"Poor Nash. He's beside himself with worry. I feel so bad for him. And he really does love my mother."

"Yes. He does."

"My father—Wilton—didn't, I don't think. Maybe at one time, but from everything I remember of him, he was drunk and violent most of the time. Any little thing could set him off, and he always took his anger out on Mom."

"Did he ever hit you?" Creed asked.

She shook her head and swallowed what had turned out to be a delicious sandwich. "Not that I remember. I remember the yelling and hitting, Mom crying. There were a lot of times when she'd send me to my room so I wouldn't see what was going on, or take me away from the house for a while until the worst of one of Wilton's rages had blown over. Then one day, she sat me down, explained that my father had died, and told me we were going away."

"Where did your mother take you when she wanted to get you away from your father's temper?" he asked before biting into a crunchy chip.

"Different places," she said with a shrug. "It was always off the reservation, because if we'd stayed there and he came looking for us, he would have found us in no time. So she would take me to the library in town, or sometimes to the park. We didn't have much money, so anywhere we went had to be extremely cheap or free."

"The town outside the reservation," he murmured. "Would that happen to be one of the small towns we drove through yesterday on the way there and back?"

"Yes, I think so," she told him slowly. "Why?"

"We didn't check there. There was no reason to. But if Patricia is running scared, hiding from Wilton, maybe she went to one of the places where she used to feel safe."

A lump formed in Maya's throat, and she didn't think she could take another bite if she tried. Laying her sandwich carefully on the plate, she used the napkin from her lap to wipe her hands.

"Do you really think so?"

"I don't know," he replied, mimicking her actions

and then reaching into his pocket for his wallet. "But it's worth checking out."

He threw a large bill on the table, more than enough to cover the cost of their meals and a generous tip, before sliding out of the bench seat. "Were you finished?"

Even if she hadn't been, she suspected he probably would have dragged her out anyway. But she nodded eagerly and hurried to her feet, any sense of hunger or weariness gone in her anxiousness to get back on the road and check the two new places her mother might have gone.

It took them nearly an hour to reach Delmont. The Yankton Indian Reservation was only a few miles farther southwest, but they weren't going that far.

Driving slowly down the main street of town, Maya studied all the shop fronts and side streets, racking her brain for memories from the past. Some things looked more familiar than others, but she couldn't be sure if it was from her childhood or because they'd driven through only the day before.

"Do you remember how to get to the library?" Creed asked, keeping a hawk's eye on the sidewalks and people bustling by.

"No. It's been too long. Maybe we could stop and ask someone."

Instead they drove around a while longer until they spotted a blue-and-white sign with an arrow and the image of a person reading a book. Two signs later they were at the library.

It was a small brick building with brightly colored flowers lining a short concrete walk. The parking lot was large enough for only about three cars, and the tires of Creed's Mercedes ground loudly on the gravel as they pulled up.

"Looks like it's open," he said as they got out of the car and spotted the hours of operation posted inside one of the windows.

He pulled open the swinging glass door, then held it while she stepped inside. Although it had been many years and the setup of the library had changed, memories of being here with her mother flooded Maya.

Like libraries everywhere, the room was hushed and quiet. There was a woman sitting behind a long counter, carding books, and a couple of kids on the floor in one corner, flipping through picture books while their mother perused cookbooks at a nearby table.

"You look over there," he whispered, pointing to the right. "I'll check things out over here."

Moving in opposite directions, they walked up and down the rows of neatly lined stacks and peeked into several auxiliary rooms. They met back where they'd started, each shaking their head to show they hadn't found Patricia.

"Let me ask the librarian if she's seen your mother."

Striding to the circulation desk, Creed smiled as the woman stopped what she was doing and stood.

"Can I help you?" she asked.

"Yes. I'm looking for someone and wondered if

you'd seen her." He pulled a photo from the back pocket of his pants and showed it to her.

The woman studied it for a second, her brows knitting together in contemplation. "I don't...well, maybe. Yes, yes, I think she might have been in here. The hair isn't quite right," she continued, handing the picture back, "but if this is the woman I'm thinking of, she comes in quite a bit. She never checks out any books, but she'll sit right over there and read for hours, and sometimes she takes one of our on-your-honor paperbacks. She always brings them back, too, before taking the next."

At the woman's words, Maya's heart picked up its pace. She moved forward until she was standing directly beside Creed, whose own tall frame fairly vibrated with excitement. On top of the counter, his long fingers curled into fists while she twisted her hands together at her waist.

"When was the last time she came in?" Creed wanted to know.

"This morning. She only stayed for a bit, and took another book with her."

"Do you have any idea where she might have gone?"

"No, I'm sorry," the woman said, shaking her head sadly.

"All right," he said with a sigh. "You've been very helpful, thank you."

Putting a hand on Maya's back, he steered her toward the door and outside.

"What do we do now?" she asked, going to the passenger side of the car and sliding in as Creed did the same.

"I say we drive around, looking for her, maybe stop and ask a few more people if they've seen her. If nothing turns up, we can always come back here and stake out the place. Patricia's bound to come back to return that book she borrowed."

Her stomach was doing flips and she couldn't seem to stop fidgeting. "Do you really think the woman the librarian has been seeing is Mom?"

"I don't know," he replied, starting the engine and pulling slowly out of the parking lot, "but we're going to stick around until we find out for sure."

For the next thirty minutes they drove around town, up and down every street, looking for anyone who looked even remotely like Patricia. They stopped several times to double-check women they saw on the sidewalk, and even more often to run into small businesses to flash Patricia's picture and ask if anyone had seen her recently.

Frustration started to seep through her again, but she fought it off, reminding herself of Creed's plan to stake out the library, if necessary.

She was scanning the area, turning her head from one side to the other, when something caught her attention.

"Stop!"

Creed slammed on the breaks, and only after the car came to a screeching halt did Maya bother to glance in the side mirror and heave a sigh of relief that no one was driving behind them.

"What?" he wanted to know. "What did you see?"

"I'm not sure, but…" She raised a hand and pointed out the windshield. "I think that might be the park she used to take me to."

It was straight ahead, tucked along a side street and taking up about two full blocks. As they pulled closer and eased into a parallel parking space along the curb, she saw a swing set, jungle gym, sand box and even a small basketball court.

A dozen children ran around, playing, yelling, having a grand old time. Teenagers in ratty clothes and backward baseball caps dribbled balls, rode skateboards and sat in small clutches sneaking cigarettes. The number of adults was at a minimum, and she suspected those belonged more to the younger kids than the older ones.

As soon as Creed cut the engine, she unbuckled her seat belt and jumped out. He met her at the front of the car.

"Do you see her?" he asked.

She scanned the park's inhabitants again. "No. But the park is pretty large, and she probably wouldn't want to be close to all this noise and activity, anyway. Let's walk around."

She was getting used to him touching her, both casually and with firm intent, so she didn't think anything of it when he placed a hand at the small of her back and let her move ahead of him. But when that hand slid to her elbow, then down her arm to clasp her hand, she nearly jumped. Holding hands *wasn't* something she was used to, not with Creed.

Now wasn't the time to analyze the gesture, though. She could do that later, after they'd—God willing—found her mother.

Still holding his hand, she started forward, entering the park and immediately beginning to scan faces. They passed the main play area and walked toward a more secluded spot with small trees, decorative flower beds, and benches where people could sit to read or enjoy the nice summer weather.

Several yards ahead, there was a woman sitting on one of the benches, her back to them. She was slender, with short dark hair, and wearing a pale-pink light-weight sweater over a white blouse. Both looked well worn and oft washed. As they passed, Maya noticed the woman was reading a thick paperback novel.

They were getting closer, she thought with a tiny sigh. They'd found the park her mother had brought her to as a child, and they'd found a woman reading a book. If they were lucky, maybe the next reader they came across in this park would be Patricia.

Unfortunately, as they finished searching the park fifteen minutes later, she had to give up any hope of getting lucky. Her mother was nowhere to be found.

Following the same path they'd taken through the park, they once again passed the woman reading. She didn't pay any attention to them, but as she lifted a hand to turn to the next page of her book, the thin gold bracelet on her right wrist glinted in the afternoon sun, and Maya stopped in her tracks.

"Oh, my God. *Mom.*"

Nine

If it hadn't been for the bracelet, which Maya identified as one of Patricia's favorites, she never would have recognized the woman sitting on the bench as her mother.

Her hair was both darker and much shorter than it had been before she'd run away. Patricia had always kept regular salon appointments, her stylish bob almost a trademark.

But since she'd been gone, she'd apparently cut her hair herself. It was spiky and a bit uneven, and looked as though she'd colored it—two shades darker than her natural tone—with one of those box kits sold at every drugstore.

Maya squeezed Creed's fingers once, hard, before

releasing him and racing forward. At her breathless exclamation, the woman on the park bench raised her head and gasped, eyes going wide, book sliding from her limp hands to fall to the ground.

"Mom! Oh, my God, Mom, we've been so worried." She threw her arms around Patricia, hugging her tight.

They sat that way for a very long time, laughing, crying, rocking together. When they finally pulled apart, Maya wiped the tears from her face with her sleeve, refusing to let go of her mother's hands for even a second, afraid she would slip away again.

Patricia's own face was damp and blotchy, twin trails of wetness continuing to roll down her cheeks.

"What are you doing here?" her mother asked, her voice rough with emotion. "How did you find me?"

Maya turned her gaze to Creed, who stood only a few inches away. She could see the relief in his eyes, along with a light furrow to his brow and the line of concern thinning his lips.

Turning back to her mother, she said, "We've been looking for you for weeks now. We've all been so worried, and Nash is beside himself."

Patricia's own lips quivered, her lashes glittering with fresh tears. "You shouldn't have come. I can't go back, and I don't want you to get involved."

"It's all right," Maya assured her, patting the back of her mother's hand. "We know everything. Or almost everything. We know about Wilton—that he's still alive and has been blackmailing you. That is why you ran away, isn't it?"

At Maya's revelation, Patricia shuddered, the moisture gathered in her eyes spilling over. She threw herself once again into her daughter's arms and cried as if her life was ending.

When she finally calmed enough to straighten, her breathing was ragged, her chest hitching as she tried to compose herself.

"I'm sorry. Sorry I lied to you and ran away, and… I'm so sorry for everything."

"It's all right. We understand." She cast a quick glance over her shoulder at Creed to make sure he was still there, still offering his complete support. "No one is mad at you, I promise. We were all just worried about you, and afraid for you, and missed you very much."

Creed stepped forward, taking a seat on the bench on the other side of Patricia. "It really will be all right, Patricia. We're here to take you home."

"No, I can't," Patricia said resolutely. "Nash will hate me when he finds out that I lied about being widowed. And Wilton is still out there. He could ruin me, ruin us. You don't understand—"

"Nash doesn't hate you, Mom," Maya told her. "He loves you very much and wants you to come home."

"And Wilton Blackstone won't be bothering you anymore," Creed put in firmly. "We know about the blackmail. We have proof of it, and he's been arrested.

We'll see that he's punished and make sure he never comes near you again."

He reached out to touch her, his large hand dwarfing Patricia's slender, sloping shoulder. "I give you my word, and the word of the entire Fortune family. We'll see that you're protected."

Patricia looked at Creed and then Maya, studying their expressions for the truth in their words. Her tears had dried, her breathing regulated and interrupted only by the occasional sniff.

"But Nash—"

"Nash loves you," Maya said. "He could never hate you. He might be upset that you misled him, and about your marriage not being valid, but he won't hate you. And I think that if you explain things to him, he'll understand."

"Do you really think so?" Patricia asked in a watery voice.

Before Maya could answer, Creed said, "Absolutely. We all love you, Patricia. Let us take you home so we can show you how much."

When they reached Sioux Falls, Patricia asked if they could stop at Maya's house first so she could clean up before returning to the Fortune Estate.

They'd stopped at the small house in Delmont where Patricia had most recently been renting a room, to collect her meager belongings. Since her clothes were now looking quite faded and threadbare from having been worn and washed so many times during the months she'd been missing, Maya helped her find some things from her own closet.

Patricia was quiet the rest of the way home, staring out the window and holding her hands together tightly in her lap.

Maya understood her anxiety. Her mother was about to see her husband for the first time in months, having to bare her soul and admit that their marriage of thirteen years had never been legal. Her own stomach was churning; she could only imagine how terrifying the prospect must be for Patricia.

Of course, her own discomfort wasn't due entirely to what her mother was going through right now. She was equally distracted by thoughts of the effect Patricia's return might have on her relationship with Creed.

As much as she'd missed her mother and worried about her while she was missing, Maya had to admit she'd enjoyed the change in Creed's attitude toward her and the time he'd been spending with her recently. But now that Patricia was back and the crisis of her disappearance was passing, there would be no reason for him to drop by her house anymore or call just to check on her.

Swallowing hard, she blinked until the stinging behind her eyes dissipated. She would miss him, miss having him in her life in a capacity other than surly stepbrother.

To say nothing of how much she would miss sharing her bed with him.

Creed made a right turn off the main road onto the long, circular crushed stone drive that led to the Fortune Estate. Her insides began to tighten as soon as the sprawling mansion came into view, almost as though her body sensed the sand in the hourglass of her happiness running out.

When Creed pulled up in front of the house and cut the engine, they all got out and slowly walked inside without bothering to knock. Silence surrounded them, and for a moment they simply stood in the middle of the foyer, no one making a move to go farther or look to see who might be home.

At her side, Patricia squeezed Maya's hand so hard, the fingers were starting to tingle.

"It's all right," Maya whispered, returning the pressure and patting Patricia's arm. "Nash will understand, and Creed and I will stay with you the entire time, if you want us to."

Creed added a supporting hand to Patricia's back as they started forward.

They hadn't taken more than three or four steps when a noise at the top of the wide double stairwell caused them all to look up.

Nash stood frozen on the landing, staring down at them, a look of utter shock on his face. A second later he raced the rest of the way down the stairs.

"Patricia! Oh, dear God, Patricia. I thought I would never see you again."

Patricia released Maya's hand and flew across the

foyer, meeting Nash halfway. They kissed and hugged, both crying with delight at being together again after such a long and stressful separation.

Maya felt tears well in her own eyes, and sniffed to hold them at bay. Beside her, Creed was grinning, rocking back on his heels with his arms linked across his chest.

He knew as well as she did that there were still a few bumps in the road ahead for her mother and his father, but right now, at this very moment in time, there was only happiness, relief and cause for celebration.

When Nash and Patricia finally parted, they were bleary-eyed and sniffing, but smiling from ear to ear.

"Where have you been?" Nash wanted to know, holding her by the shoulders.

The question made Patricia tense, and Maya took a single step forward, ready to support her mother. But before Maya could come to her rescue, Patricia steeled her spine and looked Nash straight in the eye.

"That's something I need to explain," she told him, "and I can only hope you don't hate me afterward."

Concern wrinkled Nash's brow, but his response was nothing less than Maya would have expected.

"I could never hate you, darling," he replied adamantly.

"Yes, well…" Patricia dried the undersides of her eyes with one thumb, then tucked a long strand of hair behind her ear. "You might want to wait until you've heard what I have to tell you before deciding that for sure."

Nash didn't look convinced, but Maya suspected

his spirits were too high at having his wife safely home to argue.

"Let's go into the library," Patricia said, taking him by the hand and leading him in that direction.

Maya's feet itched to follow. Her mother had been so worried, so frightened to come clean with Nash about everything, that Maya didn't want to leave her to face those fears alone.

Now that she was home, however, Patricia seemed more herself. It had taken only one glimpse of Nash for her mother to remember the love, the dedication, the man he was and the years they'd spent together.

Whatever his reaction to what Patricia was about to tell him, Maya had no doubt that his adoration for her mother would overshadow it all. If not immediately, then eventually.

When they reached the library, Patricia turned back in her direction and offered a small smile. "Thank you for everything, but I'll be fine now. You two go on."

Before Maya could respond, her mother closed the heavy pocket doors, leaving her alone in the wide foyer with Creed.

"Well," he said with a shrug, "I guess our job is done."

She nodded absently, her gaze still locked on the library door as though she could see through the thick wooden panel. Even though Patricia had told them it was okay to go, it didn't feel right to Maya to simply take off. Not yet. Not until she knew for sure that

everything between Nash and her mother would be
all right.

Taking the decision out of her hands, Creed took her
by the shoulders and physically turned her in the
opposite direction.

"Let's get something to drink, then call the rest of the
family. They'll all want to know Patricia is back and okay."

They made their way to the kitchen, where several
members of the household staff were busy preparing
dinner. Creed asked for drinks to be brought to the great
room, then steered Maya in that direction.

"Do you think Nash will forgive her?" she asked,
standing awkwardly in the doorway, keeping her hands
in her pockets to avoid the urge to fidget.

"Yes, I do."

At the conviction in his tone, she lifted her head and
met his eyes. They hit her like a ton of bricks, as always.
And as always, she felt her limbs go weak, liquid heat
pooling low in her belly.

"If there's one thing you can be sure of," he went on,
"it's that my dad loves your mother. He may not be
happy that she lied to him from the beginning, and continued to mislead him throughout their marriage, but
he'll understand. They'll work it out."

Their drinks arrived then, and Maya had to move
farther into the room to get out of the servant's way as
the young woman carried a tray of iced tea to a nearby
table.

"You use that phone," Creed said, pointing to the

sleek princess land line across the room. "I'll use my cell. We'll reach everyone faster if we divvy up the calls. Which ones do you want?"

After agreeing which Fortune family members they would each call, Maya took one of the glasses of tea and began dialing, spending the next half hour informing Creed's siblings that Patricia was home. The news was met each time with joy and relief, and every single one of the family members wanted to know where they'd found her, where she'd been and why she'd left in the first place.

Maya could hear bits and pieces of Creed's conversations, and knew he was promising them the same thing she was—that they would fill in the blanks as soon as they were all together. It certainly beat telling the same story over and over again, and until Nash and Patricia came out of the library, they weren't confident of exactly how things would end.

Twenty minutes after they finished making the phone calls, they heard car doors and then the front door slam open as Fortunes started pouring into the house. Leaving their empty glasses to be refilled when drinks were brought for everyone, Maya and Creed made their way back to the foyer to greet the others.

Creed placed a hand at the small of her back as they walked, and Maya couldn't decide if she found the gesture comforting or disturbing. Maybe a little of both.

Comforting because she was growing used to his presence, used to the place he'd made for himself in her life.

And disturbing because she wanted so much for him to remain in that place, even though she knew it wasn't possible.

As they neared the entryway, she felt Creed's touch fall away. She missed it immediately but was sharp enough to realize that he'd pulled back because he didn't want any of the rest of the family to notice anything out of the ordinary.

It hurt, which Maya found ironic, considering that she didn't want anyone else to know they'd been involved, either. It would just complicate matters that were already plenty complicated enough.

She wanted Creed, but couldn't have him. And he didn't want her at all, not really.

Unrequited love, she was unfortunately learning, was both painful and illogical.

Sadness lying like a stone at the bottom of her stomach, she pasted a smile on her face and hugged both Gina and Case, who were the first to arrive.

Gina's face was flushed with excitement, and Maya thought she saw a tell-tale rim of red around the woman's eyes, as though she'd recently been crying. Gina wasn't a Fortune by blood—of course, neither was Maya, so they had that in common—but she'd been just as worried about Patricia's disappearance as everyone else.

She also had pregnancy hormones running rampant through her system, probably adding to the ease with which she burst into tears. According to Case, something as simple as running out of milk could cause a near breakdown these days.

Eliza and Reese, Blake and Sasha, Skylar and Zack, and Diana and Max all showed up in short order, within minutes of each other. Each time a new couple burst through the front door, it was a repeat of the first— embraces all around, damp eyes and a thousand questions about where Patricia was and what was going on.

Once things had calmed down a bit and everyone who was expected to make an appearance arrived, Creed took command, drawing everyone into the great room, calling for refreshments, then explaining the entire situation in a low, even voice. He started by telling them about the information the investigators had uncovered, followed by their own personal search for Patricia and how they'd finally found her.

He left out any mention of the time he'd spent at her house recently…or in her bed…sticking strictly to the facts of the search and Patricia's return.

The news of Maya's father still being alive and Patricia's marriage to Nash being illegal and invalid stunned them all, Maya could tell.

But just as Creed had been understanding and supportive of the situation, so were the rest, which added to her sense of relief. She didn't want anyone thinking less of her mother for something that had not only gotten its start a decade before, but that Patricia had felt was her only option at the time.

Creed finished by informing the group at large that

Nash and Patricia were locked in the library, having a long-overdue discussion and hopefully working things out between them.

"I don't know about you," Case said, raising his glass of pale brown tea, "but I could sure go for something stronger than this."

Creed, who was standing beside him gave his own glass a gentle shake, sending ice cubes clinking. With a harsh laugh, he said, "No kidding. Tell you what, when Dad comes out of that library, we'll crack open a bottle of scotch. I'm guessing he'll need a drink by then, too."

"Deal."

Without planning or conscious thought, the women gathered in one corner while the men drifted to another. Conversation was stilted and uncomfortable; they were all trying to act normal and upbeat, but a cloud of uncertainty hung over the room.

Even so, Maya was struck once again by how these people—whom she'd never felt close to before—seemed to come together as a single unit for a mutual cause. They were, in a word, family.

A lump formed in her throat as she thought of how she used to consider them cold and distant. She certainly couldn't pin those labels on them now. They were anything but aloof as they struggled to maintain a sense of regularity and put each other at ease.

And she had to wonder: Had they changed—or had she?

From the time she and her mother had moved into this giant house with the Fortunes, she'd felt like an outsider, but they definitely weren't making her feel like one now. She was one of them, included and cared for.

She took a sip of tea, as much to wash away the emotion threatening to overwhelm her as to buy a little time to put her rapid-fire thoughts in order.

Looking back now, she realized this wasn't the first time she'd been included by the Fortune siblings, made to feel as though she truly belonged. She'd simply been so used to feeling left out that she assumed she was, even when these people were trying their best to help her fit in.

No, that wasn't it, either. They weren't trying to do anything…they just *were.* They were treating her like family because to them she *was* family.

A wave of love and appreciation washed over her so keenly she nearly fumbled the glass in her hands.

They were family, and she was a part of it. They were *her* family, and she loved each and every one of them with a strength and devotion she hadn't even realized she possessed until this moment.

It was a revelation, and she thanked God for it.

If only her relationship with Creed could be as quickly and easily resolved, but she had a feeling that would take twenty years to puzzle itself out, too.

She was about to sigh with resignation when the entire room went quiet as a tomb. Noticing the direction of the others' gazes, she turned to find Nash and Patricia standing in the doorway.

Her mother's face was streaked with tears, and Nash's eyes were bleary, as though he, too, had been crying. Their hands were joined, she noticed, which had to be a good sign.

All the same, Maya held her breath, waiting to hear what they would say.

Nash cleared his throat. I'm glad you're all here," he said. "Patricia and I have some things we need to tell you."

The good news was that Nash and Patricia were going to be all right. Nash had been more upset with Patricia for running away instead of trusting him enough to tell him the truth than he was that she'd lied to him to begin with. She was now strictly forbidden from ever keeping anything from him again, to which she'd chuckled and tearily agreed.

Once the family had been assured that everything was okay and life would likely be returning to normal, they'd celebrated in true Fortune style. Bottles of wine and scotch had been uncorked and passed around, and platters of cookies and cakes and other finger foods had been served.

Creed took another long swallow of the hundred-year-old Scotch that was his father's favorite, letting it burn a trail down his throat.

He should be relieved. Hell, he should be celebrating right along with everyone else…. God knew he had more to be grateful for. Not only for Patricia's safe return and an end to the mystery of where she'd run off to for so long, but his freedom from whatever spell Maya had woven around him the past few weeks.

There wasn't a hope in hell of breaking free of the spell she'd cast over him for the past twenty years, but after sating his initial passions with Maya, he'd only continued seeing her, continued *sleeping* with her, because she'd needed someone.

That's what he'd told himself, anyway.

He'd also told himself that as soon as Patricia was safe and sound back home, he'd put an end to his secret, clandestine affair with her daughter.

Well, they'd found Patricia and brought her home, so that's exactly what he intended to do.

All might not be perfect or completely settled, but it was good enough that Maya didn't need him anymore. With her mother back, and the truth of Wilton's blackmail out in the open, she was no longer vulnerable, no longer worried, no longer in need of a strong shoulder to lean on.

Or anything else he might have to offer.

This was good. Better than good; it was great. It had been the plan all along.

Now all he had to do was stick to it.

And he would, although his body seemed to have other ideas.

While everyone else was crowded around Patricia, welcoming her home and promising to stand by her through thick and thin, he'd made the mistake of glancing in Maya's direction. She'd been watching the scene, her eyes sparkling with emotion, the hint of a smile on her lips.

It was the first time he'd ever seen her look quite like that around his family. Serene, at ease…happy.

He wanted to think it was her expression that had stirred him, but he knew it was much more than that. *She* stirred him. Her strength, her poise, her quiet beauty. All the same qualities that had stirred him from the time she'd hit puberty, maybe earlier.

But now he knew so much more about her. He knew what she looked like naked and the noises she made in the throes of passion. He knew what made her toes curl, her nipples pucker and her eyes flutter closed on a sigh of ecstasy.

He knew, and he damn well couldn't forget. Would never forget.

Which was only going to make walking away that much harder.

He tossed back the last of the scotch, hoping it would dull the ache throbbing at his temples and his gut.

Walking away wouldn't be easy, but then, he'd known that from the start.

Just like living under the same roof with her all these years hadn't been easy. He'd watched her grow up; watched her blossom; watched her fail and succeed, make mistakes and soldier through them. It hadn't been easy to be forced to see her on a regular basis, even after they'd both moved away from the Fortune Estate, and to be slapped in the face with the fact that she was family—his stepsister, for God's sake—when he wished she could be so much more.

It was enough to make a man want to crawl into a bottle and never come out. And since his glass was currently empty…

He pushed himself up from the wing chair where he'd been sitting, listening with only half an ear to the conversations going on around him, and headed to the bar for a refill. Just as he was recapping the bottle of hundred-year-old scotch, Blake sauntered up.

Creed tipped the bottle in his half brother's direction and lifted a brow, silently asking if Blake wanted some before he put it away.

"No, thanks, I'll stick with what I've got," Blake said, gesturing with his still-full glass.

Creed replaced the scotch in its spot amongst the other assorted bottles on the bar, then took a sip while he waited for Blake to say whatever was on his mind. And from the look on his face, it was obvious there was something.

"I thought you should know that my mom has managed to lasso herself another rich husband," Blake told him, speaking of his mother and Nash's second wife, Trina Watters Fortune. "They're jetting off to Europe as soon as the ink is dry on the marriage license."

"I guess that's good news," Creed said. "At least she seems to have given up on trying to get Dad back and will be out of everyone's hair over there."

Blake nodded grimly, taking a drink before continuing. "Look, I want to apologize for the mess she made of everyone's lives. I didn't want to believe she was capable of some of the things she was doing, but, well…I was wrong, and I'm sorry I didn't see that sooner."

"Apology accepted," Creed replied easily. "But only if you'll accept mine for making you pay for Trina's manipulations. You weren't responsible for your mother's actions, even though I treated you as though you were." Regret narrowed his eyes and thinned his lips. "You can't know how sorry I am for that, and I hope you can forgive me. I'd like for us to start over and be real brothers from now on." Glancing over at Nash, his other brother, and his brothers-in-law, along with the women who had just begun to trickle back into the room, Creed offered a small smile. "A man can never have too much family."

For a second Blake didn't reply. Then he cleared his throat and held out his hand. "I'd like that," he said, his voice rough with feeling. "A lot."

Creed shifted his drink to the opposite hand so they could shake on it. Before letting go, though, he couldn't resist giving his younger brother a last, serious warning.

"One more thing," he said, his tone somber as he tightened his grip. "You'd better take good care of Sasha."

Even though they'd spent a good amount of time dating, Creed had never really had a romantic interest in Sasha Kilgore. They'd gone out and pretended to be seriously involved only to keep other, cloying women away from him.

She'd done him a favor in that, and they were friends. Good friends. He didn't want to see anything happen to her.

Not that he thought Blake would ever do anything to intentionally hurt his new fiancée. Blake was entirely too smitten with the gorgeous redhead.

Creed couldn't blame him, but a word of caution was still in order.

"She's a hell of a woman," he continued. "She deserves only the best, and if you make her cry, I'll have to pound you. That's what big brothers do."

"Don't worry," Blake said, casting a glance at Sasha as she entered into the room carrying a tray of hastily made hors d'oeuvres.

She was grinning broadly at something Skylar had said, waddling along pregnantly at her side, and Blake's eyes filled with a glint that could only be described as complete and total adoration. "I intend to take very good care of her."

Creed lifted his drink to his mouth to cover a smile. "Glad to hear it."

"For the record," Blake said, dragging his gaze from the woman he loved, "I think Maya is a pretty terrific woman, too. She'd be good for you, if only you'd see it and take the initiative to do something about it."

Creed froze, the scotch in his mouth trickling a burning path down his throat as he struggled to swallow and then breathe. When he finally managed, it was with a cough, and his voice was strained when he tried to speak.

"What are you talking about?" he demanded.

"I know," Blake said, shaking his head, "we're all supposed to pretend we don't know that you're attracted to her. Unfortunately, no one in this family is blind. We've all seen the way you look at her, and though we've never talked about it, I think everyone would agree that it's time you stop moping around, watching her from afar, and just went for it."

A low throb was beginning to pound behind Creed's eye sockets. "Don't be ridiculous," he snapped. "She's our sister."

"Stepsister," Blake corrected. "Related only by Dad's marriage to Patricia, which is no true relation at all. And, hell, it turns out they're not even married now. You need to stop worrying so much about that sort of thing and focus on what's important. If you care about her—and I think you do—then you need to do something about it. Toss her over your shoulder and drag her to bed, then marry her before some other lucky bastard beats you to the punch. She'd make you a great wife."

Blake chuckled and took a small sip of his drink. "Think of it this way," he added. "At least you don't have to suffer through the misery of meeting her parents and introducing her to your own. Or dealing with in-laws. That's all a done deal, and we know and love her already."

With that Blake drained his glass, set it down on the sideboard and walked away to join Sasha.

Creed stood there, watching as his brother slipped a hand around his fiancée's waist and leaned in to press a kiss to her temple. Sasha tipped her head to smile up at him, utter happiness shining in her green eyes and emanating from every pore of her body.

Blake's words echoed through his head, making the pounding even worse and keeping time with the frenetic beat of his heart.

He stood there for what seemed like forever, observing all the couples in the room. And suddenly he was envious. Everyone had someone. Everyone was happily married, or on their way to it.

Everyone, that was, except him.

He'd never thought of himself as being the marrying kind before, never thought in terms of a serious, lasting relationship or settling down with one woman. *The* woman, who seemed to suit him like no other, who fit into his life and his world as comfortably as an old pair of jeans.

But he wanted it, he realized.

It was like a flash of lightning in the night sky, hitting him hard and fast right in the solar plexus.

He wanted that, and he wanted it with Maya.

Ten

Creed was unusually quiet on the drive home, and since Maya was both physically exhausted and emotionally drained from the day's events, she was more than happy to remain silent herself. She let her head rest against the back of the seat and watched the scenery outside the side window, hoping the tension running through her body didn't show.

The trip back to her house also gave her time to decide exactly how to tell Creed it was over. Whatever had been going on between them these past few weeks, she needed to break it off, be done with it, stop letting him tie her up in knots.

She'd been wondering what would happen to this so-called relationship they'd been having, until she'd

looked over at him earlier this evening during the celebration of her mother's return. Glancing in his direction,
she'd caught him watching her. The look in his blue
eyes had sent her heart rate into triple digits, but it
hadn't lasted long.

He'd blinked, and the heat was gone, replaced by a
cool, impassive expression. Arching one dark brow,
he'd lifted his glass of scotch to his lips and turned
away.

It was the same way he used to look at her, the same
way he used to act toward and around her. So it seemed
that whatever had passed between them these past few
weeks wasn't going to grow, wasn't going to blossom
into something deep and meaningful.

That's when she'd realized she needed to call it
quits…while she still had her dignity and a chance to
put the pieces of her upside-down life back together.

She might not like it, and it wasn't how she would
have chosen to have things turn out, but she also wasn't
surprised. Whatever had compelled him to take her to
bed in the first place was obviously temporary, as she'd
known it would be.

It was probably even for the best. Now maybe she
could move on, get her life back to some semblance of
order and possibly develop a *normal* relationship with
another man, crossing Creed Fortune off her list of even
the most remote of possibilities.

And she was going to do it before he had the chance.
The end was near, she could feel it, but she would be

damned if she'd stand there and let *him* tell *her* all the reasons they couldn't be together anymore, all the reasons it would never work.

Ten minutes later Creed pulled the Mercedes up to the curb in front of her darkened town house and cut the engine. Without waiting for him to come around to her door, she got out and started up the steps, relieved when he followed her.

She stepped inside and flipped on a light, waiting for him to close the door behind him.

He didn't approach her, for which she was grateful. If he'd stalked toward her with that look in his eyes that said he couldn't wait to strip her bare and make love to her again, she wasn't sure she'd have been able to stand her ground and make him listen to what she'd decided she had to say.

But he simply stood there, just inside the closed front door, and watched her.

Setting her purse on the kitchen table, she wrapped her fingers around the back of one of the chairs for added support and said, "Thank you for all your help in finding my mother."

His expression didn't change, but he nodded almost imperceptibly. "You're welcome."

She swallowed, forcing herself to press on. "Creed, there's something I need to tell you."

His gaze flickered slightly, his eyes going a shade darker, but he said nothing, waiting for her to continue.

"I don't think we should see each other anymore."

She said the words in a rush, needing to get them out before her courage failed her.

She didn't know what type of reaction she'd been expecting from him, but it hadn't been complete silence. An argument maybe, or a creatively muttered curse. Instead, a muscle jumped in his jaw and he crossed his arms over his chest as he stared at her.

"We both know we've just been...passing time," she told him when the silence stretched out between them, jumbling her already strained nerves. "It was never going to last, and now that my mother is home, there's no need to continue spending time together. We'd only be...fooling ourselves and drawing unwanted attention."

Seconds ticked past while she waited for him to respond. She would take anything—a shout, a shrug, a string of expletives.

Eyes narrowed and mouth set, he dropped his arms, then said, "You're probably right."

Her stomach tightened at his calm acquiescence. She hadn't realized until that very moment that she wanted him to fight for her. Argue with her, yell at her, demand she not give up on them so easily.

Declare his undying love.

But, of course, that was never going to happen. She should simply be glad he wasn't going to make this any harder on her than it already was.

"I guess I'll see you, then," he said, turning to open the door.

She nodded, taking a step forward as though to see him out, even though there was no need.

"I promised my mom I'd attend Sunday dinner at the estate," she told him, then wanted to kick herself for letting him think she was counting the hours until she would see him again.

He stared at her a moment before inclining his head and walking away.

Closing the door behind him, she watched through the window as he walked down the sidewalk and around the hood of his car to slide in behind the wheel. Her lungs hitched, and she felt a tell-tale prickling of tears, but she didn't cry. If anything, she felt numb.

Breaking things off had been the right move. The only move, really, considering his lack of emotion about their relationship and the complete impossibility of a future for them.

But the young woman in her wept for the loss of a decade-long dream of true love, while the adult woman hardened her heart and steeled her spine to face a lifetime of loneliness.

Almost a week passed while Creed fluctuated between being relieved that Maya had ended things when she did…and being furious that she'd cast him aside so carelessly.

Hadn't he just begun to think that maybe he was ready to settle down and to do it with Maya? Not two hours before, hadn't he decided to sit her down and tell her flat-out that he thought they should continue seeing each other and find out where it would lead them?

Then she'd pulled the rug right out from under him by telling him she didn't want to see him anymore. That whatever they'd had was fun while it lasted, but she was ready to put it behind her.

At first he'd thought it was for the best. Had even been grateful he hadn't had to come up with the words to tell her much the same.

But the longer they were apart, the harder he tried to put the pieces of his life back to the way they'd been before he'd given in to temptation and taken Maya to bed, the less appreciative he became.

He missed her, dammit. Missed seeing her, talking with her...making love to her.

And as much as he'd fought it, he was no longer certain he wanted things to return to the way they'd been. He didn't want to see her at the estate, at Sunday dinners, and pretend she was nothing more than family, when he could close his eyes and picture her standing naked before him. Or feel the silk of her bronzed skin beneath his fingertips.

He ended up firing his receptionist twice while his brain tried to make sense of what he was feeling. Thankfully, she was used to his moods—which sometimes turned black and foul during business dealings, too—and chose to ignore him.

It was Case, though, who finally came to his office and told him to snap out of it. He suggested rather strongly that Creed either do something about whatever was making him such a bloody bear to deal with lately or get over it and stop being an ass.

Creed wasn't sure how to go about doing either, but he knew his brother was right.

Leaving work early, he went up to his apartment on the top floor of the Dakota Fortune office building and changed out of his standard business suit to a pair of tan chinos and a dark blue shirt.

Even though it was a bit early to start imbibing, he fixed himself a good, stiff drink of bourbon, then wandered restlessly around the penthouse. His blood felt too hot for his veins, simmering just below the surface, threatening to boil over.

The alcohol now sitting at the bottom of his stomach didn't help, either. Instead of calming him, it seemed to put him more on edge.

With a curse, he set his almost-full highball glass on a nearby credenza and grabbed his keys. Riding the elevator down to the underground parking garage, he climbed into his Mercedes and passed through the security gate onto the street.

He hadn't intended to drive to Maya's house, hadn't consciously thought to aim the car in that direction. But a few minutes later he found himself cruising down her block.

His fingers tightened on the steering wheel, twisting against the leather until his knuckles turned white. His stomach churned again, but this time it had nothing to do with the few sips of bourbon he'd consumed.

He eased to the curb, coming to a stop behind another car parked directly in front of Maya's town house. The black Lexus looked familiar, but he couldn't place it.

Cutting the engine, he sat there as the seconds ticked by, staring at her closed front door. He considered getting out of the car, walking up and ringing the doorbell, but he had no practical reason for being there. If anything, he should be avoiding her, except when that was impossible because of family functions.

But damned if he didn't want to see her again. Feel the satiny strands of her hair between his fingertips, smell the light, feminine scent that seemed to invade his pores whenever he was around her.

His hand was on the ignition—whether to turn the key or pull it out and take it with him, he wasn't sure— when Maya's front door opened and a man stepped out.

Brad McKenzie. And Maya was close on his heels, her hand resting lightly on his arm.

Creed saw red. Heat crawled up his neck and burned in his gut. His hands balled into fists.

What was that bastard doing here?

With Maya.

Touching her.

He was out of the car before he'd completed the thought, his vision still blurred with fury, his knuckles itching to make contact with the other man's jaw.

His strides ate up the yard or two of sidewalk between him and where Brad and Maya now stood.

"What the hell are you doing here?" he charged, startling both of them into spinning in his direction.

"Creed," Maya began.

But his attention was focused on Brad, whose own gaze narrowed and darkened when he saw Creed barreling toward him.

He recognized that expression—it was the look of a possessive man. A man who wanted to stake his claim, mark his territory.

And that territory was Maya.

Well, he couldn't have her. As far as Creed was concerned, she was already spoken for, and McKenzie could go take a flying leap. Over a very steep cliff, if he had his way.

Before another word could be uttered, Creed had McKenzie by the shirtfront, pushing him back a couple of steps as he raised his right arm, ready to throw the first punch.

"What are you doing?" Maya shouted, her eyes round with terror as she threw herself in front of Brad, shoving both hands at Creed's chest.

With Maya in the way, he couldn't pound the other man as he'd have liked. He lowered his arm but kept his hand balled in McKenzie's shirt.

"Stop it," Maya demanded, still pushing at his chest and now yanking at his arm to get him to let go of McKenzie. "Stop it, Creed, I mean it."

For long minutes time stood still. The muscles in Creed's arms bulged, and his teeth ground together. McKenzie didn't make a move against him, was just standing there. But he didn't look intimidated or afraid. If anything, he looked as if he'd enjoy it if Creed hit him, so he'd have an excuse to hit him back.

Taking a deep breath, Creed loosened his hold and dropped his arm to his side. Maya inserted herself more fully between them, and he retreated half a step to give her more room and keep her from being pressed up against Brad.

She was breathing heavily, her eyes flashing fire. But instead of laying into him, she stared at him for a moment, then turned to face McKenzie.

"I'm sorry, Brad, but I think you should go."

The man stood perfectly still for a beat, his gaze remaining locked on Creed. Then his eyes flicked to Maya and he nodded.

"I'll talk to you later," he said softly.

As soon as Brad was in his black Lexus and driving away, Maya hit Creed square in the chest.

"What is *wrong* with you?"

"What the hell was *he* doing here?" he growled in response.

"That's none of your business." Crossing her arms over her chest, she turned and headed back to the house.

"It damn well is my business," he told her, dogging her every step.

She didn't try to slam the door in his face, which surprised him. Instead she moved to the middle of the kitchen before twisting to face him, leaving him to slam the door himself after he'd stepped in behind her.

"Why? Why is it your business?"

"Because," he answered, his temper flaring before he'd fully formed his response. "It just is."

"No, Creed," she said, her voice turning low and calm. "It really isn't."

A shiver of dread ran through him, turning his blood icy as he watched her turn and walk out of the kitchen through the second entryway that led to the dining room and the rest of the house.

He'd spent the last decade pretending he didn't care about her and was pretty sure he'd spend the next decade kicking himself for all the time he'd wasted, all the time they'd lost because of his stubbornness and stupidity.

"Maya, wait."

He caught up to her at the base of the stairs and had to fight not to grab her up then and there.

It would have been a simple matter to wrap his fingers around her arm and drag her to him as his gut was urging him to do. But he didn't think he-man tactics were what the situation called for. He'd used quite enough of those over the past few weeks, and while they'd gotten him into Maya's bed, he didn't think they would win her over for a lifetime.

Sticking his hands deep into his front pockets to keep from reaching for her, he asked, "Do you want McKenzie? Is that it?"

With a sigh she said, "I don't know what I want. Brad's a nice guy. He really cared about me. But I've treated him terribly, and your little display of aggression out there certainly didn't help."

She rolled her eyes at him before continuing. "Which is why I was breaking up with him. He came over so we could talk, but I think we both knew we were never going to be more than friends. I don't think I'll ever be able to be more than friends with any man, thanks to you."

Her already-stiff posture turned even more rigid. "Happy now?"

It didn't take him a heartbeat to respond. "Yes."

Huffing out an angry, frustrated breath, she spun around and started to stomp up the steps.

"Don't you want to know why I'm happy?" he called after her.

"No, I really don't."

He followed her, climbing the stairs slowly, one at a time. Determination marked his every move.

She'd reached her bedroom, slamming the door behind her in an effort to shut him out, but he didn't let that stop him. Twisting the knob, he opened the door again and stepped inside.

Maya was on the other side of the room, standing with her back to him as she rummaged around in her closet, making an obvious effort to ignore him. Not that it was going to work.

"I'm in love with you," he said, the apprehension in his belly easing slightly when she froze in midmotion.

"I'm glad you broke things off with McKenzie. And I'm glad I've ruined you for other men if it means you'll be more likely to stay with me."

Seconds ticked past while he waited for her reaction, his lungs burning with the need for oxygen while he held his breath. Slowly she lowered her arm from where she'd been reaching for a top shelf of the closet and turned to face him.

"You don't really want me," she said, licking her lips to help get the words out. "You only slept with me to get me out of your system, remember?"

"I remember everything. Including the fact that I've wanted you since you started to change from a spindly kid to a full-grown woman."

"That's not true," she charged, her voice wavering. "You barely knew I existed."

"Oh, I knew. I treated you pretty badly back then— ignoring you a lot of the time, teasing you, censuring you. I was a jerk. I know that, and I'm sorry about it. My only excuse is that I wanted you. Even then, when you were too damn young to know the difference and I was definitely old enough to know better.

"I shouldn't have been attracted to you, though, and the guilt and frustration of the entire situation made me angry. More often than not, I took that anger out on you. I was a moody bastard, that's for sure," he said with a harsh laugh. "And I made your life miserable."

"Yes," she choked out, still looking shocked and numb, "you did."

"That was a long time ago, though. And now we've got this…" He waved a hand between them, indicating some invisible thread that seemed to tie them together, keep them bound, even when they each tried their best to break away. "Connection. This insatiable hunger for each other that isn't going away, no matter how much we might wish it would."

"You make me crazy," she said, shaking her head. Her lashes fluttered and her chest hitched slightly as she drew a breath. "You claim to be in love with me, then say you wish you weren't. You tell me you've wanted me for years, but until recently you acted like I was nothing more than a thorn in your side. Which is it, Creed? I'd really like to know so I can move on with my life."

He grinned at the sassy remark and took a step forward. Then another, until he was close enough to grasp her by the shoulders.

"That night a few weeks ago," he began. "You reminded me on the phone of the night when you were seventeen and I caught that boy trying to take advantage of you in the back seat of his car. I said some things after that—some nasty, hurtful things that you've been carrying around with you ever since. But I want you to know I didn't mean them."

His thumbs moved in small circles on the flesh of her upper arms, left bare by her short-sleeved top.

"None of it. I was furious that anyone would dare touch you like that, treat you like that. I wanted to kill that kid," he snarled, one corner of his mouth curling upward the way it had all those years ago.

"I was also sick with jealousy that you were dating at all. Because at the same time I didn't want any other boys near you, I couldn't come clean about wanting to be with you myself. But I'm older now, and I know what I want. I also know what I'm willing to risk to have it."

His grip on her arms tightened and he dragged her closer, until she was pressed to his chest, her face only inches from his own.

"I was so damn worried about what others would think and with protecting the Fortune family's reputation, that I almost let you get away. But I don't care about any of that anymore. I love you and want you to marry me."

He paused for a moment, sliding his hands from her shoulders to her temples, running his fingers through her hair and tipping her head back to meet her sparkling eyes.

"And I think you should," he added with a cocky grin.

Maya's heart was pounding so hard inside her chest, she thought it might explode. She'd never thought to hear anything close to *I love you* from this man, let alone what amounted to a marriage proposal.

And as much as she wanted to stay mad at him for all he'd put her through—not only these past weeks, but the past years—she couldn't. She loved him, too. Truly, madly, deeply, and until the end of time.

He might drive her to distraction at times, but she'd been ready to love him quietly and from afar, just as she always had. Now he was giving her the chance to scream it from the rooftops. And, more, he was telling her he felt the same about her.

Suddenly her eyes filled with tears, and she took a deep, gulping breath, fighting to keep her pulse from galloping out of control.

"Of course I'll marry you," she said in a watery voice, her cheeks growing damp as her emotions spilled over. "I've always loved you, and it killed me to think you'd never see me as anything more than your annoying, unwanted younger stepsister."

"You were always wanted," he told her, his own eyes turning suspiciously bright a second before he pulled her to him and crushed her in his firm embrace. "*Believe me.* I've spent the better part of my life doing my level best not to let anyone see how very much I *did* want you."

She cried into his shoulder for a moment, pure happiness bubbling inside her until it overflowed. "I wish you had said something sooner, instead of making me miserable all these years."

Leaning back, she fixed him with as stern a look as she could manage while all her dreams were coming true.

"Why didn't you?" she demanded, slapping him in the chest. "Even if you couldn't bring yourself to say anything before, you certainly could have said something when we started sleeping together."

He shook his head, a wry smile curving his lips. "Definitely not. I was still deep in denial and only sleeping with you to get you out of my system, remember?"

She arched one dark brow, fighting the laughter that threatened to burst past her lips. "Did it work?"

"Not by a long shot. You were under my skin long before the first time I let myself touch you. But after that, the more I had you, the more I wanted you."

He ran his fingers through her hair again, wiping the trails of wetness from her cheeks with the pads of his thumbs.

"I'll always want you, Maya," he said softly. "And now that I know you love me, too, I'm never going to let you go."

She leaned into him again, her hands at his waist as she absorbed his warmth, strength and love. "Promise?"

"Promise," he whispered, then captured her mouth for a searing kiss.

When they broke apart, they were both struggling for air. Her fingers bunched in the material of his shirt while his ran down her back to cup the curve of her bottom.

"We're going to have quite an announcement to make at Sunday dinner with the family, aren't we?" he said, his hands caressing everywhere they could reach while his lips nibbled at her throat and the sensitive hollow behind her ear.

"Mmm-hmm. How do you think they'll handle it?"

she asked, the smallest trickle of worry wending its way through her bubble of contentment.

Creed lifted his head to gaze down at her, his eyes serious. "I think they'll be surprised, but they're Fortunes—they'll handle it. I also think they'll be happy for us, despite what the media and the outside world might make of our relationship."

She thought about that for a moment, then began to grin. "I think so, too. I can't wait to tell them."

With an arm around her waist, he lifted her off her feet and turned for the bed. "Neither can I, but since Sunday's a couple days off and we just happen to have this nice, soft bed in front of us, I say we make good use of it."

"Oh, by all means," she replied in as serious a tone as she could manage while pure joy coursed through her veins.

Creed tossed her onto the wide mattress, following her down and covering her body with his own. And all she could think was that it had been a bumpy road, with more than a few potholes and pitfalls, but at long last she was exactly where she'd always wanted to be.

She was finally perfectly and deliriously happy, and knew she would remain that way. Forever.

Epilogue

One Year Later

"A toast!" Creed moved around the room, topping off glasses of champagne from the bottle in his hand.

"Uh-uh, none for you, love," he said with a smile, setting down the bottle and handing Maya, who sat on a nearby chair, a glass of punch instead. Before straightening, he leaned in to press a kiss to her forehead and pat the bulge of her hugely pregnant belly.

She was so big now she felt ready to explode. Her husband, however, seemed to love it. He would lie in bed at night, stroking her giant beach ball of a stomach and talking to the baby growing inside.

And anytime she complained about her size, her waddle or the inability to find clothes that both looked good and fit her, he was always quick to tell her how beautiful she was and to remind her that soon—very soon now, since she was a couple of weeks overdue—they would have an adorable baby boy or girl to show for all her discomforts.

Truth be told, she couldn't wait. She was scared and nervous and anxious, but also happy and excited.

This baby would be a living, breathing tribute to her love for Creed, and his for her, and hopefully possess traits that exemplified the best of them both.

They'd been married less than a year, and as Creed had predicted, the press had had a field day when their engagement was announced. He had been wrong about their relationship causing a scandal, however.

The papers and gossip magazines had certainly tried to make a big deal of their being brother and sister, but once it had come out that their only family connection was through the marriage of his father to her mother, with no blood ties between them, the entire story had died down and disappeared within a few weeks.

And, frankly, the Fortune family had begun to get used to the bevy of stories floating around about them, since the frenzy had been going on fairly regularly from the time Nash's and Patricia's lack of a legal marriage certificate had become public knowledge.

They'd had a beautiful, if somewhat hurriedly

planned wedding, and flown off to Jamaica for a luxury honeymoon.

That's where she'd gotten pregnant, to everyone's surprise and delight. Now, if only their reluctant child would decide to make an appearance.

"To Dad and Patricia," Creed continued, breaking into her thoughts as he raised his glass and his voice. "May you forever be as happy as you are at this moment, and may *this* marriage be valid, legal and last forever."

Chuckles spilled through the room, everyone in attendance aware of the circumstances surrounding today's events.

Maya's father, Wilton Blackstone, had been sent to prison for extortion, thanks to Nash and the boys throwing the considerable weight of the Fortune name and reputation behind his prosecution. Knowing that any luck he'd been having had come to a firm and final end, Wilton had also been more than willing to grant Patricia a divorce.

Soon after, Nash and Patricia had started planning a second wedding, where their vows would not only be renewed, but finally, truly legalized.

It had been one of the most talked-about events of the season in Sioux Falls, overshadowing even Creed's and Maya's nuptials, and everyone who was anyone in South Dakota and beyond wanted to attend.

But Patricia and Nash hadn't wanted a big or flashy

wedding, especially this time around. They'd trimmed the guest list down to include only family and a few close friends, and now only immediate family remained, gathering in the great room for a private celebration.

Case and Gina were there, of course, with their six-month-old son, Clive. He was the most adorable thing Maya had ever seen, and she couldn't wait to have one of her own to bounce on her knee and dress in cute little outfits.

Skylar and Zack were also in attendance, making a habit of splitting their time between their home in New Zealand and the Fortune estate so nine-month-old Amanda could grow up knowing her grandparents and cousins.

Max and Diana had also flown all the way from Australia for the occasion, and had dropped hints that they were thinking about starting a family soon, as well.

"Here, here!" everyone agreed in response to Creed's toast.

Patricia laughed, passing her glass of champagne to Nash as little Amanda stretched out her arms, wiggling in her mother's hold as she reached for her grand-mother. With a roll of her eyes, Skylar handed her daughter over.

Maya couldn't wait to see her mother holding *her* child like that, but she was happy just to see the con-tentment on Patricia's face these days. It certainly beat the strain and pallor she'd worn for so long before her first husband had been dealt with and put firmly out of their lives.

Eliza, who was sporting a slight pregnancy bulge of her own, stepped forward and cleared her throat, drawing everyone's attention. Reese stood with her, both with kooky, crooked smiles curving their lips.

"I don't know if this is the right time to make this announcement," she said, "but Reese and I wanted to share the news that…"

Her smile widened as she glanced at her husband. He lifted her hand to his mouth, taking over when she didn't seem capable of finishing. His voice was lower and a bit more controlled, but his pleasure was obvious in the brightness of his eyes.

"We just found out we're having twins."

Cheers and ecstatic exclamations filled the room as everyone rushed forward to congratulate them. Maya shifted back and forth, working to hoist herself up from her seat, which was becoming increasingly difficult these days.

"I've got you," Creed said, appearing at her side to relieve her of her punch glass and pull her to her feet.

"Thank you," she said a little breathlessly.

"You're welcome. Now smile," he cajoled, slipping an arm around the spot formerly known as her waist, "or you'll send poor Eliza into a panic over having to carry two of these."

The idea of being twice as pregnant as she already was sent Maya into a bit of a panic herself, so she did as Creed suggested and planted a wide smile on her face as she waddled forward to add her congratulations to the rest.

After things had calmed down, Nash placed his hands on his hips and focused his gaze on Blake and Sasha, who were cuddled close together, still acting like the newlyweds that they were.

"So," he said, rocking back on his heels. "Everyone else is taken care of. When are you two planning to start a family?"

Sasha blushed to the roots of her auburn hair, but Blake merely shook his head at his father's pushy antics.

"Give us a break," Blake told him, "we just got married."

"And…"

Blake rolled his eyes. "Don't worry, we'll get started on grandkids for you soon enough, I promise. Not that you don't have enough to keep you busy for a while," he added, cocking his head at all the babies and pregnant bellies in the room.

"There's no such thing as too many grandbabies," Nash persisted, his tone gruff despite the happiness of his expression.

Just as the group of Fortunes started to break away, heading for the different chairs and sofas in the room and refilling glasses, a sharp pain slashed low through Maya's abdomen and around her back.

"Oh!" she cried, reaching for Creed, who was right there beside her.

He took her hand, lines of concern bracketing his mouth. "What is it? Are you all right?"

It took her a moment to catch her breath and straighten. "Yes, I'm fine. I think—"

Another pain hit, and she knew she *wasn't* all right. It suddenly occurred to her that maybe the ache she'd had in her back the past couple of days and all of today hadn't been just another fun side effect of her pregnancy, but was actually a sign that the baby's arrival was imminent.

Clutching her belly, as well as Creed's hand, she said, "I think we're about to add another member to the brood of grandbabies."

Chaos broke out around them, but Creed simply swooped her into his arms and strode from the room.

"I can walk, Creed," she complained, knowing she must weigh a ton.

"Hush. I'm carrying my very pregnant wife to the car so we can drive to the hospital and have a baby. Don't argue."

Considering the tightness at her waist and the throb in her lower back, she decided to keep her mouth shut and let him get her to the hospital as quickly as possible.

Behind them, the entire Fortune clan poured out of the house, rushing to their respective cars, strapping babies into car seats and calling out words of encouragement.

Maya took a moment to smile over the flood of family that was about to descend on the local hospital…

and felt more than a modicum of sympathy for the staff there, who would likely be harassed and harangued within an inch of their lives.

"We'll be right behind you, darling," her mother promised, leaning into the car as Creed settled her into the passenger seat and fitted the safety belt around her wide girth. "Don't worry about a thing. We love you."

She kissed the tips of her fingers, then placed them on Maya's brow before stepping back and letting Creed slam the door closed.

Maya's eyes filled with tears and she sniffed.

"Hey."

She turned her head to look at her husband. He started the engine and put the car in gear before reaching over to take her hand.

"Don't cry. I'm nervous enough as it is, and just barely managing to hold it together. If you lose it, we're in trouble."

As always, he knew just what to say. She chuckled and squeezed his hand.

"I won't lose it," she promised quietly. "And I'm nervous, too."

"We'll get through it together, okay? We've also got a hell of a lot of backup," he remarked, sparing a glance for the rearview mirror, where she suspected a procession of Fortune vehicles was trailing behind them.

At the end of the long driveway, he stopped and turned to face her.

"In case things get crazy once we get to the hospital,"

he said, "I want you to know that I love you. I've never once been sorry that I threw caution to the wind and took you as my wife."

She blinked and held her breath, fighting the wash of tears that threatened to spill over. "I love you, too. But if you keep talking like that, I might break down, after all."

He simply smiled, then leaned over to kiss her firmly on the mouth. "Okay. Let's go have a baby."

* * * * *

Watch for Heidi Betts's next book,
Christmas in His Royal Bed,
on sale this December from Desire™.

MILLS & BOON

Blaze

On sale 4th April 2008

JUST DARE ME...
by Stephanie Bond

Gabrielle Flannery isn't the outdoor type. But she soon discov
that nothing stimulates a sexual appetite like a sinfully
gorgeous man, fresh air, a tiny tent and a whole lot of libido

JUST ONE LOOK
by Joanne Rock

Warren Vitalis is meant to be protecting Tabitha Everheart
but instead of focusing on the job at hand, he can only
think about getting her into his bed!

THE MAN TAMER
by Cindi Myers

Rachel Westover has no problem taming men. But Garret Kel
is an exception; he's hers to command between the sheets,
but outside there's more of a battle...

DOUBLE DARE
by Tawny Weber

Audra Walker is the ultimate bad girl. And to prove it,
she accepts a dare – to hit on the next guy who comes throug
the door. He's sex on legs. Unfortunately, he's also a cop...

MILLS & BOON®

INTRIGUE

proudly presents:

Nocturne

sensual tapestry of spine-tingling passion with heroes and
heroines guaranteed to be out of the ordinary

Coming in February 2008 starting with

The Raintree Trilogy

As an ancient foe
rises once more,
the rejoined battle
will measure the
endurance of the
Raintree clan…

Raintree: Inferno by Linda Howard – **on sale February 2008**
Raintree: Haunted by Linda Winstead Jones – **on sale March 2008**
Raintree: Sanctuary by Beverly Barton – **on sale April 2008**

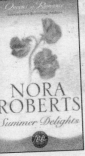

FREE!

2 Books
and a surprise gift!

We would like to take this opportunity to thank you for reading this Mil• Boon® book by offering you the chance to take TWO more specially selec titles from the Desire™ series absolutely FREE! We're also making this offe introduce you to the benefits of the Mills & Boon® Reader Service™—

- ★ FREE home delivery
- ★ FREE gifts and competitions
- ★ FREE monthly Newsletter
- ★ Exclusive Reader Service offers
- ★ Books available before they're in the shops

Accepting these FREE books and gift places you under no obligation to b you may cancel at any time, even after receiving your free shipment. Sim complete your details below and return the entire page to the address bel You don't even need a stamp!

YES! Please send me 2 free Desire books and a surprise gift. I understa that unless you hear from me, I will receive 3 superb new titles ev month for just £4.99 each, postage and packing free. I am under no obligat to purchase any books and may cancel my subscription at any time. The fi books and gift will be mine to keep in any case.

D8

Ms/Mrs/Miss/Mr .... Initials ....
                                                                                          BLOCK CAPITALS PL♦

Surname ....

Address ....

....

.... Postcode ....

Send this whole page to:
UK: FREEPOST CN8I, Croydon, CR9 3WZ